BLOOD MOON

ALSO BY ALICIA MONTGOMERY

THE TRUE MATES SERIES

Fated Mates

Blood Moon

Romancing the Alpha

Witch's Mate

Taming the Beast

Tempted by the Wolf

THE LONE WOLF DEFENDERS SERIES

Killian's Secret

Loving Quinn

All for Connor

THE TRUE MATES STANDALONE NOVELS

Holly Jolly Lycan Christmas

A Mate for Jackson: Bad Alpha Dads

TRUE MATES GENERATIONS

A Twist of Fate

Claiming the Alpha

Alpha Ascending

A Witch in Time

Highland Wolf

Daughter of the Dragon

Shadow Wolf

A Touch of Magic

Heart of the Wolf

THE BLACKSTONE MOUNTAIN SERIES

The Blackstone Dragon Heir

The Blackstone Bad Dragon

The Blackstone Bear

The Blackstone Wolf

The Blackstone Lion

The Blackstone She-Wolf

The Blackstone She-Bear

The Blackstone She-Dragon

BLOOD MOON

BOOK 2 OF THE TRUE MATES SERIES

ALICIA MONTGOMERY

ABOUT THE AUTHOR

Alicia Montgomery has always dreamed of becoming a romance novel writer. She started writing down her stories in now long-forgotten diaries and notebooks, never thinking that her dream would come true. After taking the well-worn path to a stable career, she is now plunging into the world of self-publishing.

 facebook.com/aliciamontgomeryauthor

 twitter.com/amontromance

bookbub.com/authors/alicia-montgomery

Sisters before the misters, and so this book is dedicated to my most loyal sisters of the heart, J, L, M, and Z!

PROLOGUE

"Please, Master! Don't!" the man pleaded, getting on his knees and cowering in front of the tall, pale figure dressed in black robes.

"You know the price of failure, Gregor." The master's voice was raspy, but cold and imposing.

"But Master, I didn't know! The poison was supposed to work!"

"Do you think I care about your excuses?" The voice sent chills down the man's spine.

"Lord Stefan, give me another chance! I'll find a way! I'll cut off her head if I have to!"

"Shut up, you fool! You've had two chances, and it's too late now!" Stefan's voice thundered through the dark, almost empty hall. "She has found her

True Mate and is well on her way to spawning more of those disgusting creatures!"

Gregor flinched at his master's words. He tried to plead his case, but all that came out of his mouth was a short shriek. He knew what was coming next.

Stefan stood tall over Gregor, his finger pointed at the man on his knees. "Goodbye, Gregor."

With those words, the man burst into flame in mere seconds, the blue fire burning hot as it consumed his body until it left nothing but dark ashes smeared on the floor.

"Idiot!" Stefan roared. With a snap of his fingers, the ashes disappeared, leaving the floor clean as if Gregor was never there.

"We should have struck and struck fast."

Stefan looked to his left. "Are you saying I was mistaken, Daric?"

The figure on the left stepped forward from the shadows, revealing a tall, imposing man with long blonde hair. "No, of course not, Master. But Gregor was a fool."

"But he was loyal," Stefan countered. "Perhaps my most loyal lieutenant."

"Yes. Loyalty is hard to teach, but so is intelligence."

Stefan almost smirked. "And you would have attacked the Lycans, Daric?"

The man shook his head. "Of course not. But Gregor's plan was too convoluted. Trying to blame another Lycan for the death of the girl. Pitting them against each other while we hide in the shadows. What would that have done? It's inevitable the Lycans would know of our existence anyway. His plan was too random, and the girl herself is smart. We should have gotten rid of her, before she became too significant, too precious to the Alpha and her True Mate. Killing her now would only mean taking on the entire Lycan society."

Stefan tapped one of his thin fingers on his chin thoughtfully. "I suppose a more direct approach would have been better. But it doesn't matter now. We will do what we can and take the next part of the plan into action."

"Yes, Master." Daric bowed his head respectfully, but his jaw set tight. "What should we do?"

"You already know the next part," Stefan reminded him. "But first, bring her in."

CHAPTER ONE

C ady Gray sighed softly as she watched the newlyweds on the makeshift dance floor. Alynna threw her head back and laughed as Alex picked her up and twirled her around. She smiled as the young couple embraced and began to slowly dance when the DJ put on a more subdued love song.

Was it really just five weeks ago when Alynna Chase arrived in their lives? The young private investigator had thought she was fully human for twenty-two years, and she believed she was virtually an orphan. Alynna was at Blood Moon, a club that catered to Lycans, when she met Alex Westbrooke. Apparently the young woman transformed into her Lycan form accidentally upon meeting the young man and ran away, but Alex tracked her down. Of course she was brought in to see Grant Anderson, the leader and Alpha of the New York Clan. They initially thought she was an intruder, someone from another clan who had come into their territory without permission. They discovered, however, that not only was she a full Lycan, but also Grant's half-sister by his father Michael and his True Mate, Amanda Chase. Unfortunately, Michael died in a car accident before he could bring Alynna into New York Lycan society. Although it was a difficult adjustment for the young woman, she managed it masterfully. It also turned out Alex was her True Mate.

It was a beautiful reception, and Cady had to give herself a mental pat on the back since she put everything together in about two weeks. Alynna had left all the planning to her, giving her free reign over the decorations, music, and food – except for her strange pie request. Cady went to work the moment the couple came back from Chicago and announced their engagement. There was much to be done, and she had some help from Callista Mayfair, Grant's mother, who was more than happy to lend a hand. The older lady seemed disappointed Alynna didn't want a big wedding with all the fanfare, but was quickly appeased when she learned why the couple didn't want to wait months to get married. She was overjoyed at the prospect of being a grandma, which Alynna had confessed weirded her out still, given that the baby would technically be her former husband's grandchild by his mistress.

Cady was truly happy for Alex and Alynna, not just because they were True Mates, but because they found each other and what seemed like real happiness. They also were already expecting a Lycan pup - with instant pregnancy an effect of being True Mates. Although Cady might have projected a pragmatic image, she was a romantic at heart. Would she ever find someone of her own? Not necessarily another person who would hold the other half of her soul, but someone she could come home to after a long day, and maybe a child or two to bring more joy into her life. She shook her head. *No, I shouldn't think about it.*

"You look like you're still working."

Cady froze at the familiar voice. One that never failed to make her nervous. Or giddy. Or both. "I am working. Aren't you?" she answered without taking her eyes off the dance floor.

"Of course." Nick Vrost stepped up to join her where she stood. He was dressed smartly in his formal black suit, cut in an Italian style that suited his long and lean, but powerful, frame. His blonde hair slicked back with gel, though a tendril had fallen over his forehead. "My work is never done. But that's the nature of being Beta and head of security."

"We are in The Enclave," Cady replied, turning her head up to look at him. "I'm sure you can relax while we're in here."

Ice blue eyes regarded her. "I will if you will."

She laughed. "Fine. I'll have a glass of champagne." Cady turned to head toward the refreshment table, but a warm hand wrapped around her upper arm. "Actually, I was thinking we could dance, Ms. Gray."

"Oh," Cady gasped quietly. In all their years working together, she couldn't remember Nick Vrost ever touching her. His large hand was calloused and warm, the grip strong yet gentle on her arm. The sensation of his bare skin touching hers shot tingles through her, spreading heat along the line of her body. She sucked in a breath, his cologne filling her nose. She thought back to that night he brought her home after the incident at Blood Moon. *Hmmm ... fir trees?* She wondered what brand he wore that made him smell so ... different and sexy. The scent reminded her of Christmas, her favorite time of the year.

Suddenly, a dizzying feeling overtook her. Her

knees buckled slightly, which only made Nick grab her with his other hand, his arm wrapping around her waist. "Are you okay?" he asked. His face was mere inches from hers.

"I'm fine. Just overwhelmed, I guess." Cady straightened up, which only brought her closer to Nick's broad chest, giving her another whiff of his cologne.

"Not too overwhelmed to dance with me, Ms. Gray?" Nick asked hopefully.

"No. But only if you call me Cady. Which I think you can do after all these years."

"Ten years, to be precise, Ms. – er, Cady," he faltered. "All right, but you should call me Nick, then."

Her name sounded strange coming from his mouth. She realized he had never said her first name aloud.

"Of course, Nick," she replied, giving him a smile. She let him lead her to dance floor, and when they found an open spot, he placed his left hand on her waist and took her small hand in his right one. They swayed in time to a slow song the DJ had just put on. Small tingles shot along her left palm where their bare skin met.

Nick was a surprisingly good dancer, able to keep rhythm and lead Cady along. "I didn't know you danced, Nick," Cady remarked. "I'm usually at the same parties you are. I don't think I ever saw you dance with anyone."

"We hardly have any parties where I'm not working. Didn't think it was appropriate."

"And now?" the redhead inquired.

"As you said, there's nothing to be worried about. We're inside The Enclave, and we are here as Best Man and Maid of Honor. I think it's actually our duty to have a good time." Nick twirled her efficiently, and when he pulled her back, Cady found herself pressed up against him even closer.

"You do that quite well," she breathed out slowly.

"Thank you. My grandmother insisted I learn to dance when I was younger," he said wryly.

Cady was a little surprised at the revelation. That was perhaps the only personal thing Nick ever revealed to her in all the years she worked alongside him. "Well, I'll have to thank her for making sure you didn't step on my toes."

Nick cracked a sad smile. "She passed on some time ago."

"Oh, I'm sorry." When she saw the sadness in his eyes, she couldn't help herself and touched his cheek softly.

He turned toward her hand and closed his eyes, his lips barely touching her palm, his breath warm tickling her skin. Her head felt light, and she was afraid she'd faint. Cady swallowed a gulp of air, trying to steady herself.

"It's all right, it's been a while. She –"

"Can we cut in?" A bright, cheery voice interrupted Nick. Alynna Chase, now Westbrooke, and her new husband stood behind them.

"How could I say no to the bride?" Cady quickly disentangled from Nick. She was partly relieved, feeling somewhat nervous at how close she and Nick had been. But a small part of her was disappointed.

"Thanks, Cady." Alynna turned to Nick. "May I have this dance, Nicky-boy?"

The taller Lycan gave her a wry smile. "Of course, Mrs. Westbrooke."

Alynna laughed. "C'mon and show me those moves."

Cady watched as the young woman took Nick's hand and dragged him away to the center of the dance floor.

"Sorry, you're stuck with me for a bit, Cades," Alex joked. "I'll try not to step on your toes too much."

"You should have warned me. I would have put on my hiking boots!" Cady laughed as the younger man took her hands.

The DJ put on a slightly faster song this time, much to Alynna's delight. She laughed aloud when Nick spun her. Nick was an excellent dancer and twirled her around expertly.

"You're not half bad," Cady remarked to her current dance partner. She and Alex had an easy friendship, and she had been drawn to his good nature despite him being an outsider.

"Yeah, well I'm no Nick Vrost," he teased. He turned his head to watch his new wife and his Best Man slash boss dancing. "Did you know he could dance like that?"

"I didn't, actually." *There's lots of things I don't know about him*, she realized.

"Really? After all this time?" Alex seemed surprised.

Cady shrugged. "I was as clueless as you are."

"Not that clueless." Alex smiled down at her. "But you can be slightly dense."

"What?" Cady asked incredulously.

"I'm joking, I'm joking," Alex defended. But then his voice turned serious. "But you know, if there's something you want, you should just go for it." He looked over at the other dancing couple.

Cady's eyes widened and then her mouth opened to say something, but she quickly shut it.

A spark lit in Alex's eyes. "So you do have feelings for him?"

"I don't know what you're talking about," Cady retorted in a slightly deflated voice. Despite not truly knowing Nick Vrost after almost ten years, she couldn't help it. She guarded herself and her feelings carefully, and even though his disposition toward her all this time remained formal and chilly, she knew it was too easy to fall in love with him - if she wasn't halfway there already.

———

"We shouldn't," Cady whispered, closing her eyes as she breathed in his wonderful scent.

"Why not?"

She held her breath as he pressed his long, lean body against hers, her back against the wall.

"You know why, Nick," she said breathlessly. She placed her hands on his chest, as if to push him away, but he countered by gripping her wrists and pinning them over her head with one hand.

"I want you. You want me. It's that simple," he murmured as he nuzzled the column of her throat with his lips.

Cady gasped, but bent her head back as if offering her neck to him. Nick responded by grazing her delicate skin lightly with his teeth.

"Nick!" she cried out softly.

Nick pushed one leg between her thighs, pinning her harder against the wall. She responded by pushing her hips against him, seeking out the friction that made her body shiver deliciously.

"I can smell you, Cady. You're wet ... I can make you feel so good. Make you scream out my name as you come over and over again," he promised.

"Nick ..." she whimpered, riding his thigh harder. Her pussy flooded with wetness, soaking her silky undergarments. He released her wrists and placed one of her hands between his legs, over the bulge in his pants.

"See what you do to me, Cady? I only have to think about you like this, warm and wet against me, and I get rock hard. Hell, I only have to smell you ..."

He lifted the layered fabrics of her skirt, grabbed the waistband of her panties, and pushed it down her thighs. Warm fingers trailed up higher, between her legs as he touched the slick seam of her nether lips. His fingers ran along the damp seam, pushing between them as he found her clit with his thumb. Pushing one finger, and then two inside her, he rubbed her clit and thrust his digits into her slick, tight passage.

A small cry tore from Cady's throat as Nick fucked her with his fingers harder, and it didn't take long before her body tightened then convulsed in a small, yet powerful orgasm.

"Oh god!" she managed to call out before Nick covered her mouth with his to muffle the noise ...

Cady's eyes flew open. Startled by the darkness, it took her a second before she realized she was in her own bed alone. She let out a groan and rolled onto her stomach, hugging her cool pillow to her overheated body.

The dream was so vivid. She could still remember the way his lips felt, his strong, callused hands gripping her delicate wrists, and the smell of his delicious aftershave. She took a deep breath, willing her brain to find traces of him, but she could only smell the usual lavender-scented linen spray she used on her sheets.

While Cady was pretty sure it was a dream, her body wasn't quite convinced. She squeezed her thighs together, and realized she was wet. Her body burned from the imagined orgasm, and she was craving for more. Tempted to reach down between her legs to give herself some relief, she resisted and instead rolled over her side to look at the clock on her bedside table.

5:15 a.m. The party had ended about three hours ago. She went to bed sometime after the last guest had left, slightly disappointed that after their dance she hadn't seen any trace of Nick. In fact, he all but disappeared. She supposed he'd been caught up in other business and so had she. After all, she had to make sure all the guests were taken care of, caterers paid, and everything packed and cleared away. The couple had been whisked away to their suite at The Plaza, and she supervised the last cleanup effort.

Cady closed her eyes, willing herself to go back to sleep. Maybe she'd pick up where the dream left off, but only darkness overtook her as she fell asleep.

CHAPTER TWO

"Are you all right, Nikolai? You're sitting in front of me and yet you seem not to be here."

Nick blinked twice, then focused his eyes on the older man across the table. "Apologies, grandfather. I've been busy and have a lot of things on my mind."

He picked up the teapot and poured some tea into the empty cup. His mind was occupied by a lot of things. *Well, one thing, actually*, he thought, but kept that to himself. The wedding had been a week ago, and since then he found it harder and harder to stop his mind from wandering to that night when he had a free moment. Since the wedding, even his dreams were filled with things he didn't dare think out loud. Dreams so vivid, he'd wake up aroused and frustrated, craving for soft skin and that sweet scent. So, in true Nick Vrost fashion, he plunged himself into work and avoided anyone except the Alpha and his security team. By the end of the day, he was so exhausted he slept like a rock.

"Nikolai, let Garret do that." Vasili Vrost motioned to his butler, who had quickly stepped forward to try and take the pot of tea from Nick.

Nick gave the distinguished older man a stern look, and the butler stopped halfway, seemingly trapped between the two men sitting down to tea. "It's okay, Garret, I've got it." His face softened as he looked at the kindly old butler, who had been his favorite playmate when he was much younger. "Will you please give my grandfather and me some privacy? We'll ring when we're done."

"Yes, Master Nick." The butler bowed his head and exited the library.

"I can't believe you're still having him serve tea. He must be over sixty, grandfather," Nick admonished.

"Well," the older man took a sip of the tea. "And what would you have him do? Go back to England or retire in a cottage somewhere? He would grow old within months and wither away."

Nick admitted silently to himself that his grandfather was right. Garret was old school, educated in England. He had been with the Vrost family since he was eighteen, and Nick saw him take a vacation only a handful of times. Forcing him to retire – and that was the only way they'd get rid of him – would be an insult to Garret, the equivalent of kicking him out into the street even with the generous retirement fund they would provide him. No, Garret would probably die happily shining the family silver or with a pot of tea in his hands. He and Vasili were cut from the same cloth. Even though his grandfather was seventy-five, he was still managing the family estates and businesses in the United States and in Europe.

"And stop changing the subject, Nikolai." Vasili put the cup down gently, but his voice was stern. "What is on your mind that you can't even listen to an old man ramble on?"

"Just a lot of work. Especially since I'm down one man on my security force and making sure the Alpha's sister and her husband are secure while on their honeymoon," Nick supplied quickly.

"Ah yes. True Mates. Fascinating, but more important, gives all of our kind some hope." He took another sip of his tea. "Did you give my apologies to the Alpha for missing the wedding?"

"Of course. He accepted your apologies grace-fully and sends his regards," Nick replied. "Now, what was so urgent that you asked me to tea in the middle of the week? You know I never miss our monthly dinners."

Though Nick was busy with his role as the Al-pha's second-in-command, and Vasili split his time between Europe and the US, they always met for dinner at the end of the month, whether that meant Nick flew to wherever his grandfather was at the moment or Vasili arranged his schedule to be in New York. It had been that way since Nick left for college when he was eighteen, when his grand-mother insisted on those monthly dinners. Even though she was gone, the two men made it a point to always keep that date.

That's why he was surprised by the call from the older Lycan, asking him to tea at the Hudson estate in the middle of the month. Nick never de-nied Vasili anything, and he cleared his schedule so he could drive up, to visit with the man who practi-cally raised him. Besides, he loved being at the old mansion and it brought back a lot of good memories.

Vasili took a deep breath. "Nikolai, as you know, I'm getting old."

Nick sighed inwardly. *Not this again.* "Yes,

grandfather, but you said during your last physical that your doctor pronounced you fit as a fiddle."

"Bah." He waved his hand dramatically. "Yes, for someone my age. But I feel it in my bones. I can't recover as fast as I used to, and it's only going to get worse. I've already started reducing my travel schedule. I'd like to stay in New York for longer periods."

"It happens to everyone. Even Lycans."

"Yes, and that's why I asked you to tea today."

Nick lips tightened, his jaw setting in a hard line. Losing his grandmother had been hard. He couldn't think of what it would be like to lose his last living relative and parental figure.

"Nikolai, please, I've been begging you for years. I want to see your children, my great grandpups. I want to be strong enough to play with them, talk to them, and tell them about our family."

"Grandfather, I told you ..."

"And I've been telling you," Vasili interrupted, his voice quavering slightly but gaining strength. "I'm tired of waiting. Yes, you're the Beta, a great honor for our family, the first to serve in any capacity to the Clan. And you're busy, too busy to find a Lycan girl to marry. But the longer you wait, the shorter my time and my patience gets. You've forced my hand."

He was taken aback by his grandfather's words. "Please, grandfather, calm down."

"No, you listen," the older Lycan was almost shouting. "I've decided that if I don't see any progress in the next two years, I will leave everything to Dmitri. Including this house."

Nick's jaw tightened. Dmitri Karkarov was a distant relative, maybe a third or fourth cousin. He was a good man, and actually helped Vasili run their Eastern European estates and holdings. But he was not a Vrost. "Grandfather, that's rather drastic, isn't it?"

"Well, I'm getting desperate," Vasili declared. "And, in any case, he's married to that nice Lycan girl. If you don't produce any offspring, most of the holdings would have gone to him and any heir he produced once you are gone."

Nick balled his fists in anger, but kept his emotions in check. He wasn't worried about the money - he certainly was well-paid by Fenrir, both with salary and equity, and he could retire comfortably right now if he wanted to. Plus, when his parents died, they'd left him a sizable trust. But the house belonged to the Vrost family. His grandfather was trying to get a rise out of him and they'd clashed many times in past years over many things, from his choice of schools to his line of work. Even though Nick loved his grandfather, he'd never show the older Lycan he was rattled. But what was he supposed to do with this news?

"You can't expect me to produce children in two years. You know it doesn't work that way, not with us." Lycans always had problems producing offspring. Many couples failed to get pregnant even after many years and if they did, they rarely had more than one pup.

Vasili nodded. "Yes, I know. I would have wanted more than one child but I was blessed with your father. And so were your parents with you. Which is why I want to see you try. Married or engaged. I'd be happy for a child out of wedlock at this point, as long you can prove it's yours."

Nick felt a headache coming on. He rubbed the place between his brows with two fingers, trying to soothe it away.

"Well?" Vasili asked.

Nick slumped back in his chair in defeat. "What do you want me to do?"

The Lycan smiled. "There are many eligible young Lycan women in New York and all over America. Many of them from great families, their lineage traceable back to the first wave of Lycans from the old country. Or you can even expand your search to Europe, Africa, Asia, any continent that has Lycans. You can have your choice."

"But you've already made yours?" Nick asked, anticipating the answer.

"I've made a list." Vasili produced a piece of paper from his coat pocket. "Let's begin, shall we?"

Nick groaned inwardly. This was going to be a long afternoon.

———

Tea with his grandfather had turned into dinner, and after hours of talking, Nick truly felt exhausted. He appeased Vasili somewhat by listening to his suggestions and telling him he'd consider meeting all the eligible Lycan ladies on his list. But he made no indication he would call any of the women or ask them out on a date any time soon. Meanwhile, he'd bought himself some time, maybe enough to convince Vasili to forget his plan or ... what the alternative was, he wasn't quite sure.

He drove his black Mercedes into his private garage at North Cluster in The Enclave on one of the basement levels where he kept his other vehicles. Walking into the elevator, he pressed the button for the Penthouse. He scowled and crossed his arms over his chest when the elevator stopped at the ground floor. Maybe whoever was on the other side of the door would be intimidated and opt to take the next elevator.

The doors opened and he breathed in a familiar scent, one he could never forget. Candy apples and caramels, favorite treats from his childhood, and a scent that was unique to Cady. Humans didn't normally smell so strong or distinctly to Lycans, but some did. Mostly, humans smelled like sweat and certain pheromones, and most Lycans could tell a human apart from other Lycans because of their lack of a distinct scent. But maybe Cady had a Lycan ancestor, which was not unusual for someone in her position. Nick thought it was curious she could smell like a Lycan and human at the same time, but still, he never thought to mention it as it really wasn't his business.

"Mr. ... er, Nick." Cady's beautiful indigo blue eyes grew wide as she looked at the elevator's occupant.

"Cady, good evening," Nick greeted and put his arms down to his sides. "Working late?"

"As usual." The redhead nodded as she stepped into the elevator. "And you?"

"Out on a personal matter," Nick said casually.

"I see," Cady replied as the doors closed and she pressed the floor to her own apartment, a few floors below his own. A heartbeat passed and the car began to ascend.

"What have —"

"Did you —"

Both of them stopped awkwardly as they spoke at the same time.

"Go ahead." Nick nodded.

"No, you go," Cady began. "I just wanted to —" She gasped and stopped suddenly when the elevator car was plunged into darkness.

Nick cursed softly, then reached out to touch Cady on the shoulder reassuringly as his eyes quickly adjusted. "Are you okay?" he asked as his hand tightened around her shoulder. He felt her shiver slightly as the lone emergency light overhead flickered.

"Yes, I'm okay, just startled." Her voice was slightly shaky, and he could smell the anxiety coming off her in waves.

He wanted to ask her what was wrong, but he knew it was more important to find out what happened. Nick buzzed the emergency button on the elevator panel. "This is Nick Vrost. What's going on? Who's on duty?"

"Mr. Vrost, sir," came the crackly voice from the speaker. "This is Johnson from security, team Epsilon. Sorry, sir. There's a power outage in parts of the building. The generators are taking longer to kick in. I just called in the maintenance guy, but he's still coming from downtown."

"And how long will it take to fix it?" Nick asked impatiently.

There was a long pause. "It'll take him at least thirty minutes to get here, he said, sir."

Nick let out a defeated sigh. "All right, well, do what you can."

"Yes sir," Johnson's voice crackled through the speaker followed by hollow silence.

Nick leaned back against the wall and closed his eyes. Of all the people to get trapped with in an elevator. He turned to his companion. "Looks like we'll be here awhile."

Cady nodded meekly, but Nick could tell her unease was rising by the minute. A surge of protectiveness grew in him. "Are you all right, Cady?"

"I'm ... I ..." She opened her mouth, but no sound came out. She began to heave, as if she couldn't breathe.

"Cady!" Nick took her hand and pulled her closer to him. This seemed to only make her more anxious, so he loosened his grip. "Breathe, Cady. Don't worry, we'll be fine. I'm here."

Cady nodded, even as she broke into a sweat. "I

can't ... I don't like..." Her eyes grew wide as she looked around the elevator car.

It was obvious to Nick that she was having some sort of panic attack from being in an enclosed space. Nick placed his hand on her back, rubbing up and down slowly. "Close your eyes ... that's good ..." he soothed. He kneeled down on the floor and tugged at her hand, making her sit down next to him. She sat obediently, tucking her legs under her.

"Now, just keep your eyes closed. Imagine we're somewhere else. Like the beach on a moonlit night or a park." He continued to rub her back soothingly, and soon Cady's breathing became normal. They sat together for a while, and at some point Cady had naturally moved closer to him and placed her head on his shoulder. He breathed in her delicious, sweet scent, and he started feeling slightly anxious himself. He wasn't quite sure what he'd do if they were left alone much longer. *Probably something I'd regret,* he thought.

"I'm sorry," Cady finally spoke. Her eyes remained closed with her head on his shoulder. "I hate small spaces. Always have. It's not so bad, but being in the dark like this makes it worse."

"Don't worry," Nick assured her. "Everyone has something they're afraid of."

She gave a small laugh. "Even you?"

He smiled in the dim light. "Even me. When I was young, I was always scared of storms. I used to jump into my grandparent's bed when there was thunder and lightning outside."

"Your grandparents?" Cady inquired. "What about your parents?"

"They died when I was young, so I was left in my paternal grandparent's care."

"Oh," Cady's voice fell. "I'm sorry. I didn't mean to pry. It's just that it was the second time you mentioned them, your grandmother at least."

"It's all right; I was very young when it happened." Nick shrugged. "I've accepted it, and my grandmother and grandfather gave me more than enough love growing up."

"Still ... I mean ..." Cady's voice drifted. "I'm being silly, getting all worked up about being in an enclosed space." She took a deep breath. "It's getting hot in here, though," she declared. She unbuttoned the top three buttons of her blouse and began to fan herself.

Nick's heartbeat spiked when he saw a bit of lace and cleavage. His keen senses picked up her scent again, giving him a heady feeling. Willing himself to calm down, he loosened his tie, discarded his jacket, and rolled up his sleeves, exposing his muscular forearms. "I'm going to check in with security." He stood up and pressed the call button. "What's going on there? I need a status report, Johnson."

"Sir," the voice burst through the speaker. "Maintenance guy just arrived. You're the only ones we know of trapped in the elevators, so he's gonna work on getting the power back right now. Five minutes, he says."

"Good," Nick said gruffly, then sat down on the floor again next to Cady. "Are you okay? Can you hang on for another five minutes?"

Cady nodded. "I'm good now. Thank you."

The Lycan nodded and said nothing, but leaned back against the wall of the elevator. The five minutes passed quickly in comfortable silence, then the lights overhead flickered to life, and the car began to move.

"Finally!" Cady sighed in relief. Cool air began to pump through the vents, and she took a long, deep breath.

Nick stood up, offering his hand to her, which she took with a grateful nod. Cady smoothed down her skirt, fixed her blouse, and put her stiletto heels back on. Watching her in such an intimate manner made something in him growl with hunger, and he pictured her doing the same thing after a delightful afternoon romp in his bed. *Where the hell did that come from?* Before he could act on his thoughts, the elevator doors opened to her floor.

"Thank you, Nick." She smiled weakly at him. "Glad I wasn't stuck in there alone."

"You're welcome," he answered automatically.

"Good night." She waved casually at him, and all he could do was watch her walk away as the elevator doors closed.

CHAPTER THREE

I t was a cool fall morning as Cady laid the flowers on the gray slab of stone. The marker wasn't fresh, as the elements had worn away much of the polish and shine it once had. It read "Luther Gray, beloved father and loyal friend." The second date etched on the stone was exactly nine years ago.

"Hello, Dad," she greeted as she touched the stone carefully. She never failed to show up on this date every year, and this was the one day she disconnected from Fenrir and the rest of the world, turning off her cellphone and tablet. Though the pain of his death had slowly reduced to a dull ache through the years, his last day on earth was still fresh in her memory.

. . .

Nine years ago ...

Cady wrung her hands nervously as she waited for her father to come home from work. She arrived late last night from Paris, so she barely saw her dad, only giving him a kiss goodnight before stumbling into bed and goodbye this morning before he went to work. She spent the day in their apartment – well, his apartment, as she had left some time ago – unpacking and sleeping, but mostly practicing what she would say to him. Luther was a busy man, being Human Liaison to one of the most powerful Lycan clans in the world, but tonight he promised her he had cleared his schedule so they could have dinner uninterrupted. So, after a quick trip to the market, she started making dinner - a simple salad, pasta, and steak, medium-rare, her dad's favorite.

"Now this is a nice sight to see!" Luther declared as he entered the kitchen. He was a tall, thin man with graying hair and blue-violet eyes which he had passed on to his daughter.

Cady ran up to her dad and gave him a big hug. "Welcome home," she greeted.

"Welcome home," he greeted back and gave her a kiss on the forehead.

"Go and wash up, and we can start dinner," she said, ushering him toward the sink.

Soon, they sat down to dinner, talking and catching up. They last saw each other three months ago, when Cady had graduated from Sorbonne. She was eighteen when she moved to Paris, did a year at Oxford, and then finished her studies back in Sorbonne, graduating with top honors five years later with an undergraduate in International Business and a combination fast-tracked MBA. After the ceremony, they had dinner much like this one, but at her favorite bistro in the Latin Quarter, not far from her flat.

"So, Bug," he said, using his childhood nickname for her. "You seem to have a lot on your mind. What's going on?"

Cady was looking at her lap when he spoke, and her head shot up so fast it made her head spin. "How did you know?"

"How could I not?" Her father's eyes twinkled. "You're my daughter, of course I know."

She took a deep breath. "Dad, I've had an offer to stay in Paris. Working at Le Claire Industries as a marketing associate." She looked her dad straight on, their matching indigo blue eyes meeting.

Luther's face broke into a wide smile. "Le Claire? They're the biggest conglomerate in Europe! That's wonderful, Cady!" He reached over, grabbed her hand and gave it a squeeze.

Her breath caught in her throat in shock, and she promptly burst into tears. Her father frowned, stood up, walked around to her side of the table, and put an arm around her shoulders. "Bug, what's wrong?"

Cady dried her tears with the back of her hand and looked at him. "I thought ... I thought you'd be mad ... because I wasn't going to come back and ... and work for Fenrir."

"What?" Luther sounded shocked. "Why would you think that? I mean, of course I'd love for you to move back to New York. Bug, I miss you. But this job sounds like it would be amazing for your career! You could be AVP in five years and maybe VP in a decade!" He frowned. "Unless you wanted to come back? You know Grant will find a place for you anywhere in Fenrir."

"No! I mean ..." She bit her lip. "I just ... I guess I know how important your position is to our family and to the Anderson family. We're the last of the Grays. Growing up, I've always heard I would be taking your place when you retire. And you're almost sixty, so I thought ..."

Luther shook his head. "Come, let's go and sit on the couch." He tugged her towards the living room and sat down with her on the comfy leather couch, much like they did when she was growing up. "You know, one thing I've learned ... sometimes the more you try to hold on to something, the more it will want to leave you." There was a sadness in his eyes, and Cady knew what he was thinking when he said those words. Or rather, who he was thinking of. "Cady, I would never stop you from pursuing what you want. Of course Grant will be disappointed - he's missed you all these years you've lived in Paris and London. He'll also be disappointed to be losing you to the competition." He laughed. "But I would never want you to fill my shoes as his executive assistant or Human Liaison, not if that's not what you want."

Cady sighed with relief. "Really?"

"Really."

"Thank you, Dad." Cady embraced her father tightly.

"Of course," Luther said. "Besides, me retire? What would the Clan do without me?"

Cady laughed. "They'd fall apart in an instant!"

The two of them continued to talk long into the night, finishing a bottle of red wine Cady had brought from France. They talked about Cady's plans, including when she'd be back – Luther's birthday, Thanksgiving, and Christmas through the New Year – and when Luther would visit her on her birthday and sometime in the spring when the weather was nice. They discussed going to Portugal or maybe Spain on vacation. Finally, Luther declared he was tired and went to bed.

The next day, Cady got up early, prepared eggs, toast, and a fresh pot of coffee to surprise her dad with breakfast in bed.

"Dad?" she called softly as she padded into his room, tray in hand. "I have breakfast for you."

She froze in her steps as she looked at Luther lying very still in bed, the sunlight from the window streaming down over the sheets. Her mouth went dry and she dropped the tray, sending the dishes and coffee pot crashing to the floor.

Dr. Faulkner said it was an aneurysm in his brain, and he went peacefully in his sleep. Cady wasn't sure what happened next. In fact, the next days were a blur to her. But she remembered hardly eating, sleeping, or even getting out of bed. The Lycans and Fenrir staff took care of all the funeral arrangements; all she had to do was show up for the funeral and shake hands with everyone, then get into the limo for the drive up to the cemetery. She remembered watching numbly as they lowered Luther's coffin into the earth.

The support came even after the funeral. Food, supplies, and even a cleaning lady came to her door regularly. Grant would come to her after work, beg her to get out of bed, have a bite of food, or even take a shower, when all she wanted to do was lie in bed the whole day. Dr. Faulkner and his wife came by to talk to her, and countless Lycans and Fenrir employees would knock on her door, asking how she was or if there was anything they could do for her. Condolences from all over the country and the world came, and she read notes and letters from old friends and colleagues of her father, offering all kinds of support. Cady was overwhelmed - she knew her father was loyal to the New York clan and the Lycans, but she never thought of *their* loyalty to Luther. Her father was well-loved in the Lycan community and Fenrir, and part of her had always resented that she had to share him with them. But when he died, she truly felt he was part of the community.

A month later, she made her decision. She called up the recruiter at Le Claire and told them she was turning down their job offer. She moved into one of the apartments in The Enclave, since she couldn't bear to live in Luther's place, even though she grew up there. She began to learn the ropes of being Grant's Executive Personal Assistant and Human Liaison for the Lycans.

Present day ...

"Goodbye, Dad." Cady rubbed the top of the cold, gray stone one last time. "I'll be by again soon." From here, she'd do the same thing she did every year for the last nine years - go home, have a glass or two of the same red wine she had with her dad that last night, and then go to bed. The next day, she'd wake up fresh and ready to face the day.

With one last sigh, she turned to walk back to her car. Suddenly, she felt the hairs on the back of her neck stand up, and she froze when she heard a voice call to her.

"Hello, Cady."

Cady slowly turned around. *I'm dreaming. This isn't happening. It can't be.*

"How are you, Cady?"

The woman who stood by her father's grave was wrapped in a long red coat, almost as red as her hair. Pale skin, green eyes, and only a little bit taller than her - she was almost Cady's doppelgänger, though years older.

"Mother?" Cady could hardly believe the word came out of her mouth, much less the fact that after leaving twenty-five years ago, Victoria Chatraine was standing in front of her.

"Yes, dear, it's me." The older woman smiled. "How are you?"

Cady was frozen on the spot. "What? How am I? What are you doing here?" Her voice was tense and nervous.

"That's all you have to say to your mother?" Victoria came close to her and envelope her in a hug.

"What would you have me say?" Cady pulled away, anger bubbling inside her. "You leave, don't make contact for almost three decades, and then expect me to welcome you back with open arms?"

"Cady, please." Victoria walked closer to her. "You don't understand. You were too young."

"I was seven when you left," Cady said bitterly. "Yes, I was too young."

The older woman flinched at her words. "It was … complicated. I need to explain to you –"

"Dad explained it when I was older," she interrupted.

"What lies did he tell you?" Victoria's tone became angry. "That I ran away with another man? That I didn't want to be your mother?"

Cady shook her head. "When you left, he said you were unhappy and he was sorry he couldn't give you what you wanted so you would stay."

She paused, thinking back. Luther had been needlessly kind to her mother, never saying a bad word about her. Luther had loved Victoria immensely, and her father never really got over her. It was Cady who was angry and bitter towards Victoria. Growing up without a mom was incredibly difficult, not to mention awkward during her teen years when she was surrounded by males. One day when she was fifteen, they had a terrible fight and she blamed Luther for Victoria leaving. Luther was visibly hurt, but he sat her down and explained everything to her, revealing the one secret she could never say aloud.

"He ... he ... told me the truth. You were a witch. And you couldn't live surrounded by Lycans."

Witches and Lycans simply didn't mix. They had a long-standing rivalry, which had turned into an intense war and necessitated a truce a few decades back. However, it was no secret that both factions still hated each other. Cady had asked her father how he could have fallen in love with a witch, and he confessed he simply didn't know until it was too late and Victoria had gotten pregnant. They decided to keep it a secret, but Victoria couldn't stand living in The Enclave.

Victoria's face remained stoic. "That's partly true. I *am* a witch," she corrected. "And my blood runs through yours as much as your father's."

"I'm not a witch," Cady declared. "You knew that when you left us."

"That's not why I left, Cady. Please know that." She touched Cady on the shoulder, and the younger woman visibly flinched. "Yes, you didn't manifest any powers or talent growing up, but I loved you – love you – just the same. But you're still the blood of my blood."

"What do you want?" she asked.

"I want you back," Victoria declared.

"What, a couple of lunches, maybe some shopping and we're all good?" Cady replied bitterly.

"What was I supposed to do?" Victoria protested. "Even after your father's death, you surrounded yourself with Lycans! Ingrained yourself in their world. I thought I had lost you to these –" Victoria stopped short. "To them. I couldn't approach you, but I know you come here every year by yourself."

"And now what?"

"Now, you must join us. Take your true place with our coven and leave the wolves."

"What?" Cady asked incredulously. "Why would I do that?"

"Because it's your destiny!" Victoria proclaimed. "You're not one of them. You will never be one of them."

Victoria's words were like a knife stabbing through Cady's heart. Yes, she knew that. Although she was one of the highest ranking humans in the New York clan, she would never be a Lycan or accepted fully as one of them. Maybe she would grow to become as respected as her father after a few decades, but she would always be on the outside looking in. That was the truth of her position.

"But our coven will accept you fully, powers or none. Your blood alone makes you one of us, our lineage traces back to the most powerful witch and warlock families from the olden times."

"You're joking, right? I won't be part of any coven!" Cady turned to walk away, but Victoria grabbed her arm, pulling her back.

"You will be one of us. One way or another," Victoria threatened.

Real fear shot through her, chilling her blood. "What do you mean?"

"When they find out, when the Alpha finds out

who – and what – you are, do you think your precious Lycans will tolerate you?" Victoria's eyes
blazed. "They'll toss you away like yesterday's
garbage."

"You wouldn't dare!" Cady tugged her arm
away. She squared her shoulders and looked her
mother straight in the eyes, but a pit was growing in
her stomach. "The witches and Lycans have had
peace for decades." It was more of a tenuous truce,
both parties having decided that with the world
modernizing, neither side had anything to gain by
continuing their war. However, the witch and
Lycan world remained separate.

"I'll do anything to have you back, Cady, by any
means possible," the older woman stated. "And
you'll understand when you join us. You'll find your
real family."

"You will leave me alone and never come near
me or the Clan!" Cady turned away, and walked
toward her car. She could feel Victoria's gaze following her, and she took a deep breath, trying to
calm herself. *Dear lord, what was Victoria planning
to do?*

CHAPTER FOUR

Cady couldn't sleep a wink that night. Victoria's words haunted her, and the fear of her secret coming out to Grant, to the rest of the Clan, hung over her head. When she went to work that morning, she was unfocused, flighty, and even her assistant was flustered that the normally organized Cady couldn't concentrate on her work. Finally, the day was over. While Cady normally worked late, she had enough of this day and all she wanted to do was go home.

"Suzanne." She buzzed her assistant. "Who's available to drive me back to The Enclave?"

"Let me check, Ms. Gray." There was a pause and then Suzanne's voice piped back in. "Greg will be waiting for you at the lobby, Ms. Gray."

"Great, tell him I'll be down in five minutes." Cady grabbed her briefcase and purse, then shut down her computer.

She rode the private elevator down to the lobby, where the Lycan driver was waiting for her. "Good evening, Ms. Gray. Leaving early tonight?" The young man was twenty years old and had only been with Fenrir for six months, but he was bright and friendly and Cady liked him. He was enthusiastic and wasn't shy about his aspirations to become part of Grant's elite security team, training with the more senior members whenever he had the chance.

"Yeah, just feeling a little under the weather today, Greg."

"Sorry to hear that, Ms. Gray. You are looking a little pale. You know, whenever I was sick, my mom ..."

Cady smiled and nodded as they walked to the car, not really paying attention to what he was saying, but let him ramble on anyway. Greg opened the door of the black town car to let her in and then walked to the driver's side.

"I hardly get sick, but when I'm feeling homesick, I make sure I always get myself some chicken soup! It's not the same my mom used to make, but just the smell of it makes me feel better, you know?" Greg looked at her through the rearview mirror.

"Sounds like a great idea, Greg," she replied.

"Want me to stop by a deli and get you some soup?" the young Lycan asked brightly.

"I think I have some soup at home, but thank you." Cady smiled.

"No problem, Ms. Gray." Greg nodded. "I'll have you home in no time."

As Greg kept his eyes on the road, Cady settled back into her seat. She closed her eyes, hoping to get a quick nap before they reached The Enclave. She felt herself drifting off to sleep, but the car suddenly swerved and her eyes flew open. "Greg?" she called out, before pain shot through her arm and the world went black.

CHAPTER FIVE

"And how was tea with Vasili?" Grant Anderson asked his Beta as he leaned back into this chair. They had just finished their usual end of day meeting, wrapping up whatever Lycan and Fenrir business they had for the day.

Nick frowned.

"Now *that's* not a good sign." Grant grimaced. "What is it this time? More begging for you to get married and have a pup?"

"You know me so well," Nick replied glumly.

Aside from being his Beta and right-hand man, Nick was also Grant's best friend, and they'd been inseparable since they met in college. Despite both of them being from prominent New York Lycan families, the two had never met before then, Nick having grown up in the Vrost mansion on the Hudson, then attending boarding school in Connecticut and Europe, and Grant remaining Stateside. The two actually met at Harvard of all places and became fast friends when they discovered their connection. Nick was the natural choice for Beta when Dr. Faulkner announced he wanted to step down from the position once Grant had finished his MBA.

Grant let out a laugh and stood up. He walked over to his bar and poured some amber liquid from a decanter into two glasses, then handed one to his friend. In front of other Lycans and Fenrir employees, they always projected a pure business-like relationship. But when they were alone, they were more casual and friendly.

"Thanks." Nick took the glass and downed it in one go.

The Alpha was taken aback. "It's that bad?"

"This time, yes." Nick relayed the story of what had happened during his tea with Vasili.

"Wow." The dark-haired Lycan sat back down in his chair. "He really threatened to cut you off?"

Nick nodded. "I don't need the money or the businesses, you know that. But the mansion ..."

Grant took a sip of his drink. "You love that place."

"Dmitri might let me buy it off of him."

"For the right price."

Nick scowled. "Yes."

Grant sighed. "You know if it comes to that and you really wanted it –"

"Don't even say it," Nick interrupted his friend. "You probably could buy the mansion ten times over, but even if I could afford it on my own, that would be like ... cheating."

Grant understood. The Hudson mansion was Nick's legacy, the place where he grew up and made happy memories after the tragedy of losing his parents. To have to buy it off of another relative would be an insult and for Vasili to threaten such a thing meant he was deadly serious.

"Then what do you want to do?"

Nick stood up and poured himself a second drink. "Get married. Have a child to appease the old man."

"Better make that one a double, then," Grant laughed. Nick was even more averse to marriage and commitment than he was. He wasn't quite sure why and thought it was strange that his friend never mentioned dating or even sleeping with women in the past years.

At Harvard, Nick had his choice of girls and he took full advantage of it, bedding some of the most gorgeous women in the Ivy League school and around Boston. But when he took on the position of Beta, he never even glanced at all the beautiful, rich, and eligible women throwing themselves at him. Grant himself had no time for serious dating, but that didn't mean he didn't take advantage of both the female human and Lycan company his position afforded him. He wined and dined various women, took most them to bed, but never had a dalliance last more than a few weeks. Usually his "relationships" ended with Jared or Nick letting the young woman down easy, maybe soothing hurt feelings with a nice shopping spree on Fifth Avenue, or even in Rome, Paris, or London if need be. Few women could understand what his life was like and the tremendous responsibility of being a CEO and Alpha to one of the most powerful Lycan clans in the world. But usually, Betas had more free rein and time. If Nick did date or sleep with various women, he was very discreet about it.

A persistent knock on the door interrupted them.

"Is Jared knocking?" Nick's brow furrowed. The normally reserved Lycan assistant was usually calm and reserved and used the intercom to communicate with this boss.

Grant shrugged and walked to the door.

"Primul," Jared called, using the honorific title for Lycan Alphas. "I'm sorry, but you need to take this." Jared practically shoved the cordless phone in Grant's face. "It's Mercy Grace Hospital."

"Thank you, Jared." Grant took the phone from the younger Lycan. "Hello ... yes this is Grant Anderson. Yes, I'm her contact ..."

Nick watched his friend's face change from confused to worry and then turn pale.

Grant's jaw set in a hard line. "I'm headed there now. What about the driver? Yes, I know I'm not related to him, but he's my employee. At least tell me if he's ... okay good. Yes, please go ahead and call them. You have their number? Good. And thank you." He handed the phone over to Jared. "Call the garage and have whoever is on duty get the car ready. Now." His voice was pure power and command and Jared nodded, rushing back to his desk.

"What's wrong?" Nick had a terrible feeling in the pit of his stomach.

"It's Cady. She's been in an accident. The ambulance brought her to Mercy Grace Hospital."

Nick shot up to his feet. "I'll drive, it'll be faster."

He didn't bother to wait for Grant, but instead darted toward the door.

Grant followed his friend, stopping by Jared's desk and instructing him to call Dr. Faulkner and take care of Greg's family. When he got to the elevators, Nick was pacing impatiently. The doors dinged, and he held the doors to let Grant enter first.

———

Nick jabbed the floor to the private garage, willing the elevator to go faster. There was a buzzing in his head as anger, worry, and anxiety threatened to pour out of him, but he took control. *Be calm*, he told himself. It would serve no good if he got into an accident while driving to get to Cady. A deep, protective growl came from within him when he thought of her. He pushed back thoughts of what could have happened – Cady, bloody and broken while she lay underneath twisted, burning metal. The elevator doors opened, and Nick didn't bother to wait for Grant as he strode to his car.

"The car swerved and hit a barrier," Grant supplied as he climbed into the front passenger seat. "That's all they told me for now. Greg's pretty

banged up with a broken leg, and Cady's unconscious but only sustained minor injuries."

Cady was alive. Nick felt some of the tension
leave his body as he drove out of the garage and
headed downtown.

The trip to the hospital was quick, with Nick
driving effortlessly through New York traffic, taking
a few shortcuts here and there. After parking the
car, the two men headed to the front desk where the
receptionist sent them to the East wing.

"I'm Grant Anderson," Grant said to the nurse
at main desk. "Where's Cady Gray?"

The dour-looking older nurse clicked a few keys
on the computer. "Wait here." She eyed the notes on
the screen. "The doctor will be with you in a
moment."

"What room is she in?" Nick asked, leaning over
the desk and staring down the woman. "We want to
see her now."

The nurse stared right back at him, unfazed. "I
said you have to wait. The doctor wants to talk to
you first."

Nick opened his mouth to speak, but Grant
clapped him on the shoulder. "C'mon Nick, let's
wait for the doctor." He nodded a small apology towards the nurse, who looked more bored than of-

fended. "I'm going to make a phone call," Grant told him. "Just wait here, okay?"

Nick nodded and watched Grant walk away. He crossed and uncrossed his legs, his hands unable to stay still, his eyes darting around the room, waiting impatiently.

Finally, a tall, older man in his fifties wearing a medical coat approached them. "Mr. Anderson? I'm Dr. Marks. Please come with me." Both men stood up, but Dr. Marks shot Nick a stern look. "Sorry, family or emergency contacts only."

Before Nick could protest, Grant spoke up. "Nick is my bodyguard, and he needs to go where I go," Grant explained. "And I just spoke with Paul Goldman, your hospital's CEO. We serve on a few boards together. He said he would extend every courtesy to me and my staff. I assure you, we're all discreet."

Dr. Marks looked conflicted, but relented. "All right, come this way."

The two men followed the doctor down one of the corridors, away from the main public area. "Ms. Gray was in a vehicular accident. As far as we could surmise, the driver suddenly swerved off road, hitting a traffic barrier. It was a good thing the car she was riding was built like a tank, and she sustained minor bruises and cuts, including one on her forehead. So far, the MRI shows no signs of a concussion, but we'd like to keep her at least overnight." They stopped outside a door with the number 405 in front. "She's in there resting now."

"Is she awake?" Grant asked.

The doctor shook his head. "No. We had to give her some drugs for the pain, which is why she's out. Plus she needs lots of rest. You can check in on her, but I assure you she won't be waking up until morning."

"What about the driver?"

He looked at his file. "I'm afraid I'm not the attending physician, though I was told his injuries are more severe but not life threatening. His legs, unfortunately, bore the brunt of the crash."

"Could you find out where he is?" Grant requested. "He's my employee, and I need to meet with his family as well, to reassure them we will be taking care of him."

"All right, I'll check for you, Mr. Anderson." The doctor turned back to the nurse's station.

"We'll be right behind you," Grant called. When the doctor was out of sight, he turned to Nick. "You know we have a big problem."

Nick rubbed his forehead, another headache coming on. "Once the doctors see Greg healing in a few hours, they'll know something's up."

"Right. Dr. Faulkner should be on the way. I'll do what I can with the administration to make sure we can take him back to The Enclave as soon as possible." Grant ran his fingers through his hair. "Can you check on Cady? I'm going to go talk to Greg's family. We'll have to get her out of here too and try to cover up any accident report, but she's human so it's not a problem if they want to keep her for observation."

"Of course." Nick nodded his head. "Call me when you decide what to do." He turned and walked back to room 405.

Slowly, Nick opened the door and peeked inside. He walked toward the bed where Cady was lying frightfully still, his heart stopping at what he saw. The overhead light did nothing for her complexion, which was even paler than usual, her cheeks marred with bruises that would surely turn purple by morning. Her red hair was pulled back and a bandage was plastered over her right eyebrow.

"Cady," he called softly, willing her to hear him. Her faint, candy apple caramel scent played along his nostrils. He reached out and grabbed one of her small hands, wrapping his own larger one around it. It took him years before he even let himself touch her, and now it was like he couldn't stop, like he needed to feel her warm skin all the time. The bruises on her face made him wince in pain, but he had to remind himself that she was safe and didn't have any serious injuries. He picked up the steadiness of her breath with his keen hearing, confirming she was sleeping deeply. Pulling up the chair next to the bed, he sat down and continued to watch the rise and fall of her chest, while her eyes remained closed in slumber.

CHAPTER SIX

Cady felt like she was floating. She tried to moan, but her dry throat produced a short, raspy sound. Slowly, she opened her eyes, only to be assaulted by the harsh overhead light. She shut her eyes quickly.

Where am I? Nothing felt or smelled familiar. The sheets were scratchy, the pillows lumpy, and there was an antiseptic smell in the air all around her. *Hospital*, she realized as she slowly opened her eyes. Her vision was blurry and her lids felt heavy, but she forced them open anyway.

It looked like a standard hospital room, white walls, fluorescent light overhead, a single window covered with a green curtain. The car spinning out of control and then ... nothing. Why couldn't she remember ... she was too sleepy and distracted. Her father's grave. Victoria. A chill went through her. She couldn't shake that strange feeling in the pit of her stomach that these events were connected somehow.

Suddenly, the door opened and a tall, large nurse dressed in colorful scrubs walked in with a tray.

"Well, good mornin' sleeping beauty!" she said cheerfully, her smile revealing a set of pearly white teeth made even whiter against her dark complexion. "I thought you'd never wake up!"

"What time is it? Where am I?" she panicked. She racked her brain, trying to remember what happened. It all flooded back into her. "Greg! Where's Greg?" she shouted, then winced when she tried to sit up. "Oh god, it hurts."

"Calm down, Cady." The nurse set the tray down and walked toward the bed. "You're at Mercy Grace, and I'm nurse Ellen. Is Greg that boyfriend of yours?"

"No, he ... he's the driver of the car I was in." *An accident. Must have been an accident.* "Is he okay?"

Nurse Ellen patted her arm reassuringly. "Ah yes, the other patient." She leaned down and lowered her voice. "Now, I'm not supposed to be telling you this, but ... I heard he was being transferred to another hospital. They want to do some special surgery for his legs, some state-of-the-art procedure."

Cady sighed in relief. "Thank god."

"Now, let me go get the doctor. Oh and your boyfriend, I think he said he was going to make a phone call. He'll be glad to know you're up."

"Boyfriend?" Cady looked, confused. "I don't have a boyfriend."

The nurse frowned. "You don't remember him, honey? How bad were you hit in the head?" Nurse Ellen placed her hand on Cady's forehead gently. "'Cause if that tall, blonde drink of water was my boyfriend, I'd never forget him! Mmm-hmm!" she joked.

"Tall ... blonde?"

"Yes, the one that likes to wear them tight suits and pants that show off his cute butt?" She nodded to the empty chair beside the bed. "Stayed here all night. Had one of the night nurses bring him a pillow and a blanket, too."

Nick Vrost? Last week he acted like he couldn't stand to be in the same room as her, and now he stayed with her the whole night? Maybe the nurse was mistaken, though she didn't know any other tall blonde men who wore Italian-cut suits. "Can I have some water, please, nurse Ellen?"

"Of course, sugar." The older woman patted her arm. "I'll grab a glass while I get the doctor. I think we might have to get you more painkillers, too." With that, the nurse left the room.

Cady found the controls to the bed and inclined it forward so she was sitting up in bed. She fidgeted for a while, trying to find the right position that didn't cause her any pain.

"What are you doing?"

She looked up toward the door where Nick was standing, regarding her with his usual cool stare.

"I'm trying to get comfortable which is proving to be very hard, considering I'm wearing and lying down on cold paper sheets." She fiddled with the controls again.

Nick strode over to her, reaching her bedside in a few steps. He took the pillow he had been using and placed it behind her, then wrapped the soft blanket over her shoulders. "Better?" he asked, tucking her in.

"Thank you," she sighed, snuggling into the soft warmth of the blanket. "How's Greg?"

"I just spoke with the Alpha. They moved him back to The Enclave early this morning, before any of the doctors noticed how fast he was healing. Dr. Faulkner said his broken legs should be fine in a couple of days." Nick sat down on his chair.

"Good. I was worried when I woke up and I couldn't remember ..." she drifted off. "What happened? Do they know?"

Nick shook his head. "Greg is still under sedation, which should help speed up his healing, but that means we can't question him for another day or so." He frowned. "What do *you* remember?"

The redhead wrinkled her nose delicately as she searched her memories. "Honestly? Not a lot right now." She paused. "I was falling asleep in the back seat, then the car swerved ... that's about it." When she winced in pain, Nick got to his feet.

"Are you all right? Do you need anything?"

She sucked in some air, breathing deeply. "Meds are wearing off ..."

"Where's that doctor?" Nick muttered.

"I'm fine," Cady protested. "I shouldn't be having all these painkillers. They're making me feel sluggish and groggy. I need to get to my e-mails or they'll pile up."

"You need rest," Nick stated.

"I have work to do."

"If you think Grant will let you go back to work in your condition –"

"I'll work from home," she retorted.

"I'll cut off your internet and confiscate your phone." Nick crossed his arms over his chest.

"You wouldn't dare!"

"Try me."

Before Cady could protest any further, the door opened. Dr. Marks and nurse Ellen walked in.

"How are you today, Ms. Gray?" Dr. Marks asked. "I'm Dr. Marks."

"Fine," Cady sulked. "When am I leaving here?"

The doctor regarded her carefully. "Ms. Gray, you were in a major car wreck. The only thing that saved your life was your seatbelt and that reinforced vehicle. You've got bruises all over your body and face, and you're lucky you didn't get any fractures."

Cady gasped at his words, touching her cheek where a bruise was blooming. "Oh my god!" She looked like she was going to cry.

"It's not that bad, honey, don't worry." Nurse Ellen took her hand and patted it. "Nothing a little makeup won't fix." She looked knowingly at Nick. "And your boyfriend doesn't seem to mind, right, sugar?"

She opened her mouth to tell the nurse Nick wasn't her boyfriend, but before she could say anything, Nick took her other hand and kissed it. "You look gorgeous, sweetheart."

Tingles shot through her hand where Nick's lips grazed her bare skin. She was almost glad her bruises hid her blush.

The doctor stayed a while longer, explaining what needed to be done and that she would need some serious medication in case her cuts became infected and of course, pain meds. Cady said she wanted the least amount of pain meds possible, and the doctor agreed they would dial back and eventually she would only need them to sleep at night and get rest. He ordered another night of observation and at least a week of rest at home.

"I can't believe they want to keep me here longer." Cady pouted as soon as the doctor and nurse left. "I feel fine. Fit as a fiddle."

"I don't suppose you'd like to go dancing?" Nick smirked. "I'll take you out into the hallway right now, and we can prove Dr. Marks wrong."

Even thinking about getting up made Cady wince, and she fell back into bed. "Fine. I'll stay another night. But I'll need my cell phone."

"Sorry, Cady," Nick said in a smug tone. "Your phone and pad were destroyed in the crash."

Cady groaned and pulled the covers over her head. This was going to be a long week.

CHAPTER SEVEN

Flower, gifts, and cards poured into Cady's hospital room. Tate Miller had brought over a bag with some clothes and personal items, telling her that Mr. Vrost had asked Suzanne to pack the items which she thought Cady would need. She was practically giddy with relief when she saw her robe, favorite cotton nightgown, and face soaps and creams in the bag.

Still, after getting cleaned up and refreshed, Cady had way too much time on her hands, and without her phone or pad, she pretty much didn't know what to do. She wished she could talk to someone - anyone - about what happened. Guilt consumed her at the thought of poor, innocent Greg. What if the accident was Victoria's doing?

Was her mother attempting to kidnap her on the way home? The thought of the young Lycan in pain because of her was too much to bear.

Grant came by at around lunchtime, checking up on her and giving her a status report on Greg, but other than that, he refused to talk Fenrir business with her, even ordering Suzanne to stay away. He assured Cady everything would be taken care of and there was nothing urgent that needed her attention. Cady, meanwhile, begged them not to tell Alynna or Alex about the accident while on their honeymoon. Since the couple would be returning in a week's time anyway, there was no need to worry them. She also asked if she could do anything for Greg or his family, but Grant said they were taken care of.

For the rest of the day, Cady drifted between sleep and lucidity, the drugs making her tired and loopy. Weird visions came to her - Victoria, telling her she would do anything to get her back. Dark, swirling clouds consuming her. Frightful creatures surrounding her. Also, as she drifted in and out of consciousness, she could have sworn Nick was hovering around her, holding her hand, and then apologizing when he had to leave. The scent of his aftershave lingered, and she wasn't quite sure if it was all a hallucination, but sometime in the middle of the night, she woke up lucid and saw she was alone in the room. She was disappointed, but perhaps Nick found something better to do than play nursemaid to her.

In the morning she woke up, feeling much better though very much alone. *There's nothing more you can do*, she told herself. Greg was recovering, no one else was hurt. Maybe it was the drugs that were making her paranoid. *It had to have been an accident, right?*

Dr. Marks came by to check up on her, and when she said she wasn't in much pain – downplaying it as much as she could – he said she could switch to over the counter painkillers. He also had more good news for her - they were releasing her into Dr. Faulkner's care, but only if she promised to stay at home and rest for a week and follow all their orders.

"All right, honey," nurse Ellen said as she helped Cady into a pair of loose black pants and a sweater. "There, you look gorgeous. I'm sure that cutie of yours will be happy to take you home."

"He's not ... er –" Cady stopped herself short. Nurse Ellen seemed to be giddy at the idea of Nick being her doting boyfriend, and she couldn't bear to tell her otherwise. "Thanks."

"Hope he doesn't give you too much trouble

though! I'm sure hussies are always throwing themselves at him," nurse Ellen clucked. "How long have you been together? Is he going to propose soon, you think?"

"Um ... not very long ..." she supplied, mentally crossing her fingers at the lie.

"Well, I'm sure it'll be soon! You know, he only has eyes for you, even with all the pretty nurses flirting with him for the past two nights. I know a man head over heels and that boy's over the moon for you!"

Cady flushed at the thought. She wished ... she pushed away those thoughts and decided she'd should just be glad she was going home.

"Oh, speaking of which," the older lady nodded towards the door.

Nick walked in, dressed more casually today in a black, long-sleeved shirt that molded to his toned upper body, dark jeans, and light fall coat slung over one arm.

"I'll go get the wheelchair," nurse Ellen winked at her and left, but not before giving an appreciative glance at Nick's behind.

"What are you doing here?" she asked. Why did Nick hover over her for hours and then just disappear? She suddenly felt irritated at the hot and cold treatment from Nick Vrost.

"I'm taking you home," he stated.

"You don't have to," Cady sighed. "You know you could have asked Miller or someone on your team to fetch me."

"Grant wanted to be here." Nick picked up her overnight bag. "But he got caught up in a meeting, so I volunteered to come and take you back to The Enclave."

"Fine, if you want to waste your time this way." She pouted.

Nick tsked and shook his head. "So testy today."

"What?" she shot back at him.

"Oh nothing."

The awkward silence was finally broken when nurse Ellen came in with a wheelchair and her discharge papers. She helped Cady into the chair, and then pushed her out of the room, Nick following behind them.

With one last wave goodbye to nurse Ellen and a promise she'd come by for a visit, Cady settled into the front seat of Nick's Mercedes as they drove towards the Upper West Side

———

"You don't really have to do this," Cady said as Nick opened the door to her apartment.

"You keep saying that, yet here I am," he replied in a teasing tone. Cady could be quite stubborn, he realized, but knew it was partly her independent streak. He'd been injured once in his life, and he remembered hating it, having people hover over him. "Just go and settle down on the couch," he ordered and brought her bag inside.

Nick realized this was the first time he'd seen her apartment. He wasn't sure why, but the feel of it was exactly what he'd imagined - warm, lived-in, and welcoming. Most of her furniture was off-white with splashes of color from pillows, rugs, and throws. Personal items, such as photos of her father and herself, as well as trinkets from trips all over the world were displayed carefully and thoughtfully all over the place. It was quite a contrast to his own place a few floors up, decorated in a sleek, dark, modern style with an almost impersonal feel.

He set the bag down beside the couch and watched as Cady fidgeted on the plush cushions. "What's wrong now?"

Cady sighed. "I just ... I don't know what to do!"

"Do you do anything else but work?" he asked.

"Do you?" she retorted.

"Touché." He grinned at her. He looked around and found the remote for her flat screen TV, then sat down on the couch beside her. "What do you want to watch?"

She wrinkled her brow. "How about some football?"

"American or European?"

"What do you think?" She crossed her arms.

He settled on the couch and switched the TV on, tuning it to one of the European sports channels. They watched in silence, Cady finally settling in on the other end of the couch as far away from Nick as possible.

After half an hour, Cady was starting to fidget again. She stood up, but began to sway back and forth. She gave an unladylike yelp and prepared herself for a fall, but Nick's lightning fast reflexes kicked in and caught her just in time. His arms came around her as her body fell onto his.

"What do you think you're doing?" he whispered into her ear.

"I was going to get a glass of water from the kitchen," she replied in an annoyed voice. "I just felt a little dizzy. Stood up too fast."

He pulled her down on the couch on top of him. "You could have asked me."

"You're not my nurse," she retorted as they lay practically nose to nose. "And you can let go of me now."

Nick remained still, and he realized how much he enjoyed the feeling of Cady in his arms and on top of him. His lips were inches away from hers, and she was so soft and lovely, her slight weight and breasts pressed up against his chest made desire surge through him. He didn't want to let her go, but rather hold on to her tighter, roll her underneath him and pin her body down on the couch with his. Her sweet scent tickled his senses, and when he realized that his cock was straining against his pants, he reluctantly let her go in case she realized how much he wanted her. She quickly scrambled off of him, and he watched as she darted off to the kitchen. Nick mentally slapped himself on the forehead. *What the hell am I doing?*

Cady was his weakness, always had been since they first met. He remembered that exact moment, a year after he became Beta and Grant had asked him to pick up his "little sister" at the airport. He thought she'd be a spoiled, rich girl who was sent away to Europe to spend her days shopping and wrapping handsome Frenchmen around her little finger so they would do her bidding.

But Cady was the opposite - fresh, vibrant, and so warm and open. Sure, there was a misunderstanding, and she was annoyed when she met him and not Grant, but she charmed everyone she met, from the driver who carried her bags to the receptionist at Fenrir. She didn't need to wrap people around her finger - they naturally gravitated toward her. Now, as Human Liaison and Grant's right hand, she possessed more power than anyone else in the company, yet she used her charm and sharp intelligence to get people to do what needed to be done. The irony was, Nick thought, had she been Lycan, she would have made a great mate. He stayed away from her all these years, knowing it was too easy to fall under her spell.

When Cady came back from the kitchen with a glass of water, Nick settled back to his corner of the couch. She sulked back into her end and then pulled one of her throws over her legs.

"Nice game, huh?" he asked when the football game ended. He looked over to her side, and the only answer to his question was a soft snore. Cady had fallen asleep, her arm over the sofa. He pulled her down so she lay on the couch and put the blanket over her shoulders. She looked like she was fresh out of school again, not that she hadn't aged well. Cady was more beautiful now than before, more mature and sure of herself. *Stop.* He would not let his thoughts lead him that way. There were things that needed to be done, for him to get on with his life and ensure his legacy. Going down this path would only lead to heartbreak and disappointment. Now that she was safe, he could go back to the way things were and ignore Cady's irresistible pull.

After a few more minutes of watching her sleep, he stood up and left her apartment.

CHAPTER EIGHT

S he unbuckled her seat belt and grabbed the door handle to let herself out.

"Ms. Gray ..." Nick called, his voice low and hoarse.

Cady froze, her fingers remaining still. She turned her head. "What is it?" she asked in an impatient voice.

Ice blue eyes stared back at her, luminous in the darkness. *Wait, didn't this happen already?* Cady thought. Alynna taking her to Blood Moon. Making out with that other guy. Nick Vrost suddenly appearing at the Lycan club.

Nick grabbed her arm and hauled her to him, pulling her from the passenger side seat and onto his lap. Somehow, Nick had reclined his seat and was almost horizontal, while she found herself straddling him, her skirt hiked over her thighs. She could feel his cock pressing up against her, his pants and her silky underwear the only thing between them.

"This is what I've been wanting to do," he whispered into her ear. "You drive me crazy. And seeing you with anyone else makes me insane." He shuddered as she pressed her hips down, grinding herself down on his erection.

"Nick," she moaned. "It's only you I want. It's always been you."

He growled, a deep and guttural sound coming from deep in his chest. "And what do you want?"

"You. I want you. To fuck me hard. Now. In your car. Anywhere," she confessed.

The Lycan let out a low, throaty sound and pulled her down for a kiss. His tongue snaked along the seam of her lips, coaxing her to open up to him. She gasped when his tongue sought out hers, devouring her as if he couldn't get enough.

Nick began to unbutton her blouse, but he suddenly became impatient and grabbed the fabric, ripping it open and sending buttons flying everywhere. He pulled away from the kiss, and she watched his eyes grow dark with desire as he pulled down her white lace bra, exposing her breasts to his view.

"Gorgeous," he growled as he cupped both of her breasts in his hands. She sucked in her breath when he took one of her nipples into his mouth, his tongue teasing the hard bud.

"Nick ..." Cady trailed off. She shoved her fingers into his dark blonde hair, gripping the soft strands between her fingers. Pushing down on him, she continued to grind down on his cock, her panties already soaked. She spread her legs further, finding the right angle so her clit rubbed deliciously against his hard-on, which only made him suck on her nipples harder. She continued to grind against him as his tongue lashed her skin, the sensation pushing her over the edge.

"That's it, sweetheart," he urged as he lay back, his eyes devouring her. "Keep going. I wanna watch you come and fall apart ..." He pushed his erection up against her, seeking out the delicious friction, his hands slipping behind her, cupping the round globes of her ass as he helped her set the pace.

"Nick!" she cried out as her body shuddered with orgasm. She grabbed his shoulders and pushed down harder, her panties soaking with her juices as pleasure ripped through her.

"God, Cady." Nick gripped her arms and pulled her to him. "I want to be inside you. Fuck you for real. Not just in a dream."

"Hmmmm?" *What was Nick saying?* "What do you mean not just in a dream?"

Cady felt the dream slipping away slowly. Nick's yummy scent faded away from her senses, his hard, warm body transforming into cool sheets and pillow. She groaned aloud, keeping her eyes closed. The dream seemed more vivid this time, and if she wasn't mistaken, she definitely had an orgasm. Her pussy was slick with her juices, and her lower body felt relaxed but tired. Even her leg and thigh muscles felt fatigued, as if she'd been running. Or, apparently, straddling Nick Vrost in the driver's seat of his car.

"Ughh!" she moaned aloud. The pleasure seemed to act as a pain reliever, but as the pleasure from the orgasm ebbed away, her body began to physically ache due to her injuries. Slowly, she sat up, reaching for a pain pill and some water and tried to go back to sleep.

———

"Welcome back, Ms. Gray," Suzanne greeted as Cady stepped out of the elevator. She tried to take Cady's purse and briefcase, but was waved her away.

"That's not necessary, I'm fine," she snapped before heading into her office. In a split second, she regretted being so cross at her assistant, who was only trying to help, but Cady had had enough. After a week of being trapped in her apartment, she was going stir crazy. She begged and pleaded and cajoled Dr. Faulkner and Grant to let her do something – anything – so they agreed she could come to the office that Monday from three p.m. to six p.m. and only to read her emails and catch up with light paperwork. Yes, she was irritable and short tempered because she was bored. And not because a certain Lycan had not shown up once to check on her, again, swinging toward cold in his treatment of her.

What do you want from him, Cady? That was the question. Nick Vrost was so unreadable and bewildering. She thought they had a moment, and he was warm and caring the whole time she was in the hospital. And the way he held her in his arms when she fell, she thought her heart would burst straight out of her chest. She wanted to stay there and feel safe forever. Then he just up and disappeared with no warning. Again. *Damn him.* It didn't help that she'd been having more vivid dreams about him. *Oh god.* Thinking about them made her body temperature rise by a few degrees.

"Everything okay, Cady?" The door opened and Grant's head popped in.

"Yes, I'm fine." She put her hands over her face, trying to hide her blush. "Just ... I'm not in a good mood this afternoon."

Grant walked in and sat in the chair in front of her desk. "Are you sure you're ready to come back?"

"Yes, *Mom*, don't worry." She opened up her computer and clicked on her email program. "I promise I'll follow your orders. Sheesh, now I know what Alynna means when you mother hen her."

The Alpha made a sheepish face. "Speaking of which –"

"Cady Horace Grant!" A stern, angry voice burst through the office as the door flew open. "How could you?!" Alynna Chase-Westbrooke stormed into her office, green eyes blazing, and planted herself in front of the redhead.

"That's not my middle name!" Cady retorted.

Alex Westbrooke followed closed behind. While he seemed apologetic for the way his wife barged in, he was just as incensed at not being notified. "You were in an accident and you didn't *think* to tell us right away?"

"I was fine. Am fine," she sighed and turned to Alynna. "But not if you don't lower your voice. It's giving me a headache."

The younger woman jabbed a finger at her half-brother's chest accusingly. "*E, tu Brut?!* You should have told us!"

Grant put his hands up. "Don't look at me! Cady refused to have us call you."

"You were on your honeymoon," Cady reminded them. "How was it, by the way?" She gave both of them a knowing look. "You both sure look pale despite being on a secret tropical island for three weeks."

Alynna opened her mouth to speak, but quickly shut it, the smug look on Alex's face betrayed whatever excuse she was going to give. "We made it to the beach on the first day," he supplied, his amber eyes looking over his wife with intent.

"Ugh, I *do not* need to hear this," Grant groaned and he stood up. "I'll be in my office. Cady." He gave her a stern look before he left. "Doctor's orders, remember? I'll ride back home with you to make sure you follow them."

Cady let out an exasperated tone once he left. "I swear, I'm fine! Just getting tired of being home all the time."

"Cady," Alynna's voice softened. "I was worried when I heard. And furious that we weren't told the moment it happened. You're our friend. Our family." Cady felt a lump in her throat at Alynna's thoughtful words.

"Both of us were, Cades." Alex crossed his arms over his chest. "You can't do this again."

"Believe me, I'm not planning to get into another car accident." The couple shot her twin warning looks, and she shrugged. "Fine, fine. Next time I stub my toe, should I call you, too?"

"You know, when I first met you, I thought you were so pleasant," Alynna quipped. "Little did I know you're such a sour puss when you can't push people to do what you want. I bet you wanted to read your email the moment you came out of your coma!"

"I was not in a coma! They shot me full of drugs! Ugh, never mind." The redhead rubbed her forehead, muttering softly about stubborn Lycans. "All right, tell me about the honeymoon. I mean, the rated G-rated parts, okay? How was the villa? Did you like it?"

Alynna sat down on the chair Grant had vacated. "Oh, Cady, it was wonderful! We had a butler and staff who cooked us anything we wanted, day or night! And then ..."

———

Alex and Alynna stayed for an hour before they left to go settle into their new office. Alex had decided to leave Grant's security team and work full-time with Alynna, helping with Lycan affairs. Cady went through her emails, which were, thankfully, reduced to only about one hundred important ones, thanks to Suzanne. She went through about a quarter of them when the clock on her computer indicated it was five minutes to six p.m. Not wanting to get more grief from her boss, she shut down her computer and grabbed her things, thanking Suzanne as she left.

As she stepped out into the lobby, she suddenly froze when she sighted the tall figure next to Grant. Next to them was a much older man, one she'd never seen before but was somehow familiar. Cady looked around, unsure if she should try to look inconspicuous or run away or back into the elevator, but it was too late. A pair of cool blue eyes zeroed in on her.

Damn. Nick and his companion were also standing by the doors leading outside, which didn't really leave her much of a choice. She squared her shoulders and walked toward the group.

"Ah, here she is! Cady," Grant greeted her. "Have you met Mr. Vasili Vrost? Nick's grandfather? Vasili, this is Cady Gray, my Human Liaison."

"Good evening. How are you, Mr. Vrost?" she greeted cordially. No wonder he looked familiar. He and Nick shared some of the same features, though Vasili's hair was pure white instead of dark blonde.

Vasili gave her a nod. "Lovely to meet you. A female Liaison?" He looked at Grant questioningly, and Cady had to squash down her anger at the slight.

"I assure you, Grandfather," Nick interjected, "Ms. Gray is very good at what she does."

"Cady is well deserving of her post," Grant supplied, his voice even but commanding. He was still Alpha after all.

Vasili gave Grant a small bow of his head. "Of course, Primul. I'm sure you're very ... talented, Ms. Gray." He turned to Nick. "Are you ready?"

"Yes, Grandfather. Primul, Ms. Gray." He looked at them coolly. "If you'll excuse us, we must be on our way."

"Please, don't let us hold you up." Grant nodded. "I'll see tomorrow."

Nick gave Grant a slight bow. Cady gave them a curt nod, refusing to meet Nick in the eye.

"Sorry about that Cady." Grant gave her shoulder a reassuring squeeze. "Vasili is very old fashioned."

"I can see that," she said wryly. "Meh. I'm used to Lycan men talking over me." Still, coming from Nick's grandfather, it stung a little more than it normally did.

"Let's go home, okay? Maybe pick up some dinner?"

"I'm not really hungry. Can you just take me home?" Cady pleaded.

"All right, let's go."

———

Nick waited until they were out of Grant and Cady's earshot before turning to Vasili. "Grandfather," his voice remained respectful, but stern. "You practically insulted the Alpha's Liaison. The Grays are the most important Alliance family in New York. They've been with the Lycans for generations." He loved his grandfather, but he could be trying at times.

"Bah," Vasili brayed. "Yes, Luther Gray was an excellent Liaison. But, a woman Liaison? In my day, the men were in charge of business."

"Welcome to the 21st century then," Nick sounded exasperated. "Besides, she's capable and efficient and just as good as any man."

"And I'm sure she's good for more, too," he

leered. "Perhaps that's why the Alpha keeps her around."

Nick was pretty sure if Vasili wasn't related to him, he would have punched him right then and there. Instead, he kept his hands in tight fists, his fingernails digging into the skin of his palm. "Grandfather," he warned.

Vasili snorted. "Maybe he's not sleeping with her, but you must be blind if you can't appreciate that gorgeous face and body ... and that fiery hair! If I was twenty years younger ..." Vasili trailed off. "Don't tell me you've never thought of bedding that exquisite creature?"

"She's a colleague," Nick replied coldly.

"Well, it's too late now," Vasili reminded him. "Or you can do it later, after you father your pup."

Nick groaned inwardly. "Let's just get this over with. Who did you want me to meet again?"

CHAPTER NINE

Cady decided she needed another day to recover, which Grant was only happy to give her. She came back in on Wednesday afternoon, and since she'd been following Dr. Faulkner's orders, she was allowed a new phone and tablet so she could continue her work. By six p.m, she had actually gone through all the important emails from the time she was away and she shut down her computer.

"Goodnight, Suzanne. Thank you again for your help." She nodded to her assistant. She once again took the elevator down to the lobby, but she'd be leaving alone tonight. Grant had a late dinner meeting, and though it took a lot of arguing, she convinced him to let her take a cab since they were already short one car and one driver.

Cady didn't think she'd run into Nick again, but it was like déjà vu from last Monday. The Beta was once again standing in lobby of the Fenrir Building, but instead of his grandfather, he was talking to a woman. Not human, but Lycan. Cady seemed to have a sixth sense for telling, even from far away. The female Lycan was tall, lithe, with long brown hair that fell down her back. She was wearing a smart black suit that clung to her slim form which matched her designer bag and shoes. The woman threw her head back as she laughed at something Nick said, touching him on the arm lightly. *Damn it, did Nick have nothing better to do these days than hang around Fenrir's lobby?* There was no way she could sneak around them, so she just had to walk past them. Maybe Nick would ignore her or not see her at all.

Picking up her pace, she breezed across the lobby, and she almost made it without catching either Lycan's attention. Unfortunately, the woman chose that moment to step back, bumping right into Cady. "Excuse me, coming through," she said in a slightly annoyed tone.

"Oh, sorry. I didn't see you," the female Lycan apologized.

"Cady," Nick looked surprised to see her. "You're here."

"Yes I am," she huffed. "I do work here after all."

"I mean, I thought you'd be resting at home."

"I'm perfectly fine." *Even without your help,* she added silently.

There was an awkward beat before Nick spoke. "Um, this is Madison Crawford. Madison, Cady Gray."

The tall brunette offered her hand to Cady and smiled warmly. "Nice to meet you, Cady."

Cady thought she was even more beautiful up close, with light hazel eyes, long lashes, and sensuous lips. "Nice to meet you too, Madison. You're Senator Xavier Crawford's daughter, correct? I remember you from the Fenrir Foundation Gala last year."

"Oh yes, of course." Madison touched Cady's arm lightly, brushing away a lock of her hair, and leaned closer to her. "I remember! You're the Alpha's Liaison. You were wearing that gorgeous violet Vera Wang ball gown. I thought you looked divine."

Cady gave her a tight smile. "Thank you. How is the senator?"

"He's doing well, thanks for asking." She turned

to Nick. "Shall we head out? Our dinner reservation is at seven p.m."

"We have a few minutes," Nick stated. "Cady, are you headed back to The Enclave?"

"No," she lied. "I'm actually headed to Blood Moon. Meeting a friend of mine there. Haven't seem him in a while, we're going to ... catch up."

Nick visibly tensed. "Well, you have a good night, then," he said coolly. "Let's go, Madison."

The two Lycans headed out the door, though Madison turned around and waved goodbye to Cady.

The redhead let out a breath as soon as they were out of view, but she suddenly felt out of breath. A vice gripped her chest, and she had to brace herself against the glass doors as her knees threatened to buckle. Cady closed her eyes, opened her mouth, and forced the air into her lungs. *What the hell was that?* The physical reaction when she saw Nick with another woman was unnerving. *And why did I lie?* There was almost a perverse pleasure in watching Nick become uncomfortable when she told him she was going to Blood Moon, implying she'd be meeting a male companion, maybe even that guy she had met there weeks ago. But it wasn't like they were ... what? Nick Vrost was free to date whomever he wanted, after all. She almost wished

Madison Crawford was an awful, spoiled bitch rather than a perfectly pleasant young woman. Then it would've been easier to hate her.

"Ms. Gray!" the receptionist rushed toward her. "Are you all right? Do I need to call Dr. Faulkner?"

"No!" she said quickly. "I'm fine. I just tripped. Um, could you call me a taxi please?"

"Certainly." The young woman walked back to her station and picked up the phone.

Cady sighed with relief. She needed to go somewhere - anywhere. Certainly not Blood Moon. She knew where she wanted to go, a place where she could find peace and calm and nothing to do with Lycans.

———

"And then, after I graduated, I went to Ecuador to volunteer at an orphanage," Madison said and took a bite of her salad.

"That's nice," Nick replied absentmindedly, taking a sip of his wine.

"Then aliens kidnapped me and put me on their spaceship."

"I'm sure it was a lovely vacation." Nick looked at his watch.

"It was. I highly recommend outer space."

Nick's head snapped up. "Sorry?"

Madison started to laugh, a full-bellied sound that rang through the restaurant. Nick looked confused, which only made the younger woman laugh harder. When she started to choke, she grabbed her glass of water, taking a sip to help clear her throat.

"I'm fine, I'm fine," Madison coughed. She finally stopped, took a deep breath and dabbed her lips with her napkin. "Oh, I wish you could see your face."

Nick frowned. Madison Crawford was exactly what Vasili wanted – a Lycan from a prominent family, educated, beautiful, and of the perfect age to bear children. She was on the top of his list, and it seemed the old man had already conspired her with father even before Nick called her. He and Madison had met several times before at various functions, and he thought she was pleasant enough, certainly smart and charming. By all accounts, she would make the perfect Lycan wife.

"I think this was a terrible idea."

"I couldn't agree more." He took his wine glass and downed the rest of it. "I apologize, Madison. For this. And for pushy old men. And for not giving you the attention you deserve."

She sighed. "I'm sorry, too. I was flattered when you called me, but I should have known my father was behind this." She frowned. "He's been after me to find a nice Lycan boyfriend. I keep telling him I'm just not interested."

"In boyfriends?"

"In boys."

"Oh." It wasn't unusual, of course. Lycans had the same urges and preferences as humans. But because of the difficulty of producing pups among their kind, homosexuality was usually frowned upon, a loss to their race. Seems like although Madison made her preferences clear, her father wasn't having any of it.

"Actually," she took another sip of her water, "I was going to ask you if Cady Gray was seeing anyone. I've always thought she was gorgeous. But I think I have my answer," she said, her eyes twinkling.

"Well, she's meeting a friend tonight," Nick said glumly. The thought of Cady and that guy made his blood boil. How long had they been seeing each other? Where was he when Cady had gotten hurt?

"You should go to her," Madison seemed to read his mind. "If you wait too long, you might have to fight *me* off!"

"I don't –" Nick stopped as his phone rang. There was only one number that would trigger his phone to ring even on silent mode. "Sorry," he apologized as he fished his phone out of his pocket. "Alpha, what is it?" Nick answered.

"Nick," Grant's voice was grave. "There's been an incident. At Blood Moon."

Nick froze. *Cady.* "I'm on my way."

———

Nick apologized to Madison, saying there was an urgent matter he had to attend to. Madison understood, of course, and offered her help. He declined and saw her off as she took a cab home. He felt relief as soon as Madison's cab zoomed away, not just because he was off the hook, but now he could get to Blood Moon and Cady as soon as possible.

He probably wouldn't escape the night without at least one speeding ticket, but he didn't care. He drove like madman to Blood Moon, parking in the empty spot in front of the entrance to the club. He opened the heavy black doors and was surprised to see all the lights on and the floor devoid of dancers. In fact, the club was practically empty, except for a couple of Lycans lying down on the floor and around the couches, being attended to by various medical staff from The Enclave. He recognized a lot of them, including Tate Miller. He searched around, trying to spot any sign of Cady. When he didn't see her, he strode toward the bar where Grant, Alynna, Alex, and Dr. Faulkner were talking quietly.

"Where's Cady?" he asked in a tight voice. "She said she would be here."

Alynna shook her head. "I don't know. Actually, I haven't seen her at all. Why would she be here? She's still recovering."

Nick looked relieved. Cady never went to Blood Moon. Maybe she decided to go home, which meant she wasn't hurt. *Or she's with that guy,* a voice inside him said. He quashed those thoughts and turned to Grant. "What happened?"

The Alpha shook his head and rubbed the bridge of his nose. "Belladonna poisoning. We've got several Lycans down. A couple of humans too, but it's not lethal to them though they'll probably think they have food poisoning."

"Good thing we had belladonna antidote stocked up," Dr. Faulkner supplied. "My staff administered it to everyone who was poisoned. There are one or two who had particularly large doses, and they've already been transported to the infirmary."

Alynna looked thoughtful. "This can't be a coincidence. The attacks on me. This mass poisoning. Maybe even Cady's accident."

"Al Doilea," Alex addressed Nick by his honorific Beta title. "Two Lycans from the security team were poisoned. Tate Miller and John Patrick. And another one of the trainees."

Nick's eyes narrowed. "Were they targeted? Because they're part of my team?"

"Possibly," Alex paused. "Maybe a bid to weaken our security?"

"Someone's out to get us. All of us." Grant's jaw set in a hard line.

"We'll find out who it is," Alex gritted his teeth.

"Oh yes, we will," Nick vowed. Someone was trying to harm his clan, his family. He was going to find them and stop them.

CHAPTER TEN

"What did you find out?" Stefan looked towards Daric.

"Several of them were seriously injured, Master," the taller man replied. "We don't have any reports of fatalities though, but we definitely crippled their security force making them more vulnerable."

"Good." Stefan's lips curled into a smile. He turned to the other figure next to Daric. "Excellent work." Stefan placed a hand on Victoria's head as she bowed down before him.

"Thank you, Master." Victoria smiled. "I live to serve you. And it wasn't that difficult." She ran a finger over the empty glass bottle in her pocket.

"Those stupid creatures. A little charm spell here and there was all it took. They're none the wiser."

"At least not to *your* presence?"

"Of course," the witch said smugly. "But they'll piece everything together. At least, the way we want them to."

"And the security footage? You're sure they'll see her?"

"Yes, my glamour spell should work well enough on the cameras." Victoria tossed her hair over her shoulder. "Besides, Cady and I look enough like each other that it shouldn't be too obvious."

"Perfect," Stefan boomed. "We'll soon turn the Lycans against your daughter."

"And bring her into the fold," Victoria finished.

Stefan turned to Daric. "And as soon as you finish your part, you'll be on your way to becoming who you were meant to be. To fulfill your destiny."

"Yes, Master." Daric bowed his head.

———

"Ms. Gray, line two for you," Suzanne's voice crackled through the intercom.

"Give me a minute, okay Suzanne?" Cady sounded frazzled.

"Yes, Ms. Gray."

The redhead huffed, blowing a strand of stray hair away from her face. She was in full crisis mode, and despite the protests from her overly protective Lycan friends, she insisted on going back to work. Cady was having breakfast at home the next day when she received news. Grant had come by and told her. She was furious he didn't call her the moment it happened, but he reasoned it was already handled and she needed her rest.

Cady immediately went to work. There was much to be done, but for now she was working with Alynna and Alex to find out how the poison had spread and how to track down any humans who might have been affected.

Of course, she also had other things on her mind. Her blood ran cold when Grant told her the exact poison. Belladonna, a favorite poison and drug among witches. Also the same poison that was given to Alynna at her coming out ball. It was a good thing Alynna was already pregnant at the time she was poisoned and carrying a True Mate child; it gave her super invulnerability. Was her mother's coven behind all of this? It couldn't have been a coincidence. Victoria's warning rang through her head. It seemed her mother really would do anything, even kill Lycans, to get her back. But what was Victoria's end game? Threaten to kill Grant?

Alynna? Nick? She bit her lip, contemplating telling Grant. *No.* She couldn't bear what it would mean. She'd just have to stop Victoria herself somehow.

"Ms. Gray, line two," Suzanne reminded her.

"Right." She picked up the phone. "Cady Gray."

"Hi Cady, this is Claire Fenton, the director for Arch Manor Women's Shelter in Albany. I've been trying to reach you for days, but your assistant said you were unavailable."

"Hello, Claire," she greeted. Cady had never met the woman, but they'd exchanged a lot of phone calls and emails. "Yes, I'm sorry. I had a medical emergency." She gave the standard reason she'd been telling everyone.

"Oh no! I'm so sorry! Are you all right?"

"Yeah, a minor injury," she explained. "What can I do for you?"

"Well, I just wanted to remind you that you and Mr. Anderson are set to attend our annual meeting next week up here in Albany. We still have you on our program to receive one of our awards for helping us raise all that money. We'll be naming the new halfway house after Fenrir, of course."

Cady cursed in her head. "Oh, yes ..."

"If you can't make it because of your injury ..." Claire began.

"Oh no, no of course not!" Arch Manor was actually her pet project, a cause she had brought up to Grant which he happily offered to fund through the Fenrir Foundation. They made Grant and herself board members because of their contributions. "I'll be there, of course." She felt a headache coming on. "Can you send me the details, please? Yes, to Suzanne. Thanks Claire!"

The phone clicked off as she hung up. Cady sighed. *One more thing to add to my plate*

———

Cady was swamped with work, so she actually didn't get to telling Grant about the event until the following Monday.

"Cady, what is it?" Grant asked as soon as he picked up the phone.

"Grant," she began. "I wanted to remind you about the Arch Manor event this Friday. We're still on for that, right?"

His brow wrinkled. "Isn't that next week?"

"No, it's this Friday. Did you forget?" she asked. "They're giving us an award."

"As I recall," Grant began. "The award is for you. And you deserve it, considering all the work you put in."

"Well, it's for me and Fenrir," she said. "But you did put up the money."

Grant sighed. "Can't we cancel? Or send our regards?"

"Grant," Cady warned. "Look, I forgot about it too, with everything going on. But we can't *not* go. They're also naming one of their houses after Fenrir."

"Why don't you go?" Grant suggested. "I mean, you did all the work. I don't have to be there, right? It's just way too busy and you know the security situation will be a nightmare."

Cady paused. "I suppose I could drive up."

"Not alone, though," he said. "I'll have one our guys drive you up."

"Can you really spare them? I can always rent a car."

"Don't be silly. I'm not letting you go alone, not with what's going on. I'll take care of it okay?"

"Fine," she sighed. "Just tell them to be ready to leave by noon on Friday."

Grant put the phone down, shaking his head.

"What's wrong?" Nick asked as he entered the Alpha's office.

"Sit down." Grant motioned to the chair in front of him. "Who on your team is free to go on a trip this Friday?"

Nick took out his phone and scrolled through the screen. "Well, as it stands ... nobody."

"Absolutely no one?" Grant asked incredulously.

"Well, you know what this week is, right?" Nick answered. "It's Blood Moon on Saturday, in case you forgot."

"Oh fuck me, that's right." Grant slapped his forehead. Blood Moon was the one night Lycans could not control their shift nor what happened while they were in wolf form. All Lycans all over the world were required to go into special safe houses and safe rooms, ones built to withstand their strength. "Right. I'll have to tell Cady there's no way we can have her go up to Albany without a security detail."

"Wait," Nick said. "Cady is going to Albany?"

"We were supposed to go to this event for this women's shelter Fenrir is supporting. It was her pet project, and they're going to give her an award for her work," Grant explained.

"Well, I could go," Nick volunteered.

"That's not necessary," Grant said. "Cady'll be disappointed, but she'll understand. You don't have to go."

"It's not a big deal," the blonde Lycan shrugged. "Albany's what, four hours away? We could drive up on Friday and be back Saturday before noon if we leave early. Or take the jet back in case something happens."

"Hmm ..." Grant scratched his chin. "I suppose that could work. I'll have Jared compile a list of the nearest safe houses just in case."

"Well, it shouldn't have to come to that, but it'll be good to be prepared."

CHAPTER ELEVEN

"Is the temperature okay? Are you comfortable?" Nick asked. He kept his eyes on the road, but glanced over at the redhead in the front passenger seat.

"I'm fine," she replied. "I could have driven myself, you know."

"With your injuries?" Nick retorted. "I don't think so."

Cady grumbled and sank bank in her seat. *Damn you, Grant,* she cursed the Alpha silently. She knew they were spread thin, so she thought he might send a junior driver or trainee. To her surprise, on Friday at noon, Nick Vrost was waiting for her outside The Enclave, his black Mercedes fueled up and ready to go.

She had a mind to cancel right then and there, but she couldn't do that to Claire and Arch Manor. It was about a four hour trip with stops, plus it would only be overnight. The plan was to drive up on Friday, accept the award that evening, and be on their way back by Saturday. Surely, she could stand to be in his company for a little over twenty-four hours.

"I have to stop for gas." Nick slowed the car down and maneuvered it into the rest stop. They were about halfway there. Cady said nothing as he left the car to pay.

After a few minutes, Nick slipped into the driver's seat. When he turned on the engine, the radio began blasting.

"*And in other news, some weather stations are reporting we might actually see some snow this weekend!*" the male anchor on the radio news program announced.

"*Wow, James. This early?*" the female replied.

"*Uh-huh. No one knows yet —*"

Nick turned the volume down from the controls on his steering wheel. "Sorry. Too loud?"

Cady massaged her temple with her fingers. "It's fine. I'm fine."

"Usually when a woman says 'fine' it means trouble for the man," he quipped.

She shrugged and leaned her head against the cool window.

There was more uncomfortable silence that followed, which suited Cady just fine. It was already driving her slightly mad sitting next to him, his spicy fir-scented aftershave filling her nostrils. Nick also took off his jacket and rolled up his sleeves for the long drive, exposing his forearms. The muscles underneath shifted and flexed as he drove the car expertly, and she couldn't help glance over once in a while. It was distractingly sexy. She just hoped the next twenty-four hours would pass quickly.

Finally, Nick cleared his throat. "You've never met my grandfather before, have you?"

"No, I haven't," she said curtly.

"He's ... very traditional," Nick began. "My grandmother was definitely more forward-thinking, and she knew how to best manage him."

There was a warmth and softness in his voice that made Cady's frozen resolve melt a little bit. "How long has it been since she died?"

"About twelve years."

"I'm sorry." She truly meant it.

"It was hard on him. They'd been together for more than fifty years," Nick explained. "And in the last couple of years, he's been thinking a lot about family and legacy."

"That's normal." Cady shifted in her seat to face him. "She ... they both raised you."

He nodded. "Yes, after my parents were killed."

"Was it an accident?" Curiosity got the better of her.

"No, they were murdered."

She let out a soft cry and covered her mouth. "Oh my lord. I'm sorry, Nick." Not knowing what else to do, she put a hand on his arm. "Did they find out who it was?"

"Yes, they did. Three rogue witches chased them down while they were on vacation. I was left at home with my grandparents."

Cady's blood froze in her veins. Witches. *Nick's parents were killed by witches.* The words rang in her head over and over again, blocking out everything else.

"... And so I lived with my grandmother and grandfather."

"Um, what happened to the witches?" Did she really want to know?

"The Lycan High Council wanted justice, of course," he said. "But they weren't going to risk war, so they let the Witch Assembly deal with them. They were executed. My grandfather was there, and Michael Anderson was one of the witnesses."

Cady's vision swam in front of her, imagining

what type of execution they used. "I'm so sorry. I'm glad you got justice." Why was Nick telling her this?

"I was very young. I don't remember them." His voice was even, but had an edge. "My grandparents raised me, and I owe them ... everything."

"Of course." She nodded.

"That's why ..." he hesitated. "Well, my grandfather's getting older. He's been clamoring for me to settle down."

"Ah, I see." A strange pain ached in her chest at the thought of Nick settled down and married. "That's probably normal, right?"

"He's gotten more insistent. He gave me an ultimatum a few weeks ago. Find a mate and have a pup or else he'll give away his fortune and the only home I ever knew."

Cady's jaw dropped. "He can't do that, can he?"

Nick nodded. "Of course he can. He owns everything, from the businesses to the Hudson house. I'm not strapped for cash, my parents made sure, but since he never passed it on to my father, the house is his to give away."

She didn't know what to say, so many thoughts processing through her mind. Witches. His parents. Vasili. And then something clicked. "I'm sure Madison would make a great wife."

He chuckled. "My grandfather thought so, too. Except she's not interested in me."

Cady huffed. *Of course.* "Well, she can keep trying, but no one's tying Grant down anytime soon." She'd seen it a dozens of times in the past decade. All these Lycan women fawning over the Alpha of New York, hoping they'd be selected and become his Lupa, as one who was wife to the leader was called. They all failed, of course.

"Actually, she was interested in *you.*"

"M-me?"

"Yes." He glanced at her. "You made an impression, apparently. She's been meaning to look you up."

Cady blinked at his words. She thought back to that meeting at the lobby, the way Madison leaned toward her, touching her on the arm and hair.

"Should I give her your number?" Nick teased, noting the way Cady's cheeks turned pink.

She turned away, trying to hide her blush. "You're joking."

"Madison is a gorgeous girl. Educated, smart, and funny," he recalled.

Cady rolled her eyes. "I'm flattered, but no. Besides I don't think Senator Crawford would approve of me as an in-law. Do you think he knows?" she asked.

Nick nodded. "Sounded like it, but still expects her to do her duty to the Clan."

Cady felt sad for the lovely Lycan. "I hope he changes his mind and she finds someone."

"Not you then?" he teased again.

She laughed, and the tension around them seemed to ease. "She and I could share clothes and bags, but other than that, I don't see any other benefits!"

————

The rest of the trip passed by in more comfortable silence, though they got by on some small talk. They arrived at the Albany Spa and Resort, where the event was taking place and where they were also checked in for the night. After settling into their individual rooms, Cady freshened up and changed into her outfit, which was a simple dark blue gown and pearl earrings. She didn't want to look ostentatious; after all, this was a charity event to benefit a women's shelter and most of the people in attendance were also CEOs and business owners. Nick dutifully escorted her to the event, dressed in one of his gorgeous tuxes and was as charming as he could be.

Her speech was a smashing success, and many

of the people in the audience came to her to congratulate her on the award. She could have sworn Nick beamed at her with pride, though she was too busy chatting with other guests and encouraging them to donate more for the next fiscal year to focus her attention on him.

There was some dancing and music afterward, and though she danced with a couple of CEOs and fended off some advances, which she was used to, she never got a chance to dance with Nick. For one thing, he never asked, and for another, he seemed busy networking in Grant's stead.

Finally, when she had stayed an acceptable amount of time, she headed up to her room and got ready for bed.

CHAPTER TWELVE

"Good morning, Cady," Nick greeted as she stepped out of her hotel room. It seemed like he had been standing there, waiting for her.

Cady checked her watch. It was eight a.m. on the dot. "Good morning," she greeted back. Before she could protest, Nick grabbed her wheeled bag.

When they reached the lobby, Cady's eyes widened in surprise at the sight of about thirty people at the reception area. People were angry, pleading, and a woman was sitting in one of the chaise lounges, speaking frantically into her cell phone.

"What's happening?" Cady asked.

"Let me find out." Nick placed their bags to the side. "Stay here."

Cady stood in a corner, watching Nick make his way to the reception desk. When he got to the front, he spoke with the ragged-looking receptionist. After a few minutes, he made his way back to her. His face was dour and shoulders tense.

"It's a freak snowstorm."

"What?" Cady finally looked outside since she didn't get a chance this morning as her blackout curtains had been closed. Snowflakes whipped in the air, sticking to the windows, the trees - everything. It was a winter wonderland out there, but it seemed everyone inside the hotel was trapped in hell. "What are they saying?"

"All the main roads are out. No one's driving out of Albany or even flying out today. Airports are closed, too," Nick's voice was edgy and strained.

Shit, Cady cursed. She was stuck in Albany for at least one more night. With Nick Vrost. Squaring her shoulders, she decided to take matters into her own hands and whipped out her best weapon - her phone - and began to dial.

Cady, being efficient and well-connected, exhausted all her connections - a luxury car rental place, a private jet company, even the local Albany government. But no dice. Snow was over six feet in some areas and since no one was expecting this freak storm, the plows weren't prepared. They had only just began clearing the roads but only for emergency services and routes to hospitals. Plus, the snow continued to fall. No one was getting out of Albany, at least not for another few hours.

"Any luck?" Nick's face was pained.

The redhead shook her head. "The best I can do is get us an empty suite here, since they've already begun giving out the rooms to guests who are stuck. It'll be ready in a few hours. It's a one bedroom, but there's a pull-out couch. I can sleep there."

"We'll figure it out later, okay?" Nick took their bags. "Let's eat some breakfast and go get settled in

———

As soon as they entered the suite, Nick went straight to the bathroom inside the lone bedroom, leaving a puzzled Cady in the main room.

His hands were shaking as he turned the tap on. Rolling up his sleeves, he splashed his face with cold water. "Fuck!" he cursed, wanting to punch the mirror. "Motherfucker!" He pounded on the marble sink with his fists. Taking a few deep breaths, he fished his phone out of his pocket. Hopefully Cady was not on the phone with Grant yet.

"Nick," Grant greeted as he answered. "How's the drive? Are you on your way?"

"No." Nick gritted his teeth. "Did you see the news? There's a freak snowstorm. All the roads are snowed in, and so are all the nearby airports."

"Fuck! Nick, you can't possibly be stuck there today of all days!"

"I know." Nick rubbed his temples. "I know. Can you do anything?"

There was a pause. "Hold on. I'll call you back."

It felt like he waited an eternity before his phone rang. "Anything?"

"Sorry, Nick. All runways are closed. There's snow everywhere. I can't even send a chopper over."

"Goddamnit!"

"Nick ..." Grant hesitated. "You need to put Cady on the phone."

"No!" Nick wanted to smash his cell. He knew what Grant would say. "We have a few hours. If we can leave here by three p.m, we'll make it to New York by evening. And if not, well ... there has to be another way. Swear to me, on your father's grave, you won't call her until you find another way!"

There was silence from the other end. For Nick to invoke such a vow meant he was serious. As his friend and as a member of the New York clan, Grant could not deny such a request. "I'll talk to Dr.

Faulkner. But for now, stay away from her, okay?"
the Alpha ordered.

"Yes, Primul," Nick complied and put the phone
down. "Motherfucker!" he cursed again, and this
time, he smashed his fist into the mirror. Blood ran
down his knuckles, but he didn't care. Of all the
times to get stuck in a freak snowstorm with Cady
Gray, it had to be during a Blood Moon.

––––––––

Cady watched Nick retreat into the bedroom when
they entered the suite. *Well, I thought it was going
to be a big fight over who was going to stay on the
couch, but apparently Nick Vrost liked his comforts.*
She shrugged and settled down into the couch, unpacking a few of her things. At least it was a nice
living room, plush and well-appointed. As she
turned on the TV, she tuned in to the local news
channel which, of course, featured only the
snowstorm.

After an hour, Nick hadn't left the bedroom.
Maybe he was tired? She realized she hadn't seen
him last night after the party. Did Nick stay up all
night with some female company? The thought
brought a sharp pain in her gut. *No, can't think
about that.*

Cady had made a decision. From this point on, her relationship with Nick would remain 100% professional. She would not joke with him, tease him, and avoid any contact outside work. It was bad enough witches had killed his parents, but even if she was fully human, it wouldn't have worked out. Nick obviously was determined to keep his legacy, and fantasizing about anything happening between them would only lead to heartbreak. And when he did find his Lycan wife and have his pup, she would smile and give her congratulations, never giving away any hint of any emotion. The lump in her throat grew, but she pushed it down. Yes, she would harden her heart against Nick Vrost and move on with her life.

An hour turned into a few hours, and she clicked off the TV. Her stomach grumbled and she realized she hadn't eaten anything since breakfast. Outside, it had grown dark, though the snow had slowed down to light flurries. Walking to the bedroom, she knocked on the door. "Nick" she called. "I'm going to order some food. Do you want anything?"

"No," came the reply. "I'm not hungry."

His voice sounded shaky. and Cady knew something was wrong. "Nick, what's going on? Are you sick? Should I call a doctor?"

"Don't!" came the anguished cry.

When Cady heard his voice, she began to panic. She grabbed the doorknob, but it was locked. "Nick, open this door now!" She rapped her knuckles hard on the wood.

"Stay away, Cady. For god's sake, leave me alone. And find another room!"

"What in the world is going on? Open this door now or ..." There was some rustling coming from the inside and then she heard silence.

"I'm calling Grant!" she threatened. When he didn't answer, she picked up her cell phone from the coffee table.

"Cady, finally!" Grant sounded frantic. "What did Nick tell you?"

"Nick? Nothing! What's going on?"

There was a short pause. "Oh, fuck. He made me swear an oath I wouldn't call you, so I was hoping you would call me. Cady, tonight's the Blood Moon."

"What?!" Cady's knees buckled, and she sank down onto the couch. Why didn't she remember? Oh lord, her tablet and her phone were destroyed in the car crash; she must have forgotten to update all her apps and alerts when she got her replacement devices. Suzanne wouldn't have warned her as her assistant was unaware of Lycans. Her hands began to shake. In a few hours, there would be a fully-formed wild animal in the room next to hers, one with giant teeth and claws. "Grant, what do we do? The hotel is full of guests and staff right now."

"Jesus. I know, I know," Grant said in a frustrated voice. "Cady, we're about to head into the safe rooms and well, you won't have any contact with any of us. I'm making sure everyone goes in first, and Dr. Faulkner and I will be the last ones in."

"Grant, we have to do something! Nick could go on a rampage ..." Her mouth went dry. She had never seen Nick's wolf form. In fact, she'd only seen Lycans shift a handful of times, but she knew it wouldn't be pretty. They were risking lives and their secret if Nick were to get out or hurt anyone in the hotel. Wooden doors and locks couldn't stop a full-grown wolf.

"What can I do, Grant? Are there any safe houses nearby?" The only thing that could contain a rampaging Lycan were safe houses and safe rooms that were built to withstand their razor sharp teeth and gigantic claws. Otherwise, they would shred through wood, glass, and event drywall.

"We've been working on it all afternoon, Cady. The closest one is at least two hours away, and the roads are blocked there also," Grant explained. "We thought ... well, Nick insisted on driving you and we put all these precautions in place, but we weren't prepared for a snowstorm."

Oh god, Nick drove me because I wanted to go. It's all my fault. "There must be something we can do!" Cady panicked. There was a pause, and Cady knew Grant so well she knew he was holding back. "There is something, isn't there? Tell me now, Grant," she threatened, "or I'll call the police and have Nick locked up in the local jail because metal bars might be the only thing that can hold him. But that would mean exposing the Lycans and you better be prepared to deal with it."

Grant let out a defeated breath. "I'll have Dr. Faulkner explain it to you." There was silence as he passed the phone to the older Lycan.

"Cady," Tom Faulkner's voice was grave.

"Dr. Faulkner, tell me what I need to do," she said in a determined voice.

"Cady, dear ..." Dr. Faulkner hesitated. "You know what happens during the Blood Moon. Nick is going to start to shift soon. He'll probably try to stop it, which will cause him great pain. He might even go mad or ... he could die or attempt to kill himself to protect you, the people around him, and the Clan. He's going to become a full wolf, with no control over his actions. And he might not re-member everything once the Blood Moon is over."

"How do I stop it?" She bit her lip.

"Well, there is one sure way ... you need to give him what he wants. What his wolf instinct wants. Food, drink, and ... allow him to give into his sexual needs."

Her heart slammed into her chest, and she sank back farther into the couch. Dr. Faulkner didn't have to explain any further. "And you're sure that will stop him from shifting?"

"Yes. You might ... and I'm sorry to say this ... you might have to keep him, uh, occupied throughout the night. Until the Blood Moon wanes, which could be a few hours. It was how our ancestors dealt with the Blood Moon, before we had the technology to build safe rooms."

Cady's mouth went dry. "I understand."

"I'm sorry to ask this of you, Cady," Grant said as he came back on the phone. "I'm really, really sorry." He sounded choked up. "If there was another way ..."

"Please Grant, don't ..." She wanted to cry. "I'll ... I'll take care of it, okay? Just go into the safe rooms. I know Alynna will need you now as well. So please ... and don't tell anyone. I mean, I know you won't."

"We'll deal with the aftermath later, okay?" Grant promised. "And, whatever you want, whatever you decide, I'll make it happen. And Nick ...

he's stubborn as hell. He knew about it and refused to have you deal with it. We tried, we really did."

Another stab of hurt went through her. Of course Nick didn't want her. She should have known, but hearing it cemented the realization.

"I know you did. Bye, Grant." She put the phone down. Cady pushed away all other thoughts. Right now she needed to focus, to save the Clan, the innocent people at the hotel, and Nick.

CHAPTER THIRTEEN

Cady walked back to the door, knocking softly this time. "Nick, please open the door."

Nick's head perked up at the sound of her voice, and a growl came from within as his wolf seemed to respond to her. "No. Go away, Cady." He gritted his teeth, his hands curling into fists as pain shot through his body. He discarded his shirt as the temperature seemed to keep rising in his room, and his chest was covered in sweat. Of course it wasn't the room that was getting hotter. Spiking body temps meant the change was about to come.

"I spoke with Grant and Dr. Faulkner. Please let me in."

He could hardly stop himself as he stalked toward the door. It was a big mistake as Cady's caramel apple scent wafted through the cracks. The wolf wanted to rip the doors apart and drag her into the room. "I can do this I can stop it ..."

"You can't; they told me," she sighed. "Even if you could, you might go insane. Or die."

"I'll take that risk. I can't ... I could hurt you." His hands clawed at the thick wooden panels, and it took every ounce of his human self-control to stop from opening the door.

"Nick ... I ... I know you don't want me, and you would rather be with someone else," she choked out. "Please, I'll do anything. Don't think about me, think about someone else. Someone you want to be with."

Something inside Nick snapped at her words, and whether it was the wolf or human part he wasn't sure. But it made him pull the door open violently. "What are you talking about?" He stopped short when he saw her standing in front of him.

Cady had never looked more beautiful, and his cock sprang to attention at the sight of her. Her long red hair hung in loose waves around her shoulders and down her back. She was wearing a silky pale lavender nightgown that showed off her milky skin, her nipples straining against the thin fabric. Indigo eyes looked up at him, her pink lips slightly parted. Barefoot and barely wearing any makeup, she looked even more vulnerable than usual, standing before him, offering herself to him. Her delicious scent wafted into his senses, mixed with fear and arousal. He could barely keep himself in check.

"Grant said you refused ... to have me help you," she whispered, her face turning away from him.

"Yes, but not because ..." He closed his eyes, but the sight of her was etched into his mind, something he would never forget for the rest of his life. "Cady, it's not that I won't. I can't ... I couldn't. You were off-limits. But I've wanted you since the moment I met you."

Nick grabbed her by the shoulders and pulled her into the room with him. Slamming the door behind her, he pushed up against her, pinning her body with his. She gasped, and he bent down and pressed his lips to hers roughly.

Their first kiss was savage, with Nick digging his fingers into her hair and pulling her head back. His lips weren't gentle, but fierce and violent, practically devouring her. It was a decade's worth of pent up desire and hunger pouring out all at once. His tongue sought out hers, tasting her mouth, ravaging her. She moaned when he pressed his hips against her, his erection evident.

"Nick," she cried when he dragged his lips lower. He nuzzled her neck with his mouth, his tongue licking a path down the column of her throat. She placed her hands on his bare chest, his skin almost burning her with heat.

"Cady ... Cady ..." he repeated it like a prayer. When he reached her neckline, he paused. "I need you now. I'm sorry. I can't control it ..."

"Sorry for –" She was interrupted by the ripping of fabric as Nick tore her nightgown down the middle.

———

His face was flush and his expression pained. The muscles under his cheeks seemed to shift, at least that's what she thought she saw. *Oh god, it was starting.*

He cupped her breasts with both hands, squeezing them gently and testing their weight in his palms. Bending down, he sucked on her nipples, tasting and savoring her.

It seemed almost familiar to Cady, the way his tongue and lips licked at her nipples. But the real thing was about a thousand times more amazing, and she could feel her pussy flooding with wetness. She whimpered as he sucked a nipple deeper into his mouth.

"Please, Nick," she begged.

"I need to taste you first," he growled, the sound wild and animalistic.

"Will that ... help?" She felt almost silly for asking. For some reason, she thought it would be quick and fast.

"I have to ... listen to what the wolf wants," he gasped as he knelt in front of her. "And right now he wants a taste." Spreading her legs, he plunged a finger into her wet cunt, the small thatch of red hair already glistening with her juices.

"Nick!" she sobbed as his lips and tongue touched her core. Cady looked down and watched Nick lick her nether lips, his tongue thrusting up into her tightness. He looked up at her, and his eyes seemed to glow in the low light, twin ice blue shards that glittered with desire. She cried out as he touched her core one last time and her body exploded in orgasm, pleasure ripping through her so hard she would have collapsed were she not braced against the door.

Nick picked her up effortlessly, and in his arms she could feel his entire body humming with desire. She took a deep breath, reveling in his amazing scent. She knew it wasn't his cologne, but the pure animal magnetism he seemed to exude, calling to her. He laid her down on the bed almost reverently. Standing up, he removed the rest of his clothing, pushing his pants and briefs down to his ankles. Her eyes followed a trail from his bare naked chest covered in a light matting of hair, down his perfectly sculpted abs, lower still to the shallow dip of his hips, then finally, to his erect cock. The shaft was thick and long, jutting up and forward. She gasped quietly and forced herself to look up. Nick's gaze was naked with want. She shivered when his eyes clashed with hers, and she could feel how much he wanted her.

He joined her on the bed, leaning over her. Pushing her hair away, he bent down and kissed her again. Cady sensed a calmness in him, despite the urgency in his kisses. Skin to skin, with nothing between them, he lay on top of her, spreading her legs as the tip of his cock nudged at her entrance.

"Nick ... I ... I need to ..."

"Yes," he growled. "I need you, too."

"That's not ... I mean ... Nick!" she cried out when he pushed into her.

"Cady ..." He paused, his eyes growing wide as the tight barrier gave way. "You're a ..."

She closed her eyes and nodded. "Yes, I haven't ..." God, she was ruining this, wasn't she? But when was she supposed to tell him that she was a virgin?

"Cady, Cady," he soothed, brushing her hair away from her temples. "I'm sorry ... I can't stop ..."

When she looked up into his eyes, she saw them glow,, the pupils blowing up. She swallowed a gulp. "Please, Nick. It's all right. I'm ... please ... fuck me now. I need you. Take me. I want to come with you inside me."

Nick snarled and growled, then his eyes shifted back into something more human. He moved his hips, hands digging under her as he pressed her close.

"Cady," he whispered into her ear. "So beautiful, and lovely, and sweet ..." He thrust slowly, almost experimentally.

Her body tensed at first, but the discomfort ebbed away quickly until she could only feel pleasure. She arched up, her hips pushing at him.

"More ... Nick, please, I want more ..." she begged, her nails digging into his shoulders as she clung desperately to him.

Nick tensed and his hands slipped lower, cupping her sweet bottom and he thrust into her. Cady moaned in pleasure as he increased his thrusts, pushing his cock into her as far as he could. He moved in and out of her, building a slow and steady rhythm as her tight walls created that delicious friction he craved.

She buried her face into the crook of his neck as her body tensed one last time. "Nick ... I'm ..." Pure white heat shot through her, and she closed her eyes tight as pleasure rippled through her in waves. She clung to him, unable to do anything else as she orgasmed.

"Cady ..." Her name was low and guttural, coming from deep within. With one last thrust and as her pussy tightened around his cock, he emptied himself into her. He called her name again, and then collapsed on top of her.

Cady lay still underneath him, her mind reeling. She stroked his hair, much softer than she'd ever imagined and darker, too, under the soft lamplight. Turning her head, she looked outside. The night sky had cleared up and the snow had stopped. The moon was large and tinged with red as it hung high. Closing her eyes, she sighed, Nick's weight becoming heavy on top of her. She nudged him softly and he rolled over, but not before grabbing her by the waist and tucking her against his warm body. His arms were like vices, and though she could settle comfortably against him, she wasn't getting away. With a defeated breath, she closed her eyes and let exhaustion take over her.

CHAPTER FOURTEEN

To say Nick was insatiable was an understatement. After the first time, Cady dozed off, but it wasn't long before she felt hands roaming all over her body, a low, rumbling growl waking her up. She gasped as a warm hand slipped between her legs, coaxing them apart. He stroked her until she grew wet and Nick's hard cock nudged at her from behind. She sighed as he slipped into her, his other arm snaking around her waist as his hips thrust up into her, his fingers playing with her clit as he fucked her until she orgasmed, her body shuddering. When he finished, her name on his lips as he gave one last thrust; his soft cock slipped out of her, his seed drying on her thighs. He fell asleep again, but refused to let go of her, even in sleep.

When she woke up a second time, Nick's blonde head was between her legs. She gasped as his tongue licked at her, thrust inside her, sucking on her hard little clit until she orgasmed. With a wicked smile and a grunt, he flipped her over, so he was on his back and she was over him, impaling herself on his already hard cock. She ground down on him, setting the pace as she sought out her pleasure, sliding up and down his shaft. Cady grabbed onto his shoulders and raked her nails down his chest as orgasm after orgasm ripped through her, and Nick thrust up as he filled her again.

But she herself couldn't get enough. *It would have to be enough*, she thought. She would get what she could and keep the memories, even if there was a possibility he wouldn't remember afterward. He said nothing the whole time except her name, moaning and groaning as he sought his pleasure and kept the wolf at bay.

They had sex twice more, and by the time the sky was pink outside, Cady was exhausted. She knew the danger was over. Nick had collapsed on top of her, and she slipped out from under him. He didn't wake up or try to trap her, so she crawled to the other side of the king-sized bed, wrapping herself around a cool pillow and welcoming the dreamless sleep that took over her.

———

Cady ached all over. And she was naked. She sat up quickly, her mind foggy. *Oh. Right.* She looked around her, and saw Nick lying on his stomach on the other side of the bed. It seemed like he hadn't moved since ... this morning?

"Nick?" She shook him, but he remained still. She nudged him, but he didn't move. Placing a finger to his neck, his pulse was strong and steady, his breath even, but he just wouldn't wake up or move. "Dear lord!" She almost wanted to laugh. She literally screwed Nick Vrost into a coma.

A loud ding-dong sound snapped her out of it. The doorbell. She jumped up and grabbed the first thing she could that was wearable - a hotel robe which more than adequately covered her - and opened the door.

"Dr. Faulkner!" The older Lycan stood outside the door, his hands clasped behind his back.

"May I come in?" He couldn't look at her in the eye.

"Of course." *Talk about awkward.*

Dr. Faulkner walked in, looking a little sheepish. "Um, Grant sent me as soon as he could."

"What time is it?"

"It's three p.m., my dear."

Cady gasped audibly, not realizing how late it was.

"How ... how is Nick?"

She turned as red as her hair. "He's fine, but I can't wake him up."

The doctor nodded. "That should be normal, but I'll go check on him." He fished something out of his pocket. It was a foil packet with a couple of pills. "Cady, you know it's hard for us Lycans to conceive, but on the off-chance ... these are morning after pills. Take the first one now and follow the directions for the rest."

She numbly took the packet from the older man. "Thank you." She didn't even think of the possibility, but chances are there wouldn't be a child. And even if it happened, it would be a fully human one. However, she wasn't prepared to be tied to Nick Vrost forever. She stared at the pills in her hand and popped the first one into her mouth.

A few minutes later, Dr. Faulkner stepped out of the bedroom. "He'll be out for another couple of hours, but he'll be fine. Did you want to go home? The jet is waiting. I'll stay here with Nick until he wakes up."

Cady nodded. "I'll pack my things."

CHAPTER FIFTEEN

Cady couldn't wait to get home. Confused, tired, and overwhelmed, all she wanted to do was sit in her tub at home and soak for hours. Nick's scent seemed to permeate her skin, and it was driving her mad. Part of her still craved for him, for his touch. She had to wash it away, if only so she could think straight.

As she sat surrounded by bubbles and her favorite scented oils, she contemplated the situation. What could she do? Pretend everything was normal? Quit? The best case scenario was maybe Nick wouldn't remember a thing, and they could just go on as they did before. She sank into the bubbles farther. *Talk about being stuck between a rock and a hard place.* She would just have to take it one day at a time.

Monday came and she was actually glad to go to work and have something to do. The good news was, since it was after a Blood Moon, about half the Lycan staff would be gone. She didn't hear any word from Dr. Faulkner about Nick's condition, but she figured no news was good news. Grant didn't take the day off; he never did after a Blood Moon. As Alpha, it was luxury he couldn't afford, but she knew he was out of the office at meetings the whole day. Alynna and Alex had definitely taken the day off, but the young couple assured her in a text message that they were fine and so was the baby, but stayed at home as an extra precaution.

The next few days were a bit tricky, but she managed to avoid Grant and Nick. The Beta was probably back at work, seeing as she saw the new security rotation list. Since she had access to both men's schedules, she worked it out so she could avoid them. If Grant wanted to see her, he made no indication, only communicating with her through email. She heard nothing from Nick at all. While she was disappointed, she was also relieved. Grant's avoidance, however, almost hurt. But what did she expect, anyway? A clap on the back? An award? Of course, she knew any meeting with Grant right now would just be awkward.

In the middle of the week when she knew both men would be at the office, Cady scheduled herself to work from home and then come in later in the afternoon. Before she stepped into Fenrir's building that day though, she decided to take a walk around the block to the nearby coffee shop, where she knew the peppermint mochas were most definitely in season, even this early. She was about to push the door open when it swung out, almost knocking her to the ground.

A strong pair of arms caught her before she hit the pavement. "Apologies!" the deep, masculine voice said.

Cady brushed her hair away and looked up into blue-green eyes behind a pair of glasses. "No worries. No harm, no foul, right?"

When the man propped her back up, she realized how tall and imposing he was. He was probably three or four inches over six feet with broad shoulders. His long, dark blonde hair was tied up in a fashionable man bun, showing off a handsome face, if a little humorless.

"Are you sure you're all right?"

He had a slight accent, UK-educated maybe, but he looked more like a Viking than a Brit. She was usually good at accents, but she couldn't place this one for some reason. He was also dressed like a hipster, with ripped jeans, a tight shirt, suede jacket and a checkered scarf around his neck.

"Yes, I'm fine." She brushed imaginary dirt off herself. "Thanks for the catch."

He nodded and said nothing. "Have a good day."

Cady shrugged and went inside the coffee shop, getting in line at the counter. "One peppermint mocha, please. With extra whipped cream," she told the barista as soon as she reached the front of the counter. When she slipped her hand inside her purse, she realized that she didn't have her wallet. *Just my luck.* But before she could tell the barista to cancel her order, someone tapped her on the shoulder.

"Excuse me." It was hipster Viking. "I think you dropped this."

In his hands was her wallet. "Oh, thank god!" She grabbed it from him with a grateful nod. It would have been terrible to lose all her stuff. "Thank you so much!"

"No problem." He gave her a short nod and turned around, leaving the coffee shop.

Strange guy, she thought. Seemed nice enough. She shrugged and paid for her drink.

———

"Did you get it?"

Daric waited until he was two blocks away from the coffee shop. He whipped off the glasses and the ridiculous scarf.

"Relax," came the voice from the communicator in his ear. Some punk kid Victoria hired, who seemed to be obsessed with spy movies. "I've got the info, dude." The guy was good though. All Daric needed to do was grab Cady's wallet, place her card next to a special reader, and they had an exact copy of her access card.

"Good. I want to get out of here," he said impatiently.

"Why the rush?" Victoria Chatraine smiled wolfishly at him as she rounded the corner from where he was.

"I don't like cities and this outfit is ridiculous." Daric threw the scarf and glasses into the nearest trash can. "And I don't understand why we needed to spoof her keycard. We have magic."

"Daric, darling." Victoria placed a hand on his arm. "You know why. Magic and glamour will only take us so far. Anyone who's familiar with witches or another witch will be able to see through the glamour once they review security tapes. But," she paused, "when they see the real, hard evidence, they won't be able to deny it."

"Hmph."

"Besides," she drawled. "What did you think of Cady? Will she do?"

"Her bloodline is suitable enough, at least the Master seems to think so," Daric replied.

"But do you think she's attractive?" she asked, her bright red painted lips curling into a smile.

"That shouldn't matter, right?" the blonde warlock knitted his brows.

"I mean, if you find *her* attractive ..." Victoria stroked his arm, her voice full of meaning.

Daric's face was a solid mask of indifference. "Let's go back. The Master will want to know what happened."

CHAPTER SIXTEEN

As soon as she thought the coast was clear, Cady returned to Fenrir. She entered the building, crossed the lobby, and headed to the private elevators. When she turned the corner, she saw a familiar, tall, dark-haired figure waiting.

"Alpha, welcome to New York." She nodded reverently at Liam Henney, Alpha of San Francisco and Alynna's one-time, would-be suitor. *Ah right.* He was scheduled to meet with Grant and Alynna regarding Amata Ventures. Grant and Alynna were both funding his startup, and the latter even had a seat on the board. He was dressed in a smart business suit in charcoal gray, though his jacket was slung over one arm, a rolling case and briefcase right beside him.

"Good afternoon, Ms. Gray," he greeted back. The elevator doors opened, and he struggled to enter and drag his things in at the same time.

"Can I help you, Alpha?" she asked.

"Yes, please." Liam handed her his jacket, and Cady hugged it against her chest as he maneuvered his bags into the elevator. "Sorry," he said, rubbing the back of his head with his palm. "I'm on Amata business, not Clan business. Had to fly commercial this trip, just got in from JFK," he explained.

"Ah, startup mode, right?" Cady joked.

They made small talk, with her inquiring about his trip from the West Coast and Liam asking for restaurant recommendations for dinner near his hotel. The trip up was quick and soon they reached the top floor of Fenrir Corporation.

"Have a good meeting and rest of your trip, Alpha." Cady handed his jacket back to him, which he quickly put on.

"Thank you, Ms. Gray. I'll see you around." He gave her a nod before they headed in opposite directions.

———

"So, looks like we're ready for the next step in our project," Grant concluded as he leaned back in his chair casually. Liam and Alynna sat in the chairs across from him. "We're in good shape. Thanks for coming, Liam."

"My pleasure." Liam stood up and offered his hand to the other Alpha. "I'll be headed to San Francisco early tomorrow morning, but with the new lab results coming in, I should be back again soon."

"Excellent." Grant clasped his hand and gave it a firm shake.

"Looking forward to seeing what results we have," Alynna interjected. "You really can't stay longer?"

The San Francisco Alpha shook his head. "Sorry. Duty calls, I'm afraid."

"All right, well, let me walk you to the elevators at least." She tucked her arm in his and led him toward the door.

As soon as the door closed, Grant turned to Nick who had been standing stiff as a board in his usual spot in the corner.

"Now, are you going to tell me why you look like you're going to murder Liam Henney?"

The Beta tensed, a tick in his jaw showing how hard he was trying to keep his anger in check. "It's nothing. Nothing at all."

Grant shook his head and went to his liquor

cabinet, taking out a special key from the drawer and opening a secret compartment. Taking out a pure black quarter-liter bottle, he filled a shot glass halfway, then walked over and handed it to Nick.

"You never take out the good stuff." Nick sniffed the liquid.

"You look like you need the good stuff," Grant said.

It was Torlyncă, a supercharged version of vodka, made in secret from the old country and infused with old magic, or at least that's what Lycans believed.

Nick swallowed everything in one gulp, the liquor going down smoothly, smoother than any alcohol in the world. He felt his shoulders relax, and he sank down on the nearest chair he could find.

"Now tell me what's going on," Grant said in an authoritative manner. "Why are you so worked up?" He couldn't exactly compel Nick to talk to him, but he hoped the liquor would help loosen Nick's tongue.

"He smells like her. I could scent it the moment he walked in the door." Nick wished he had another swig of that drink.

"Smells like ...?"

"Like her. Cady. You know, like caramel apples." Nick grunted in disgust. "I don't know how, but it was like he had been all over her. Touching her."

Grant gave him a puzzled look. "First, I don't know why you think Cady has a scent, and second, why would it be all over Liam Henney? I don't think he's the type to try and get over one woman by going after her friend." Although Liam had failed to secure his sister's affections, Grant had thought the other Lycan took it in stride. He also never gave any indication he was interested in Cady.

Nick felt his head spinning. The Torlyncă was taking its effect, but thank god that with the amount he drank, it would only last a few minutes. "I don't know ... maybe I was imagining things. But goddammit." He threw the shot glass to the ground, the pieces shattering all over the hardwood floor. "Everywhere I go, I'm imagining her, seeing her, smelling her. I can't get her out of my mind."

Sitting down across from his Beta, Grant shook his head. "Maybe this is a side effect of ... I'm so sorry, Nick. I'm sorry."

"I'm not the one you should be saying sorry to."

"I know, I should apologize to Cady, and I have ... I mean, I did." Grant bowed his head. "She doesn't want to see me, either. I talked to her assistant, and it seems she's been keeping tabs on our schedules, working around it."

"Can you blame her? After what I did ..." Nick trailed.

"Did you hurt her?" Grant's voice suddenly turned edgy.

"No, of course not!" Nick stood up and walked toward the windows. "There are certain things that are hers alone to tell you, but both you and I know she was pushed into this by circumstance. She was doing her duty and protecting everyone around us and the Clan."

"If there had been another way ..." Grant was still obviously anguished by the decision.

"I know. You tried. Well, there wasn't and we can't turn back time." Nick curled his hands into fists. "I just wish it didn't have to go that way." He turned to Grant. "But I don't regret a moment of what happened between us. I've wanted her from the beginning. Since I saw her that first time."

The Alpha seemed surprised at the revelation. "Well, why didn't you do anything about it?"

Nick laughed sardonically. "After you told me she was your 'little sister'? I thought that was a warning."

"It was," Grant recalled. "I know your track record, and the effect Cady has on men."

The Beta shrugged. "And so, out of respect for you and the position you gave me, I treated her with the same respect as I would anyone in your family. I couldn't seduce her, no matter how much I wanted her."

"But all this time ...? You've never slept with anyone else?" Grant asked incredulously.

Nick shot him a look. "I'm your Beta, not a monk, Grant. I've just been selective and very discreet." He never slept with the same woman twice in the last ten years, all one night stands and outside New York City, if possible.

"Still, it's been a decade. You've changed, and so has she," Grant paused. "Why did you never go after her?"

"Does it matter?" Nick asked soberly, as the effects of the liquor began to fade. "Maybe if I did from the beginning, things might be different. Maybe we would have gotten over it and moved on. Both you and I know, in my position, it wouldn't have been appropriate."

"You ... *we* have to make this right somehow," Grant said solemnly.

Before Nick could answer, Alynna burst into the room. "I forgot my purse!" She grabbed the black bag by Grant's desk. "Whoa!" She looked at the floor covered in glass. "Who's the butterfingers?"

"I'll get someone to clean that up, Primul," Nick said before he walked out of Grant's office.

"Is everything all right?" Alynna eyed her brother suspiciously. "You two have been walking on eggshells around each other all week."

"It's all good," Grant lied and then changed the subject. "Everything okay with Liam?"

She nodded. "Yup. He says he's gonna head back to his hotel. Oh, and thanks for sending Alex off on that errand by the way. He was driving me crazy ever since I told him about the meeting with Liam." She dug through her bag, her face lighting up as she found what she was looking for - a candy bar. Apparently, incubating a Lycan pup took up a lot of energy and she was eating twenty-four hours a day. "He was starting to mark his territory." She scarfed down the entire thing in two bites.

"Jesus, Alynna." Grant wrinkled his nose. "I do not need to know how kinky you guys get."

"Not that way, you pervert!" Alynna tossed the wrapper at Grant. "I mean, he was rubbing his wrists all over me this morning. He thinks I won't notice he's trying to cover me with his scent. As if my scent hasn't already changed, being knocked up with a magical Lycan baby and all. Anyway," she gave her brother a pleading look, one that she knew he couldn't resist, "I'm starving! How about an early dinner? Think you can spare a few minutes to feed me and your ravenous soon-to-be-niece-or-nephew?" She rubbed the non-existent bump on her stomach.

He gave her a warm smile and pushed thoughts of Cady and Nick away. "Of course. Let's go."

CHAPTER SEVENTEEN

The sun had set long ago and outside her window, Cady could see the Manhattan skyline lit up. It was past nine p.m., but there was always work to be done. She turned back to her computer screen, tapping away at her keyboard, finishing up the report she had been working on for the past hour.

The door creaked open, but she kept her eyes on the screen. "Are you still here, Suzanne?" she asked without looking away from her computer. "I told you to go home hours ago."

When the lock on the door clicked she froze. Taking a deep breath, Cady slowly turned her head to see who her visitor was.

"Hello, Cady." Nick Vrost was standing in her office, leaning against the door.

"What are you doing here?"

"I work here."

"I mean," Cady narrowed her gaze, "Grant has a late dinner meeting at Le Cirque. Why aren't you there with him?"

"Are you keeping tabs on our schedule, Cady?" he asked.

"I'm just ... it's my job to know," she stated.

"I told Grant I wasn't feeling too well and I was headed back."

Cady snorted. "Right. Well, maybe you should go home then." She turned back to her computer, looking at her report. The words blurred together, not making any sense to her, but she pretended to keep reading, despite the fact that she could feel Nick's gaze boring right into her.

Finally, Nick straightened up and stalked over to her desk, like a predator tracking his prey. "And you? Working late? You know Liam leaves in the morning. That doesn't leave you much time."

"What are you talking about?" she asked in an exasperated tone. "Their meeting ended hours ago."

"I mean," he walked around her desk, "isn't he waiting for you? Maybe you planned a midnight tryst?"

Cady huffed. "I think you should leave, Nick. You're imagining things. I heard rest can do a lot of good for that."

Nick spun her chair towards him, and placed his hands on the arms, effectively trapping her. "Don't lie, Cady. It's not like you. I could smell you all over him the moment he walked in the door."

"Nick, you're delusional. Liam and I went up the elevator together. I held his jacket, that's the closest I got to him." She looked him straight in the eyes. "Now, let go of my chair and leave." Her voice was shaky, but she did her best to sound confident.

"I won't ... I can't," he growled and leaned down, pressing his lips to hers. His hands dug into her hair, pulling out the pins out and letting the long, red curls fall down her shoulders.

Cady tried to pull away from him, but was trapped. His scent enveloped her, like walking in the woods in the winter. She stopped struggling and instead, wrapped her arms around his neck. "Nick," she said in a pleading voice. Unable to control herself, she opened her mouth willingly, tasting him as his tongue invaded her mouth.

Nick hauled her up off the chair and then placed her on the desk. Cady spread her legs, grabbed him by the collar, and pulled him in between her knees.

"Fuck, I need you," he snarled as he devoured her lips again, their tongues clashing. Cady responded by wrapping her legs around his waist, pressing up against him. He was already rock hard, his cock straining through his trousers.

Cady pushed against him, sliding her legs down his body. She bit on his lip, coaxing him to step back as she reached down for the zipper on his pants.

"Cady," Nick breathed.

"Shhh ..." She pulled down the zipper and slipped the pants down his thighs. "Let me ... I want to taste you."

Nick groaned as Cady tugged down his briefs, his cock springing free. She gasped softly, wrapping her delicate fist around his shaft. Tentatively, she stroked it, feeling the soft, velvety skin over hard steel. Opening her mouth, she licked the tip, the salty taste of his pre-cum teasing her taste buds.

"Fuck, Cady!" Nick dug his hands into her hair.

Cady wrapped her lips around the tip, her tongue licking more of the salty liquid from his cock. She moved her head down, slowly taking in more of him into her mouth. Her tongue caressed the underside of his cock, then sucked back, dragging her mouth along the rigid shaft.

"I need to be inside you," he said, pulling her up.

"But I want –"

"Later, sweetheart, I promise." He reached under her skirt and pulled her panties down. Her slit was already wet, his finger sliding easily within her. "I can't wait any more. I need to fuck you now."

She cried out as his fingers sought out her core, this thumb playing with her clit as she grew slicker, soaking his fingers. Strong hands wrapped round her trim waist, turning her around and bending her over the desk.

Nick pulled her skirt over her ass, exposing the round, fleshy globes to his gaze. He bent down and gave her playful bite, making Cady yelp. She grabbed the end of her desk, bracing herself as she pushed her ass up at him.

Taking his cock in his hands, he placed the tip against her wet slit, pushing himself slowly into her warm, tight passage. "I've been wanting you for days. Dreaming of being inside you again."

"I thought ..." she moaned when he gave her a thrust, seating himself fully into her, "you didn't remember."

He scoffed. "I can't. I can't forget that night." He pulled back and slid back in. "The feel of you, your skin and your sweet body."

"It's only been you, Nick," she confessed. "Just you I want."

"Shhh ..." He bent down, pushing her hair aside and nuzzling her neck. "I know sweetheart, I know."

"Please, Nick." She pushed back against him, seeking the friction that would make her fall apart.

Nick didn't say anything else, but grabbed her hips and began to move. Slowly at first, but when Cady kept wriggling deliciously under him, he thrust himself into her, pushing all the way in and then pulling back. Her tight passage gripped him, coaxing him to go faster and faster.

"Nick!" Cady squealed as her body began to shake, her pleasure coming in waves. A rush of wetness flooded her pussy as she squeezed him.

"Fuck! Cady!" Nick thrust into her one last time, his cock twitching as she continued to grip him. He shuddered as his own orgasm mirrored hers, and he completely emptied himself into her.

Cady's body shook from her own orgasm, the release rushed through her body. It was perhaps the most powerful one she'd ever had. Nick collapsed on top of her, kissing and nuzzling her neck.

"I'm sweaty," she protested as she tried to brush him away.

"I know." He grinned against the soft skin of her neck. "And it's delicious."

She giggled when his tongue hit a ticklish spot. She sighed as he stood up, pulling her up with him.

He turned her around to face him, his arms wrapping around her.

She laid her head on his chest, inhaling his scent. "You smell good."

"So do you," he groaned, burying his nose in her hair. "Like sweet, sweet candy." He leaned down and kissed her again.

She responded eagerly, tasting him and savoring him. When he pulled away, she cupped his jaw with her small hands. Ice blue eyes stared back down, searching her face. "I'm sorry. I didn't mean ... it was stupid of me to think about you and Liam."

"Shhh ..." She put a finger on his lips. "I don't want to talk about Liam."

"Good." Nick's hands moved lower, cupping her ass. He lifted her up and planted her on the desk again. "Because I don't want to talk at all."

———

"Did you do something to your hair? Or are you using a new face cream?" Alynna asked as she plopped herself on Cady's office couch. She was munching on a donut, taken from a brown paper bag slung over her arm. The young Lycan had requested a meeting with Cady to go over a few items regarding the investigation into the Blood

Moon incident, as well as advice on a few other things.

"Oh my god, are those fresh donuts?" Cady sniffed the air and her stomach growled. "Can I have one?"

Alynna nodded and offered the bag her. Cady got up from her desk and picked up a hot donut from the bag. "Cinnamon and sugar!" She took a bite, and then another, and soon she was licking her fingers delicately. "How many more do you have?"

"I have a dozen ... in *this* bag," Alynna confessed, giggling as she handed Cady another donut. "Seriously, Cady," she peered closer, almost nose to nose with the redhead. "Your skin is glowing and ... is that new perfume?"

"Hmm?" Cady closed her eyes, savoring the warm, fried dough. "This is amazing. I'm starving!"

"I'll leave this here then." Alynna placed the bag on the couch. "I have another one in my office. Hopefully Alex hasn't eaten them all! You'd think he was the one knocked up these days. I swear if other men have pregnancy sympathy pains, he has hunger pains."

Cady eyed the bag, but held back from picking up another piece. "Thanks. These are really good."

"Now dish. I want the name of your new skin care regime or whatever pill you're popping, or I will take these with me." She motioned to the bag of donuts.

"No secret." Cady hoped she wasn't blushing. "Just ... getting more sleep."

She mentally crossed her fingers. She had actually been getting *less* sleep in the past two days. Nick was insatiable and kept her up all night long. After that evening in her office, they immediately went back to The Enclave and spent the whole night in Nick's apartment. She only went home to shower and then headed to work by herself. By the time seven p.m. had rolled around and most of the staff had left, Nick strode into her office and demanded she finish up so he could take her home. That night, they spent it at her place, which she later realized was a ploy to make sure she didn't leave him – nor could she kick him out – until the last possible moment before they both had to be at Fenrir.

They weren't exactly telling the whole world, but they seemed to mutually, silently agree to be discreet. Or maybe because it was so new and they didn't know where they were going, so they wanted to keep it to themselves. Cady had made a decision that, for once, she would think about herself. Despite the looming threat of Victoria and complications with Vasili, this was the one thing she would take and keep with her. In Nick's arms, she could forget everything else and find some peace and happiness.

"Hello, earth to Cady?!"

Alynna's words shook her out of her thoughts. "Sorry. I was thinking about, er, work."

"Oh yeah? That's the third donut you've eaten." Alynna pointed out.

Cady looked down at the half-eaten treat in her hand, startled she didn't even realize she had kept eating or that she was hungry. There was no time for breakfast that morning, not when Nick dragged her back to bed. Twice. "I was hungry. Sorry about that." She brushed the crumbs from her blouse.

Alynna eyed her friend with suspicion. "Hmm ... you sure everything's okay? Are you fully recovered from your accident?"

"Yes, I'm fine." Frankly, she had almost forgotten about her injuries. Her shoulder stopped bothering her a while back and the bruises on her body had completely faded. "Anyway, let's get on with business, shall we?"

———

"You could have waited, you know," Cady said in an almost annoyed voice as she opened the car door, cool air rushing into the Mercedes. Her heels clicked on the cement floor, and she pulled her panties up before smoothing her skirt down. "We're already in The Enclave."

Nick gave her a wicked grin, his eyes roaming her body. The front of her blouse was still open, exposing her black lacy bra, her fiery hair tumbling down her back, lips swollen and lipstick smeared away. The sight of her made desire surge through him, despite the fact he had already come inside her after giving her two orgasms. As soon as they pulled into his private garage, he grabbed Cady and put her on his lap, and she eagerly rode him in the front seat of his car. The windows of the Mercedes were still fogged up.

"Make no mistake, Cady." He stepped out of the car, zipping up his pants. "I still mean to have you when we get upstairs. I just wanted you now."

She shivered visibly at his words, which only made him want to bend her over the hood of the car.

"Besides, this is kind of a fantasy of mine. Something I've always wanted to do."

"You mean you've never had other girls in your car?" she teased as she buttoned up her blouse.

His eyes grew dark. "No. I mean, this." He spun her around and then pushed her back against the

Mercedes, trapping her. "You and me in the front seat of the car is a fantasy of mine. I've even dreamt about it a time or two." She lowered her eyes and gasped. "Now," he pulled away, "let's go upstairs before I do something else. Are you hungry? How about we have dinner at my place?"

She nodded, and they went up the elevator, keeping a respectable distance in case anyone was watching the security cameras. It was early Friday night, and so the elevators weren't busy. Only one person, a human, joined them at the ground floor, getting off on the third floor. As soon as they entered his apartment, Nick pushed her against the door.

"I was promised dinner." She pouted, placing her hands on his chest.

"Fine, fine," he relented, resting his forehead on the door.

"Good." Cady smirked, pushing him away. "So, should we order Chinese or pizza?"

Nick looked at her like she had grown two heads. "Order? No, I was going to cook you dinner."

"You cook?" Now *she* looked at him in the same way.

"I have to eat, right?" he shrugged. "Something I learned at home. C'mon."

Cady sat at the counter, finishing up some work

on her pad while Nick started to prepare dinner. However, it wasn't long before Cady had to put down her tablet as she was quite distracted. Between watching Nick work in the kitchen, his sleeves rolled up showing off his forearms and the delicious smells, Cady simply couldn't concentrate on the task at hand. So, she just watched him, fascinated as he finished preparing dinner.

"You've been holding out on me," she said, as she nibbled on a piece of bread. "You know how to cook! And ... oh my God, where did you get this bread? It's even better than the ones I had in Paris."

"Well, my grandmother insisted I learned how to make myself a proper meal before I went off to Harvard, so she had our cook teach me." Nick finished putting their dinner together - salmon and steamed vegetables - and placed one of the plates in front of her. "And as for the bread, well ... I get it delivered every other day by my grandfather's butler."

"Butler?" she asked, puzzled. "You have a butler?" She picked up her fork and took a bite of the salmon, perfectly cooked, of course.

"Yes, Garret. He comes with the house, at least that's what he says," he joked. "Seriously though, Garret has been with the family since I was a kid. He's an excellent butler and a baker, too."

Cady took another bite. "So, this house ... where is it again?"

"It's on the river, in the Hudson Valley," Nick explained.

"Wait a minute." Cady put her fork down. "So, it's not actually a house ... more of a mansion, right?" The Hudson Valley was home to some of the most gorgeous mansions in the state. She'd driven up there once or twice with her father, just to look at the beautiful historic homes.

"Er ... well, I guess. It was originally built in the 1800s by one of the robber baron families; I can't remember the name right now." He scratched his head. "Are you okay?" Cady seemed to choke on her salmon. "Did I overcook it?"

"Uh, I'm fine." Cady took a swig of water. "It's perfect, just ... went down the wrong pipe."

"Eat up." Nick gazed intently at her. "You'll need your strength."

CHAPTER EIGHTEEN

Neither of them decided that they would spend the entire weekend together, but that was what ended up happening. Friday rolled into Saturday and then Sunday. Cady was tired and sore in a good way. She did, however, threaten to go back to her apartment and lock Nick out if he didn't let her sleep before work on Monday. Not wanting to be away from her, he relented and they went to bed early on Sunday night. She'd never slept better than she did in his arms.

They arrived separately at Fenrir, and Cady went straight to her office. She was surprised to see Grant was already waiting for her.

"Grant." Her eyes widened at the sight of him sitting on her couch.

"Cady." He stood up. "How have you been?"

"I'm good. And you?"

"Fine."

She walked to her desk. "Is there something I can help you with?"

"I know you've been avoiding me. Us. Me and Nick, I mean." He sounded nervous, something she'd never seen.

She sighed as she sat down. "No. I mean, yes." She wouldn't insult him by lying or patronizing him. "I needed some space. I hope you understand. But, as I told you, I'm okay. I mean, I went into this willingly. I did it to keep everyone safe and for the Clan."

"I know and I'm grateful." Grant cleared his throat. "But I can't help but feel at fault."

"Well, don't because it's not your fault," she assured him. "It's no one's fault. And we can't change the past."

"What do you want to do now?" he asked. "I don't want to lose you as my assistant or Liaison, but if things are too awkward, then I'll understand."

"What?" Her head shot up so fast, she was almost dizzy. "Do you want me to quit?"

"No!" he protested. "Of course not. Do you *want* to quit?"

"No, I don't," Cady stated. "Nick and I will

work it out. We just need time." She contemplated telling him, but it didn't seem like a good idea. Besides, what was she supposed to say? *Actually, Grant, we're working it out by screwing each other silly.*

"Good." He stood up. "I'd hate to lose either one of you."

"You won't," she assured him. "We're all adults here."

"Anytime you change your mind," he began. "Just tell me."

She nodded. "I will."

Grant seemed slightly relieved. "Good. Now, let's go over the calendar for the next few days, okay?"

———

"The footage from the accident is arriving today, right?" Alynna asked her husband.

"Uh-huh."

"And the list of witnesses?"

"Uh-huh."

"And the list of humans who got sick?"

"Mm-hmm"

"And the footage from Blood Moon?"

"Working on it."

Alynna pushed Alex away playfully. "Hey, what did I say about getting handsy in the office?"

"That you enjoyed it?" Alex tickled her, eliciting a shriek from his wife.

"But?" She stepped away from him and crossed her arms.

Alex sighed. "We need to stay professional while in Fenrir."

"Right." She pulled down her skirt, which Alex had raised up over her hips. She pointed to his desk. "Back to work, Mister."

"You're no fun." He mock pouted and sat down on his chair.

"You know this is important," she said, her voice taking on a serious tone.

"I know, baby doll, but I don't want you to get too anxious and stress out the baby, okay?" he replied. "Plus, doesn't relaxing help you think better?"

"Is sex the only way you relax?" She raised an eyebrow at him.

"No, but it's the best way - hey!" Alex ducked when she tossed a pencil at him. He picked it up, grumbling something about husband abuse.

Alynna sat back down in her chair, staring at her computer screen, trying to put together what they had so far. She frowned. "How come we don't have the footage from Blood Moon? That was over two weeks ago!"

"Well, they don't actually have in-house security. Grant is only part owner of the club, and the decision from the management was to outsource security," Alex explained.

"Still." Alynna narrowed her eyes. "It can't be difficult to get the footage."

"According to the security company, all the footage is on an external server ..."

"And?"

"Hmm ..." Alex opened his email. "Well, they sent me this email ... having trouble downloading the server ... sincere apologies ... blah blah ... endeavoring to get it to you ASAP ..." He turned back to Alynna. "I can see the wheels in your head turning."

"It seems all too weird to me –" She was interrupted by a knock on the door. "Come in."

"Mr. Westbrooke, Ms. Chase, er, Westbrooke," It was Jared, Grant's admin. Since neither Alynna nor Alex had time to interview applicants for assistants, he was doing double-duty, which was fine for the time being since they didn't have many cases yet. "This came for you, from the NYPD." The handsome young Lycan handed her a slim envelope.

"Thank you, Jared." Alynna nodded. "And thank you, Lycan connections. I would have had to break some laws if I wanted to get this on my own as a PI."

"Did you?" Alex teased. "Break laws, I mean?"

"Hmm?" She tore open the envelope. "I have to keep some secrets to myself, right?"

Before Alex could answer, she popped the DVD into the drive of her computer and pulled him beside her. They sat in silence as they watched the grainy, black and white footage from the traffic cam. It showed a section of road on the West Side Highway, which was strangely empty for that time of the day. The black town car approached the traffic camera, which was probably mounted over-head. As it was halfway out of frame, the back end of the car fishtailed and disappeared from view.

"That's it?" Alynna frantically clicked on the computer. "That's all we have?"

"Afraid so." Alex put a hand on her shoulder. "The next camera was too far away to capture anything."

"So, whatever caused Greg to swerve was in the one blind spot between cameras?"

Alex's brows knitted together in a frown. "Seems like it."

"And Greg still doesn't remember?"

Alex shook his head. Nick interviewed the young Lycan driver as soon as he woke up from his induced coma two days after the accident. However, he had not provided any useful information, other than that he had swerved to avoid something, but he couldn't remember what it was. An examination of the car showed that it was clean and had not been tampered with.

"This is all too fishy." Alynna tapped a finger on her chin.

"Could it be all coincidence?" Alex suggested.

"You know I don't believe in coincidences."

CHAPTER NINETEEN

"Finally," Grant said as he poured himself another cup of coffee. "There's one more thing ..."

"Yes?" Cady asked, without looking up from her pad.

"I've been invited to a dinner party tonight for some visiting Lycans from Europe. Vasili Vrost is hosting. I'd like you to come as my date. I'm sorry to have to ask, but you know I don't have anyone else." It wasn't uncommon, after all, for them to go to business or Lycan-related functions together, especially since Grant had no Lupa.

Her breath caught for a moment, but she continued. "Oh. I didn't realize you had that in your calendar." Nick hadn't mentioned anything, only that he wouldn't be home tonight. She had been planning to stay in, read a book, and drink some wine.

"It was a last-minute invite. It's a bit much to ask this of you right now," Grant said sheepishly, "and I know you don't like Vasili."

She thought about what he was doing to Nick, forcing him to do something he didn't want. "Don't worry. It's fine. And I don't know him enough to like him. But he obviously doesn't like me very much."

"I think he underestimates you," he said.

"Why weren't these Lycan visitors cleared in advance?" she asked, switching topics. "Usually when you have some sort of delegation, it takes weeks to get everything together."

"Vasili requested it and he said it would be to talk business, but nothing formal. We've had some minor business in the past, but he's mostly in Europe. I have a feeling ..." Grant stopped short.

"Yes?" Cady looked up from her pad.

"Well, I shouldn't be discussing this but, maybe he wants to solidify our partnership when Nick takes over –"

"You're right, you shouldn't be discussing this," Cady interrupted. Grant would obviously know about Vasili's ultimatum to Nick, but didn't realize she did, too. Did Nick already give his grandfather an indication that he had found his potential Lycan wife? A stab of jealousy went through her.

"If it's all too much right now, I can always beg Alynna to come," Grant offered.

"Don't be silly, Grant," Cady sighed. "I'm an adult. We're all adults. Besides, I can't think of anything worse to put your sister through." Alynna hated any society-type event where she'd have to make small talk and pretend she was enjoying herself. She'd rather be at home eating pizza. "Besides if there's any Lycan or Fenrir business to be discussed, I should be there."

"Great." Grant stood up. "Pick you up at five? It's a long drive upstate."

———

Cady wasn't quite sure what to expect when she arrived at the Vrost family home, but it certainly wasn't a restored one-hundred-twenty-year-old, twenty-five-room mansion sitting on one hundred acres with spectacular views of the river and the Catskills. As she exited the town car, her breath caught as she stared up at the stately facade. All the lights were on and the mansion looked absolutely stunning. It was done in Beaux-Art style, with arched windows, cornices, and the front door was framed by four large columns topped a triangular pediment with tasteful ornamentation. This was where Nick Vrost grew up, the childhood home he was desperate to keep, and she understood why.

"Beautiful, huh?" Grant whispered as they ascended the front porch.

"You should think about getting one," Cady joked.

"I think one mansion is enough," Grant replied, referring to the Anderson mansion in Long Island.

"In New York, you mean?" Cady quipped. The Andersons owned numerous homes, some of them mansions, around the world. Still, she thought most of them – the ones she'd seen anyway – didn't quite have the character of this one.

They walked up to the front door, which was answered by an older man with white hair, dressed in a tuxedo.

"Alpha, good evening," he greeted Grant with a bow. "Welcome, please come in."

"Thank you," Grant greeted. "This is my dinner companion for the evening. Ms. Cady Grey."

Cady smiled at the older man. This must be the butler, Garret, whom Nick spoke so fondly about.

"Good evening, Ms. Grey," he said. His accent was very British, as if he just stepped off the plane yesterday, not decades ago. "How was your trip up?"

"Good evening ... Garret, right?" The older man nodded an affirmative. "It was fine, thank you."

"Excellent." He bowed again. "Please come this way. Everyone is already here, having pre-dinner drinks in the drawing room."

Grant's brows raised at Cady's use of the butler's name. "I didn't know you knew Garret."

"Uh ..." Cady cursed her slip internally. "Nick mentioned him before. I just remembered."

The Lycan said nothing more as they entered the drawing room. It was a beautiful space, well-matched to the exterior and what other interiors Cady had observed on their way there. Everything looked original, probably restored to its 19th century grandeur. It wasn't gaudy, but classy, and Cady felt like she was transported back in time.

There were already several people in the library, including Vasili Vrost and of course, Nick. He looked particularly handsome in his formal tux, and her heart skipped a beat, watching him as he spoke with his grandfather and a few other men.

"Ah, Primul," Vasili greeted as they came closer. "You honor us with your presence." He turned to Cady, and if he was surprised that she was there, he didn't show it. "Ms. Gray, you look stunning."

"Thank you, Mr. Vrost," she said with a slight blush. She had taken care of her appearance tonight, wearing a long, light blue draped jersey dress with one shoulder. The fabric hugged her curves, showing them off. Her makeup was carefully applied, but only minimally to enhance her looks, and her red hair swept to one side.

If Vasili wasn't surprised to see her, Nick sure was. He stared at her for a few seconds before he spoke. "Primul, Ms. Gray, thank you for coming," he finally greeted.

"Of course. I'm honored to receive your invitation," Grant replied. "It's always a pleasure to be invited to your home, Vasili. It looks especially stunning tonight."

"Thank you, Primul, but I'm afraid I don't deserve much credit. You know, my Ana took care of all the renovations and decorating when we bought this place fifty years ago." The older Lycan's eyes softened, and Cady guessed that Ana was his late wife. "I left everything the way it was when she passed, as she was always the expert in these matters."

"Dinner will be ready in five minutes," Garret announced as he entered the room.

"Thank you, Garret," Vasili said. "Now, why don't I introduce you quickly to our guests before we sit down? They are quite eager to meet you, Primul."

CHAPTER TWENTY

Nick took a sip of his wine, his eyes darting over the guests. And as always, he couldn't help but linger over one guest in particular. His grandfather was right. Cady looked stunning, especially under the low lights of the dining room. Her skin glowed under the soft lights, a light blush tinting her cheeks, lips full and red, her auburn locks swept artfully aside. She was the most beautiful woman he'd ever seen. And that dress. The moment she walked in wearing that dress, all he could think of was dragging her upstairs, peeling it off of her and having his way with her in one of the bedrooms. She smiled and laughed and chatted with the people around her with ease and grace. He was surprised to see her, but he should have known since Grant always took her as a default date for Lycan functions, unless his mother was in town.

"... And it really is a beautiful home!" a twittery, nasal voice said from his right. "It's like that *Pride and Prejudice* movie!"

He was jolted out of his reverie by that voice, which was not the first time that night. "Thank you, Constanza," he replied politely.

Constanza Dantis was the daughter of one of Vasili's Lycan business partners from Eastern Europe, who had tagged along for this "meeting." Of course, he knew this was one of his grandfather's schemes, a way for him to meet a suitable Lycan girl. However, it was obvious that Vasili had never even seen her. Sure, Constanza was beautiful and young, but she surely wasn't what Vasili was hoping for a granddaughter-in-law. Nick had gone to the private airstrip in Hudson with Vasili to pick up the delegation, and when she stepped out of the plane, she was teetering on five-inch heels paired with a short, bright yellow tight dress that barely covered her behind and showed off her ample breasts. Her platinum blonde hair was done up so well it didn't move even in the slightest breeze, and the cloud of flowery perfume that followed her everywhere was so thick, he couldn't tell what her scent was. Nick rode in the car with her, and all she did was complain about America and Americans, ignoring him the whole drive. The only time she did shut up was when they pulled into the mansion, and she couldn't stop talking about how big and beautiful it was, nor would she let go of his arm during the whole mini-tour Vasili had arranged. Her tone completely changed once she realized there was a chance she could become the mistress of the mansion.

"It reminds me of this tour to England I went on with Papa last year! Let me tell you ..."

He let her drone on and on about her travels and, of course, her complaints about the people, food, places, and smiled politely, not listening to a word she said. He let his eyes drift once again to Cady, who was talking to an older Lycan man, a former prince from Germany, apparently. She laughed and smiled at a joke he told her in German, which she spoke well enough, and the former prince's chest practically puffed up in pride as the young woman seemed to dote on him.

A surge of jealousy went through Nick as he continued to watch them. *Stop it*, he told himself. He knew he was being ridiculous, yet he still wanted to beat the living daylights out of anyone who touched, looked, or even smiled at Cady. Even Grant, who had walked into the drawing room with her on his arm.

Finally, Vasili, who was at the head of the table, stood up. "And now that dinner and dessert are over, I'd like to invite everyone to the music room for coffee, more dessert, drinks, and some special entertainment I arranged for this evening."

Everyone got up and filed out of the dining room and made their way to the music room. The German prince offered his arm to Cady, and she accepted. Nick, in turn, offered his arm to Constanza, who eagerly wrapped herself around him.

Vasili had invited a famous Japanese pianist to perform for them this evening, along with a string quartet. The musicians were already set up, and after a few words from the pianist, they began to play. Everyone was seated on various chairs and chaises placed strategically around the musicians. Nick's eyes immediately zeroed in on Cady, who had chosen to stand near the fireplace all by herself. He turned his head back to the performers, but kept Cady in the corner of his eye.

The musicians were halfway through their second song when he noticed Cady slip away. He waited, then followed her quietly, hoping no one would notice.

Cady was halfway down the hallway leading to main receiving room when he caught up with her. Grabbing her hand, he pulled her quickly into the alcove under the stairs and pressed his hands over her mouth.

"Shh ... it's me," he said, removing his hand.

As her eyes adjusted to the low light, her face lit up in a smile. "Nick," she said breathlessly. "I'm sorry. I didn't know ... I should have texted or called, but it was last minute."

"Sorry?" he asked, confused. "No, I'm glad you're here. I was surprised, but I should have known. Grant has no social life and no one else to take to these things. Alynna would have puked on his shoes before she let him drag her here."

She laughed. "That's what I kept telling him. I –" She stiffened when he drew her into an embrace, but then relaxed into his arms.

This feels so right, Nick thought. *Having her here.* "I missed you." He kissed the top of her head.

"You just saw me this morning," she quipped, but moved closer into his embrace. "But I miss you, too. I thought I wouldn't see you until tomorrow."

"Well, this was kind of a last-minute thing. My

grandfather conveniently 'forgot' to tell me until it was too late to say no."

She pulled away and leaned back against the wall of the alcove. "Oh, right." Her face fell.

"I'm sorry. I didn't want ... not that I didn't want you here, but I know what the old man is up to. She's barely left my side."

"Constanza?" She had been introduced to the young Lycan earlier in the evening, who had merely given her a cool nod and then dismissed her altogether.

"Yes. Her." He almost shuddered. "I don't know what he was thinking." Constanza had shown up in an even shorter silver dress, more suitable to a club in Ibiza than a formal dinner party.

"He's thinking she's got the right child-bearing hips," Cady joked. "Really, it's okay."

"This isn't what ... I mean," he looked down at her face, inscrutable but there was hurt in her eyes, despite her objections, "I don't want you to have to deal with this."

"This was a reality we both knew was lurking around the corner," Cady stated. "We have to –"

Nick couldn't stand it anymore, and pressed his lips to hers. She moaned softly as he pressed his body against her, pinning her against the wall, his arousal evident. He pressed his erection against her soft belly, letting her know how much he wanted her. Dragging his lips away from hers, he traced a path of kisses along her jawline, and then kissed the shell of her ear. "Come upstairs with me, Cady. Now." His voice was rough with need.

"Here? With all those guests and your grandfather?"

"I don't care." His hand slid up from her waist to her breast, cupping it gently. His thumb brushed over her nipple were and she gasped.

"We can't!"

"You're growing wet thinking about it ... I can smell you." Her scent and arousal mingled and was teasing his nose. "I can practically taste you." His other hand reached down and began to lift her dress, his fingers tracing up her creamy inner thighs.

Someone clearing their throat politely interrupted them. "Master Nick, I believe the last concerto is about to end," Garret's cool, collected voice cut through the air. "Perhaps it's time to head back to the music room."

Nick took a deep breath, then banged his forehead on the wall behind Cady. "Thank you, Garret." He leaned back, releasing Cady. Adjusting his pants, he turned to face the butler, whose face remained stoic. Cady, on the other hand, was red-faced with embarrassment.

"And maybe Ms. Gray would like to use the powder room on the other side of the stairs? It's well stocked with cosmetics and other items she might be able to use to refresh herself?"

Cady squeaked her thanks and scampered away.

"Thanks, Garret," Nick said sarcastically.

The old man gave Nick a knowing smile. "My pleasure." He turned around to go back to the kitchen, but then turned back around. "May I ask, Master Nick, is she the reason you asked me to double your bread deliveries?"

Nick nodded. "She said it's better than the French's."

The old man beamed with pride, but said nothing as he walked away.

Cady came back from the bathroom, arranging her hair and dress as she walked by. "Okay. I think the amount of perfume I put on could possibly rival Constanza's, but it'll have to do. Thank goodness jersey doesn't wrinkle."

Nick sniffed the air, disappointed that she didn't smell like him anymore, but they didn't have a choice. She couldn't walk into a room full of Lycans smelling like sex and him. "You go in first, and I'll follow. I'll tell Grandfather I had to run upstairs to get something from my room."

"Thanks."

"Wait." He grabbed her arm. "I can't leave tonight; I don't have a driver. But I'll drive up early tomorrow. Breakfast at your place?"

"Sure." She smiled and then turned to walk back to the music room and join the rest of the guests.

———

"What did you think of Constanza?" Vasili asked. It was the end of the evening, and all the guests had either left or retired to their rooms. The two Vrost men were sitting in the library, having a last drink before bed.

"What did *you* think of her?" Nick threw back the question.

"Eh, she needs some polishing." The older Lycan took a sip of his scotch. "She drinks and parties too much, but I think once she settles down, she'll be a good Lycan wife," he emphasized the last two words. "And her father is richer than Midas. Not as rich as Grant Anderson, but, well, it's too bad you didn't swoop in and marry his sister before that other one did."

"Grandfather, Alynna is about thirteen years younger than me. Besides, that 'other one' is her True Mate," Nick remarked. Thinking about

Alynna that way ... it would be like marrying a sister. He put down his own glass, losing his taste for liquor.

"Right, right. He's smart, getting her pregnant as soon as he could," Vasili remarked.

The younger man could only shake his head, not wanting to engage him further. "Goodnight, Grandfather." Nick stood up and headed towards the door.

"Nikolai," he called as Nick was about to cross the threshold.

Nick turned. "Yes?"

Vasili's tone changed. "I don't like the way you look at the human woman, the way your eyes follow her every move."

"I don't know what you mean."

"I'm old, not stupid." He took another sip of the amber liquid in his glass. "You will not pursue this further. You already know she won't be able to give you what you want."

You don't know what I want, Nick thought, but bit his tongue to prevent himself from saying it out loud. He gripped the wood of the door frame where he stood.

"Once you have produced my great-grandchild, you can do as you please," Vasili continued. "Sleep with her, keep her as a mistress, I don't care. But not until then. I won't risk a suitable mate or her family refusing you because you cannot control your lust for a human."

"Like I said, goodnight." Nick turned away and walked out on his grandfather.

CHAPTER TWENTY-ONE

"Cady ... Cady?" A gentle voice and hand shook her awake. She opened her eyes and yawned.

"We're back," Grant said. "Good thing there's no traffic at this time."

Cady glanced at the time on her phone. It was 1:45 a.m., and they did make it back to New York City in record time. "Oh thanks for waking me up. I'm just so tired ..." She got out of the town car with Grant's help. They were stopped in front of North Cluster.

"Don't come in 'till after ten tomorrow, okay?" Grant ordered as he got back into the car. "Work from home in your pajamas if you want, but I'll bar you from the lobby if I have to."

"Yes, *Dad*," she snickered and waved goodbye as the car drove toward Center Court. Walking into the building, she waved at the doorman and headed to the elevators.

As she prepared for bed, she heard a chirping sound from her phone. "Who could be calling me at this hour?" *Maybe it was Nick? No, he should be in bed by now, if he wanted to leave by five a.m.* Taking her phone out of her purse, she frowned at the "number unknown" on the caller ID.

"Hello," she answered.

"Cady, dear," Victoria greeted her. "It's me, your mother."

"What do you want, Victoria?" she asked impatiently. "I don't have time for your games."

"Oh, but you have time for your precious Lycans, coming home so late?"

"Are you watching me?" she asked in a venomous tone. "How can you even get close enough?" The Enclave was guarded by magic, which made anyone who walked by simply ignore or forget they had even seen the Lycan stronghold.

"My dear," her mother sneered. "The Enclave is protected by a witch's magic, which doesn't always work on other witches and powered beings."

"What do you want?" she asked again.

"Come meet with me."

"Now?" Cady sat down on the couch. "Why should I?"

"Because if you don't, I'll make a scene at Fenrir and then you can't ignore me," Victoria threatened. "Just come to the diner on Madison and 59th now. All I want to do is talk. And if you don't like what I have to say, I ... I promise it will be the last you hear from me." Her mother sounded strange, like she was sad. Or frightened.

"All right," Cady relented. "If I listen to you, do you promise to leave me alone?"

"I'll talk and you listen. After you hear what I have to say, you can decide if you want me in your life."

She paused. "Fine. I'll be there in twenty minutes."

"Thank you, Cady." The line went dead.

What could Victoria want? Why did she threaten to reveal her secret and then turn around and tell her she'd get out of her life? Cady shook her head and went to her closet to find something appropriate to wear. It didn't matter. The only thing that did was that Victoria would be out of her life soon enough.

———

Cady waited for almost hour, drinking bad coffee and waving away the young, tired-looking waitress several times. *I should have known.*

The hands on the clock over the door pointed at three and twelve. Victoria wasn't late, she just didn't show up. She duped Cady and that was that. Disgusted, the redhead dropped some bills on the table and left the diner, waving a passing cab to take her back to The Enclave. All she wanted was a shower, bed, and then Nick to come to her in the morning.

CHAPTER TWENTY-TWO

The smell of fresh coffee brewing, toast, and bacon woke her up. Glancing at her bedside table, she saw it was barely seven a.m. She smiled, got up, brushed her teeth and washed her face quickly, then bounded into the kitchen.

Nick stood by her stove, wearing a white towel as a makeshift apron, watching over a pan of bacon.

"I didn't even know I had bacon," she quipped as she came closer.

He gave her a grin and then crossed the distance between them. "You didn't." He wrapped his hands around her waist, pulling her close. "I brought it in from the house. As well as three loaves of bread, compliments of Garret." The loaves, which looked freshly-baked, were sitting on the counter.

"Smells amazing." She closed her eyes.

"Yes, and so does the breakfast." Nick swooped in for a kiss. Cady wrapped her arms around his neck, pulling him closer. She eagerly opened her mouth as his tongue sought hers, tasting her and savoring her. Unfortunately, her stomach chose that time to remind her about the delicious food.

"Sorry." She pulled away, embarrassed. "I haven't eaten since last night."

Nick patted her playfully on her behind. "Go sit and I'll serve you up a plate."

Cady obeyed and in a few minutes, Nick put down a plate heaping with eggs, bacon, and bread in front of her. She ate every morsel of it.

"Hungry much?" he teased as he bit into a piece of bread.

"Is there more bacon?" she asked hopefully, peering behind him.

Nick laughed and stood up, grabbing the last four pieces and putting it on her plate. "Here you go, eat up. Can't have you getting weak and hungry." His voice was light, but full of meaning.

She practically devoured the last pieces, her appetite finally appeased for now. She spied the last piece of bread, and Nick sighed, handing her the basket.

"Done?" he asked impatiently.

"Yes," she answered as she polished the last bit of egg on her plate.

"Good." Without another word he stalked over to her side of the table, pulled her up, and carried her bridal style into his arms.

"Wait!" she giggled. "Aren't you supposed to wait thirty minutes after eating before any activity?"

"That's swimming, sweetheart." He kissed her. "I don't think that applies to sex."

She shrieked as he dumped her unceremoniously on her bed and began to take off his clothes. Watching him with hooded eyes, she admired his long, lean body, muscled chest, and the trail of light blonde hair below his abs, teasing what was below his belt.

Nick was gentle, yet still passionate and urgent when he took her. All other times it seemed like sex between them was like a storm, loud and thunderous, leaving her spent and breathless. This morning, he seemed almost careful, reverent. He caressed and tasted her, bringing her to orgasm twice. As he thrust up into her, he cradled her face with his hands and pressed his forehead against hers, moaning out her name as he orgasmed hard and fast. He collapsed on top of Cady, then rolled to the side to gather her into his arms.

Speechless and spent, she lay there, watching as the sun began to fill her room.

"I couldn't sleep last night," he confessed, nuzzling her neck.

"Hmmm?" She turned around and touched his cheek, rubbing the slight stubble that had begun to grow. "What's wrong?"

"I was thinking," he began. "I don't need it ... any of it."

"Don't need what?" Her eyes felt droopy, and she closed them with a yawn.

"The house. The businesses. All of it. I've enough money on my own to last me a lifetime, and I'm well compensated by Fenrir and the Clan."

"Oh ... wait, what?" Her eyes flew open. "What are you talking about?"

Before he could answer, a soft chirping sound rang through the room. Cady's phone began to dance as it vibrated on her bedside table.

"Ignore it," he ordered, and then continued. "I'm talking about Vasili's ultimatum. I don't need to do what he says. Dmitri can have the house."

Cady shot up in bed. "You can't be serious?"

"Why not?" he asked, then sat up to face her. "You don't think it's selfish of him to dangle my heritage to get what he wants? I should have walked away from the beginning and refused to play his game." The phone continued to ring, buzzing insistently. As Cady reached for it, Nick grabbed her hand and turned her to face him. "They can wait."

She hesitated, but put her hand down. "But ..." Cady thought of the house, that beautiful mansion. "It's where you grew up. Where your father grew up. It would mean so much to your parents."

"My parents are dead," his tone was even. "They have been for a long time."

Cady's eyes widened. "And Vasili is your last living relative."

"And if that meant anything to him, he wouldn't have given me that ridiculous condition." Nick's expression hardened. "Why are you being like this all of a sudden?"

She turned away, hiding her face from him. Closing her eyes, she tried to stop the tears threatening to spill. *Oh Nick ... if only I had been honest.* But it was too late. It wasn't Vasili holding her back the whole time.

In a way, she was using the ultimatum as an excuse not to tell him about being a half-witch. If they never had a chance to be together to begin with, it didn't matter, so she didn't need to tell him. If she confessed now Nick would hate her forever *and* lose the one thing he held dear. She couldn't let him do that. But, before she could say anything, another ringing sound came, this time, from somewhere on the floor.

Nick's expression immediately changed when he heard the phone, turning serious and stoic. "That's Grant." He got up and grabbed his pants.

Cady took the opportunity to pick up her own phone, which had not stopped buzzing the whole time. It was Alynna.

"Alynna," Cady greeted. "Good morning. Sorry, we came in late last night and I had a hard time getting up," she lied.

"Cady!" the younger woman's voice sounded frantic. "You have to come to the office, now!"

Hearing the panic in Alynna's voice made Cady's heart speed up. She turned to look at Nick, who was on the phone with Grant, his face grim.

"What's wrong?"

"There's been another attack. Someone set off a firebomb at Fenrir."

———

The scene outside Fenrir Corp was total chaos. Fire, police, paramedic, and other emergency responders swarmed around the building, while reporters and news vans were desperately trying to get into the area.

As soon as they got off the phone, both Nick and Cady sprang into action. It was like slipping into their old skin, and now they were not Nick and Cady, but they were Grant's right and left hands. Wordlessly, they dressed and got into Nick's car, speeding downtown to Fenrir.

Grant, being the CEO of Fenrir and the face of the company, was already being briefed by their lawyers and PR firm so he could make a statement. As Human Liaison and Executive Assistant to Grant, Cady's first concern was the employees. That included Alynna, who seemed almost dazed, standing outside Fenrir watching the scene unfold. Alex stood by her side, a comforting arm around his wife. Cady knew Alynna needed to do something, so she put the young couple in charge of securing a place where they could convene. She sent them to The Hamilton Hotel to book as many rooms for employees who might need a place to stay nearby and to set up a temporary headquarters to gather and pick up the pieces while the Fenrir building was blocked off.

Cady gathered the employees who had been evacuated, telling them to go home and be with their families and wait for an announcement when they could come back, although some of them opted to stay and help. She then had to take care of employees who were hurt and possibly dead. Still, there was so much more work to do.

Nick had his hands full as well. Aside from having to piece together what happened on the scene, he was also in charge of damage control. His first call was to the Police Chief Deputy of New York and the Fire Department Chief. He didn't know the exact cause, but instinct told him that with the series of attacks, it was probably Lycan-related. If they hoped to cover up anything, it would have to be now.

By mid-morning, he was in a meeting with Grant, Police Chief Andrews, and Commissioner O'Grady, sitting around a table in one of the conference rooms at The Hamilton.

"We can't explain it." Commissioner O'Grady shook his head. "It was definitely some type of homemade explosive. We found traces of a timer and possibly a case, but with the size of the damage, the device should have been at least twice the size."

"Our CSI guy said the device was probably as big as a brick." Deputy Police Chief Andrews showed them a picture of a burned-out clock timer. "But they can't find traces of any explosive, chemical, or anything that could have possibly made such an explosion."

"Could it have been mailed to you?" O'Grady asked.

"Our security protocols are pretty strict, especially in the mail room." Nick rubbed his jaw. "Believe it or not, we have state-of-the-art x-rays and chemical detectors that examine all packages before they go into the building. We had them installed a few years ago."

"One of your people then?" Andrews offered cautiously.

"We don't allow outsiders in our mailroom, and everyone who goes in goes through the same detectors," Grant replied. "And I can't imagine who would do this. Our HR is top notch, no one slips through."

The two men looked at each other. "Mr. Anderson, this might be something beyond us." Andrews rubbed his forehead. "Perhaps something ... not of our world?"

"We can't explain it," O'Grady added. "It may be time for you to consult your own sources."

Grant nodded. "Yes, this is something we need to keep internal. Thank you gentlemen, for your help, as always."

"Of course, Alpha." Andrews stood up and

shook Grant's hand. "We've kept this to as few people as possible. Just my head CSI guy and the first responders."

"And the guys from Ladder 453 who looked through the scene. I have the list here." O'Grady pushed a piece of paper towards the Lycan, but hesitated. "You won't ... scramble their brains too much, will ya?"

Grant shook his head. O'Grady was a human ally, but they usually never needed his help for anything. "They'll be fine, Commissioner. No harm will come to them, but they may be confused for a few days. You might want to suggest to their captain to give these guys some time off."

The Fire Commissioner seemed appeased, and he shook hands with both men before leaving with the Deputy Police Chief.

"I'll make sure they all get the potion." Nick took the list from Grant. Although the higher ups in the police and fire departments were allies of the New York clan, their people were not aware of the existence of Lycans in the world. Thus, they kept a stash of confusion potion on hand for situations like this. "It might deplete our stores for a bit." The potion was notoriously hard to get a hold of, since it was made by witches who were not fond of the Lycans. Nick had to go through several channels to buy it, and by the time the potion came to him, it had already passed through so many hands that the price was exorbitant.

"But worth it." Grant let out a breath and massaged the bridge between his nose. He collapsed back in the chair. "What a mess."

"Don't you wish we had some of that Torlyncă right now?" Nick leaned back into his own seat.

"Maybe we can get room service to send us a bottle of whiskey or something," Grant sighed. "Could use a drink or five right now."

"You and me both." Nick picked up the picture of the timer. "So, a device that mysteriously appeared in our office and left no traces of an explosive or chemical and half the size it should be."

"There could only be one explanation," Grant offered.

"Magic," Nick said with distaste. Unlike The Enclave, Fenrir was definitely not protected by any sort of magical charm. It was simply too big and too busy.

"Right." Grant put his hands on the conference table. "Call Dr. Cross in."

"She'll be here today." Nick picked up the phone. "I'll get her in to examine the mailroom."

CHAPTER TWENTY-THREE

"I want those videos, and I want them now!" Alynna roared into her cell phone. "You tell your boss that the footage from Blood Moon better be on my server in fifteen minutes or he can kiss the contract goodbye ... you bet I'll make it happen, buster, don't try me!" She wished she was on her phone in the office, it would have been so much more satisfying to slam the receiver down on that whiny IT guy.

"Argghh!" she groaned in frustration. When this was over, the first thing she was going to do was to tell Grant to fire that two-bit, so-called security company Blood Moon had hired and do it in house or have her vet their next contractor.

"Please don't get too stressed out, baby doll."

Alex walked into their temporary headquarters at The Hamilton Hotel and soothed his wife, rubbing her arm.

"How can I not get stressed?" Alynna tugged her arm away. "We've been waiting for that footage for over two weeks! We're under attack, Alex, don't you care? How can you just sit there and look calm?"

Alex put his hands on his wife's shoulder. "Because panicking won't do us any good." He kissed the top of her head. "I know you're angry, and so am I. We all are. But if we have any hope of finding whoever's out to get us, then we all need to have cool heads." He gathered her into his arms, and although she resisted, she finally relaxed.

"You're so smart, you know?" she murmured into his chest.

"Well, that's why you married me, I guess." He grinned down at her.

"I'm sorry for going off on you." She pulled away and took a deep breath. He answered by stroking her hair. "Okay, what do we know so far?"

Alex and Alynna had followed Cady's directions and went straight to The Hamilton. The manager, Jake Evans, had seen the news and was more than happy to help. He cleared out the top two floors of the hotel, including their Presidential

Suite, which they had designated as their headquarters for now. They still couldn't get into Fenrir, but it was a good thing that all their servers and IT department were actually offsite in an undisclosed location in Brooklyn. It took a few hours, but their IT guys were able to set up some new laptops in the suite to mirror their computers in the office. They had access to everything, including the video and evidence they had previously gathered. They got to work as soon as they could, while Grant, Nick, and Cady took care of everything else.

"Well," Alex sat down in front of his borrowed laptop, "at exactly eight am, there was a large explosion on the 8th floor of the Fenrir Building. The mailroom and most of the south-east corner was destroyed. There were twenty people clocked in. Eighteen are in the hospital, two of them in critical condition and ..." Alex shook his head. "Two dead bodies were found. Traces of dead bodies," Alex choked, but cleared his throat. "Unidentified by the authorities for now, but when cross-checked with the records of people signed in at the time versus our people at the hospital, the only ones unaccounted for are Marilyn Wasser, a human manager, and John Burns, a Lycan mail clerk."

Alynna put her face in her hands. Dead. Two people dead. It was bad enough when it was only her under attack, but now people were dying. "We have to stop whoever is doing this! What do we know about the explosion?"

Alex's jaw tightened, but he continued. "I just spoke on the phone with Nick. He had some expert come in and examine the scene, a Dr. Jade Cross, a Lycan R and D scientist. Nick was able to sneak her into the mailroom, and she did a preliminary examination. She said it was probably some type of device using by Ognevaia."

"Okay, what's that?"

"It's a type of flammable substance. Think Molotov cocktail, but powered by magic. It explodes like wildfire, virtually undetectable by modern technology and leaves no traces afterward. And you only need a small amount to make an explosion that big. That's the only reason she thinks it was Ognevaia. Dr. Cross says it seems like the device was planted in the mailroom and set to explode at eight a.m."

"Magic?" Alynna asked.

"Yes, that's why Nick had Dr. Cross examined the room. Apparently, she's our Lycan expert on all things magical."

"So, magic meaning witches possibly?" If she remembered her crash course in all things Lycan and magical correctly, only witches could use magic.

Her husband nodded. "That's what it looks like."

Alynna sighed. "I don't know anything about witches and warlocks."

"We've had an informal truce with them for about a hundred years." Alex's brows knitted. "Why they'd start attacking us, I don't know. Grant will have to alert the Lycan High Council if it turns out the witches are violating the truce."

A ringing interrupted the couple. "Hello?" Alynna picked up her phone. "Okay, good! Yes, download it to the server. I'll look at it now." She sighed. "Blood Moon's CCTV footage is finally in!"

"Good. I have the ones from Fenrir, too. It's a good thing all our security is in-house."

"Let's get to work."

It took about twenty minutes for them to download all the footage, and they sat down on their respective laptops to start combing through the evidence.

"I'll take the Fenrir one, you do the Blood Moon," Alynna said. "I'll start going backward, from eight a.m. If you're done before I am, you can help me. If this device had a timer, it could have come in at any point in the last twenty-four to forty-eight hours."

"Right." Alex pulled up his footage.

They worked in silence. Alynna opened the files from the server, starting with the ones from inside the mailroom. It showed a bird's eye view of the entire office. She started at eight a.m., right when the feed was cut off. It was difficult to see the explosion, but she grit her teeth and watched the footage, setting it at double speed. The activity seemed normal enough, people arriving for work and going to their desks.

She scrolled back and forth, trying to see if anyone had brought in the device or walked to the blast area. No such luck. Everyone who arrived had gone straight to their desks, which were on the opposite side and most likely why most escaped with just injuries. The first one in at seven a.m. was an older female, Marilyn Wasser. Her office was on the east corner, with a view of the river. The device was most likely just behind her office, just under the camera, since the south-east corner was the most destroyed area. Rewinding further, she saw no one had entered or exited for the previous couple of hours.

"Huh?" Alynna's finger tapped on the stop button when a figure appeared in the video. She stopped and noted the time. 2:29 a.m. Scrolling back a few minutes, she played the tape forward and watched the door open. "Gotcha!" Narrowing her eyes, she could clearly make out the face of the figure. "What?" The figure entered the mailroom carrying a small bag and went straight to the south east corner, disappearing for a second, then coming back into the frame.

"No!" Alynna slammed the laptop lid down. "No!"

"Alynna!" Alex rushed to his wife. "What's wrong?"

The young woman's face was anguished. "It can't be!" She shook her head, and her body began to shake. "I refuse to believe it!"

"What is it? What did you see, Alynna?" He drew her into his arms and his wife clung to him tightly.

"It's ... it's ..." Alynna took a deep breath. "There's some mistake ..."

Alex gently pried her arms away from his waist and sat her down. He opened the laptop and saw the face staring up at them. It was Cady. "No." He looked at his wife. "There's some explanation, right?"

"I think ... what do we do, Alex?"

The young man gritted his teeth. "We need to tell Grant and Nick."

"But what if they ..."

"Well, if she did do this, then we have no choice but to tell them."

Alynna nodded. "Call Nick. I'll call Grant. Don't tell them anything, but we'll show them when they get here. I'm going to look into her background and see what I can come up with. There must be some way to explain this."

———

Alynna couldn't get a hold of Grant, which was understandable since he was still putting out fires. Nick arrived at the suite at around six p.m., looking tired and haggard.

"What's going on?" the Beta asked as he dropped his jacket on the couch. "You said it was urgent?"

Alex and Alynna looked at each other, hesitating. "Maybe we should wait for Grant?" Alynna suggested.

Nick shook his head. "He's gonna be tied up for at least another two hours. He's about to go on a major news network to make sure everyone knows it was all a gas explosion. I'm sure you can tell me now if it's that important."

Alynna bit her lip to stop it from trembling. "Nick, this is hard to say ... but we know who planted the device."

"Who?" All tiredness left Nick, and his stance tensed, as if ready to spring into action. "And why couldn't you tell me over the phone?"

"I think you should just see it for yourself." Alex gave the laptop to the other man. "Go and press play. We've seen it a million times by now."

Nick took the laptop, opened it and clicked on the play button. Alynna watched as his face turned into a stern, cold mask. The tension in the room became thick and heavy. He scrolled back and watched it once more, then another time. He stood there, motionless for a few seconds and handed the laptop back to Alex. He turned and walked toward the windows.

"Nick," Alynna began. "Say something."

The Beta turned back to them. "Do we have other proof?"

"Y-y-yes." Alynna sounded like she wanted to break down and cry. "Not just for this, but for Blood Moon as well."

"We have footage of her at Blood Moon, spiking drinks. The bartender, well, he seems to have been distracted, and she put something from her hand into a couple of trays ... I'll show you –"

"I've seen enough," Nick cut her off.

"Her keycard was used to enter Fenrir at 2:20 a.m. this morning and then exited at 2:39 a.m., which matches the footage," Alex explained further. Alynna had broken down at this point and sank onto the couch. Her husband sat down next to her, pulling her close.

"Do we have a motive?" Nick's voice was cool.

Alex looked up. "Alynna found something ... we're not sure, but it's obvious this is all connected to magic and possibly witches." He looked at his wife and she nodded. He continued, opening up the laptop again. "We looked at records of known witches who might live in and around the New York area or mentioned in Lycan records. We don't keep track of everyone of course, not since the truce, but we did find a mention of witch named Charlotte Fontaine, who tangled with some Lycans back in 1909. She married a William Chatraine in 1920 and had four children, the youngest was named Elise Chatraine. She had two kids, one a Victoria Chatraine. Victoria then married Luther Gray and had one daughter, Cady Elise Gray, before they separated." Alex paused. "She's a witch, and we didn't know."

"There has to be some explanation, right?" Alynna hiccupped. "Some ... magical explanation?

Was she hypnotized? Did the witches force her to do this somehow? Why didn't we know she's a witch?"

"We can't tell them apart from humans," Alex explained. "At least, not until they show their powers." He turned to Nick. "Al Doilea, what do we do now?"

Nick's eyes were like glinting shards of blue glass. "Keep trying to contact the Alpha. Don't tell anyone else for now. I'll take care of the rest." With that, he left the suite.

CHAPTER TWENTY-FOUR

Cady was bone tired. All the other times she had a ton of work to do, had to finish some project, or organize an event, she *thought* she was tired, but this was different. It was physically and emotionally tiring, dealing with Fenrir employees and their families. The image of John Burns' wife breaking down and Marilyn Wasser's son crying out in grief was something she'd never forget in her life. And the work wasn't done. There was still a lot to do, but at least the media and the general public seemed appeased that the Fenrir explosion was nothing more than a gas leak. Sure, there were a few fringe media outlets and blogs crying conspiracy, but the major news stations and gossip rags had moved on. Thank god for the surprise celebrity divorce between that Hollywood hunk and his starlet wife.

The receptionist at The Hamilton handed her a set of keycards to her room, which Alynna had reserved for her. She was able to sneak in two burgers from a fast-food place around the corner from the hospital after she met with the families of the employees with injuries, but she was still so famished. She asked the front desk to send her two of the fastest meals they could whip up. By the time she had finished her shower and was slipping into a robe, the room service cart was waiting outside with a dish of beef stew, a basket of bread, a hearty tuna salad, and a big slice of chocolate cake. Needless to say, she scarfed everything down in fifteen minutes.

A chirp indicating she got a message on her phone interrupted her as she finished off the last of the cake.

Where are you? It was Nick.

Room 3214, she answered.

Cady waited for a few minutes for his answer, but didn't get anything. *Hmm.* That was unlike Nick, but today was an unusual day for all of them. She pushed the room service cart to the side and reached for her pad so she could check if any more news stories had popped up. A sudden knock on the door almost made her drop her tablet. *Nick,* she thought. He was the only one who knew where she was. She hadn't had time to think about their conversation this morning, but all she wanted was to see him and have his arms around her.

She rushed to the door, opening it without looking through the peephole, not that she needed to. Launching herself at him, she wrapped her arms around his torso, breathing in his comforting scent.

Nick seemed almost surprised, and staggered back slightly, but regained his balance in time. It took a second for Cady to notice that his body was stiff as a board. *Probably from today.* Without saying anything else, she led him into her room and closed the door behind her, making sure to put the Do Not Disturb sign on the knob.

"How are you?" she asked cautiously. He had walked over to the window of her small room, which had a view of the building across from them. His shoulders were tense and his hands remained still at his side. "Is there anything I can do for you?"

He said nothing, but he slowly turned to her. His face was a stone mask, eyes like hard steel. "Nothing. Nothing at all." It took only two steps for him to cross over to where she was standing by the bed. Looking into her face, he put a hand on her cheek.

There was something off about Nick, but she didn't say anything. Though she craved his touch, she wanted to give him time to process. Closing her eyes, she felt his hands run down her cheek, to her neck, and across her shoulder.

"Nick," she gasped when his hand slipped under her hotel robe, exposing her collarbones.

"Do you like that?"

"Hmm ... yes ..." she sighed.

"You don't mind," he paused as he wrapped both hands on her arms, "that a dirty, lowly Lycan is touching you?"

Cady's eyes flew open in surprise. "What?" Her blood froze in her veins and the bottom of her stomach dropped.

"Don't deny it." Nick's hands gripped her harder. "That's how you witches view us, right? Dirty, filthy creatures?"

"No! What ... what are you talking about?" Cady tried to move away from Nick, but couldn't as the Lycan kept his grip strong.

"It's true, right? About your mother?"

"Y-y-yes ..." she confessed. "How did you ... Nick, please, listen to me –"

"Witch," he spat. "All this time, sitting right

under our noses! That was the plan, right? Worm your way into the clan and destroy us from the inside?"

"Nick, let me explain!" Cady wrenched herself away from him. "Yes, my mother is a witch. She came to me a few weeks ago and caught me off guard. She threatened me. No one knew about her, just my father. But I swear, I'm not a witch and I have no magic."

"It doesn't matter. We know it was you. All of it. The belladonna. The bombing."

"What?" Cady asked incredulously. "What are you talking about?"

"Don't deny it, witch!" he accused, cornering her until the backs of her knees hit the edge of the bed. "We have you on camera, poisoning the drinks at Blood Moon and footage of you planting the device in the mailroom. Your keycard was used to enter the building. I bet you even planned your little 'accident' to misdirect us!"

Cady looked confused. "What? What are you talking about! I would never ..." Her brows knitted. "I wasn't even at Blood Moon that night!"

"You said you were meeting your friend there," he reminded her.

She let out a frustrated groan. "I said that because you were going to dinner with Madison and

... anyway," she squared her shoulders, "I didn't go to Blood Moon, I went to The Met Museum! I go there sometimes because that's where my dad and I would go when I was growing up. We both loved the impressionists."

"Stop lying, Cady," he roared at her. "We have you on camera clearly. And the same with the mail-room bomb. It was an Ognevaia bomb you and your witch coven cooked up, but you already knew that. Your keycard clocked you in and then you planted the bomb. It's all on camera."

"There must be some mistake!" She threw her hands up and planted them on his chest. "Please, Nick, believe me."

"What were you doing between two and three a.m. this morning?"

"I ..." Cady stopped. "Oh god ..." The wheels in her head started turning. Victoria's call. The meeting at the diner. She was set up. "I swear Nick, if you let me explain, I can clear this up."

"And how will you explain, my sweet?" he mocked. "I suppose you can't help yourself and who you are."

Cady bit her lip to stop the tears from falling. Nick reacted exactly as she thought he would. Her heart wrenched, seeing him look at her so coldly and with such hatred in his eyes, when it was just this morning he was ready to give up everything for her. "Nick, I swear. I'm not a witch. I know how you feel about witches because of your parents –"

"Don't you dare mention them," he warned. "My grandfather told me that even as they were burned at the stake they kept screaming and spitting out, calling my mother and father 'filthy, dirty creatures' and that they deserved to die."

Cady let out a small cry, the tears finally falling down her cheeks. "Nick, I'm sorry ..." She reached up and touched his cheek. He flinched, but put his hand over hers.

"Are you really?" His voice was so cold, she shivered.

"I ..." Cady didn't know what else to do. She leaned in and placed her head on his chest. "I'm so sorry about your parents. But I didn't do this."

Nick pushed her back until they fell on the bed. He loomed over her, pushing her hair out of her face, his hand playing with the collar of her robe. "Tell me you didn't do it," he demanded as he un-buttoned his shirt.

"I didn't do it." She gasped when he shoved the robe aside, exposing her breasts to the cool air. Her nipples hardened instantly.

"Convince me."

Cady looked up into his eyes, seeing hurt behind his the anger. He never talked about his parents, always claiming he was too young, but it was obvious their death had left a big mark on him. Despite all the things he said, accused her of, she wanted to comfort him and take that hurt away. She did it the only way she knew how. Reaching up, she pulled him down for a kiss, pressing her lips to his.

Nick growled and devoured her mouth, his body coming down on hers. Cady whimpered when she felt his hard cock pressing up against her core, even through the thick robe. His scent filled her nose, and she breathed it in, letting it fill her and surround her. He ripped his mouth from hers. Grabbing her wrists, he placed them over her head with one hand, forcing her breasts to jut out.

"So beautiful." He stared down at her as his other hand captured her chin, tipping it up to face him. "I always thought you were the most beautiful woman I'd ever seen."

Before she could say anything, he lowered his head to her nipples, drawing them into his warm mouth. Pleasure shot through her body, and she squirmed as her pussy flooded with wetness. The erotic, tortuous strokes of his tongue made her bones melt, and she moaned in pleasure. Nick seemed like a man possessed as he continued to torment her. Her body was craving him, despite what he might think of her now, and she pushed up her hips and breasts at him, trying to get more contact. He let go of her wrists and ripped the robe open.

"Please," she said. God, she was going to die from need. She reached up and put her hands on his shoulders.

"No," he growled. "You don't get to touch."

Her hands recoiled like he had slapped her. More tears gathered in her eyes and she sucked in a breath, trying not to make them fall. A vice gripped her heart, and she thought of the betrayal Nick must have felt – his parents, knowing about Victoria. She wanted to reach out to him, but knew he wouldn't listen. This was it, this was the end. Her life as she knew it was over, and she would take every bit of what Nick could give her, what he had left. Because the truth was, she loved him, always had. And she wanted this, wanted him.

Nick shrugged off his shirt, then reached down to unzip his pants. He tugged away at this clothes until he was fully naked. His large hand trailed down her stomach, fingers tracing a path down to her thighs. His fingers delved into her soft, wet folds, and Cady gasped as his thumb found her clit, stroking it, making her even wetter. She groaned. "Nick," she pleaded.

He withdrew his fingers, which made her

whimper in disappointment. He grabbed her wrists again and pinned them over head. Positioning himself over her, he grabbed his erect shaft and pressed the tip up against her damp folds.

"What do you want, Cady?"

"You," she replied without missing a beat.

"You want this dirty, filthy Lycan inside you? Fucking you?"

She flinched at the words, but she couldn't do anything but nod as the thick head of his cock teased her clit.

"Beg me for it."

"Please, Nick. I want you. Fuck me, please!"

She cried out as he buried himself in her, pushing all the way to the hilt. He released her wrists and, risking his anger, she reached up and ran her fingers through his dark blonde hair. She pushed up closer to him, his chest hairs tickling her sensitive nipples. "Keep going," she urged.

Nick grunted as he rolled his hips forward, not even bothering to start slow. Instead, he thrust in and out of her in an unfaltering rhythm. "Cady," he whispered with a ragged breath. He pulled completely out of her and then pushed back in. "God, you're so hot and wet and tight. And completely mine."

Cady wrapped her legs around him, not

wanting to let go. He hammered in and out of her, pushing her open, her body winding up tightly as the tension built in her. Nick reached down and stroked her clit as he slammed into her.

She screamed his name, gripping him tighter as he continued to plunge into her. It was such a contrast from that morning's sweet and gentle lovemaking, his hands gripping her so tight she knew they would leave bruises all over, but she reveled in every moment, every bit of friction. Her orgasm ripped through her, exploding in a white heat that made her see stars. As she came down, she felt his body stiffen and his thrusts becoming erratic. He grinded against her, then buried himself one last time into her, body trembling as he came, his seed flooding inside of her. Bracing himself on his elbows, he remained on top of her, his head hung low as he breathed heavily.

Shame burned in her face, and she pushed at him, rolling onto her side. God, she had wanted him so bad despite what he had accused her of doing. *What am I going to do now?* Did Nick believe her? Would Grant believe her story? What else did Victoria do to convince them?

"All this time ... tell me, Cady," he leaned down and whispered in her ear. "Was sleeping with me part of the plan? Or was that an opportunity that came along at the right time? That was pretty convincing on your part. I suppose I should be thankful I'm the first one you decided to whore yourself out —"

A loud crack rang through the air as Cady's palm connected with his cheek. "You bastard!" she cried out, her face a mask of hurt. She scrambled off the bed, closing the robe to cover herself.

He didn't even flinch. "Get dressed. We're going to see Grant." With cat-like grace, he rolled off the mattress and began to put on his clothes. She ran to the bathroom, slamming the door behind her, thankful she made it before she broke down.

Heart-wrenching sobs tore through her, and she had to bite the back of her hand to stop herself and muffle the noise. She washed her face with the cold water from the tap, biting her lips until they bled just to stop herself from crying further. Taking a deep breath, she began to dress in the clothes she had left in the bathroom. Looking at her reflection in the mirror, she took a deep breath. She would not give him the satisfaction of seeing her cry anymore.

A loud shout followed by a thud interrupted her thoughts. "What the ..?" She whipped her head around. The noise came from the room. Yanking, the door open, she rushed out of the bathroom.

"What? Mother!"

Victoria was in the room standing over Nick, who was lying motionless on the ground. There was a tall, broad-shouldered blonde man behind her, who seemed familiar. "Hello, Cady."

"You!" She rushed as her mother, wanting to hurt her for ruining her life. But the tall man grabbed her by the waist and hauled her back.

Victoria tsked. "My dear, that's no way to behave toward people who have come to save you."

"Save me? *Save me?*" Her voice was high with tension. "You ruined my life!"

"I told you I would do anything to have you back." Victoria nudged the unconscious Nick with the toe of her stilettos. Cady cried out, reaching for Nick. "Don't worry, dear. Just a bit of knock-out potion. It probably won't last long seeing as I didn't bring enough, so we should get out of here now."

"Why would I come with you?"

Victoria motioned to the tall man, who let Cady go and walked toward Nick. He picked up Nick by his neck and pinned him against the wall. "Because, my dear, if you don't, Daric here will crush your precious Lycan's throat."

Cady's eyes widened. "Don't! Please don't! Put him down," she pleaded to the blonde giant. "I'll come with you," she whispered, defeated.

Victoria's face broke into a smile. "Good. And

just in case you have some bright idea of trying to escape or call for help, Daric here will be staying behind until we're safely in the car. Now," she held out her hand, "be a good girl and take my arm, and smile while you walk out with me."

———

Victoria led her out of the room, down to the ground floor and out of the lobby. They stopped in front of a blue sedan, and her mother unlocked the car, pushing Cady into the back before settling into the front passenger seat. She took out a phone, tapped on the screen, and settled back.

About ten minutes later, the tall blonde man casually strolled out of the hotel and got into the driver's side.

"I recognize you!" Cady realized. "You're the man at the coffee shop ... my wallet! Did you steal my keycard?"

The man said nothing, but started the car instead.

"Smart girl," Victoria scoffed.

"Where are we going?" Cady asked. "Why aren't you tying me up or blindfolding me? Isn't that what you do when you kidnap someone?"

Her mother laughed. "Well, my dear, first of all,

I had to make sure the staff and the cameras at the hotel saw you leaving with me willingly," she explained. "Next, I don't need to tie you up. You've got nowhere to go now, don't you see? Do you think you can go back to the Lycans after all the 'evidence' we planted? It's your face on the videos, your keycard used to enter the building. You were also in that 'accident' that almost killed a Lycan driver. You can't even explain your whereabouts when I planted the bomb because we made sure all the cameras around the diner weren't working that night."

Cady gasped, and Victoria continued. "If you do go back to them, they'll take you to the High Council, and they will find you guilty. You'd be tossed out like garbage at best and burned at the stake at worst for the attempted murder of several Lycans and killing those employees."

Cady felt her chest tighten, her stomach dropping. That was their game. She was so stupid, falling right into their hands. They weren't going to take her by force, but make sure she had nowhere else to go. Instead of taking her away, they took the Clan from her. And judging by the hatred she saw in Nick Vrost's eyes, they succeeded.

———

Grant ran a hand through his hair in frustration as Alex finished his explanation. Alynna remained on the other end of the couch, her arms crossed and her face inscrutable. "And this is what we have so far?" His eyes remained transfixed on the laptop screen, at Cady's face.

"Yes, Primul." Alex shut the lid of the laptop. They'd all seen the footage enough times now, and each time they played it, it was like being betrayed all over again.

"God, what a mess!" Grant stood up. "And Cady ..." He was obviously hurt by the betrayal, but hadn't had a chance to process it yet.

"I hate to sound like a broken record," Alynna walked up to Grant, "but can't we find another explanation?"

The Alpha shook his head. "I want to find another explanation too, Alynna." He placed his hands on her shoulders comfortingly. "I swear, I do. I would do anything for a logical explanation or one that absolves her. But all the evidence is here. I ..." he paused.

There was a loud, insistent knock on the door to the suite. Alex walked over and opened the door. "Al Doilea?"

Nick burst into the room, rushing to Grant. "I'm sorry, Primul. She got away."

"Got away?" Alynna asked. "Who?"

"Cady," he said the name with such distaste it made Alynna flinch. "I confronted her in her hotel room and then ... I don't quite remember, but I opened the door and there were two people standing in front of me. That's the last I remember. They probably hit me with a potion of some sort."

"Are you okay?" Grant asked.

"I'm fine," Nick assured him. "I woke up and I was on the floor and she was gone. I was about to take her here so we could interrogate her."

"Did she say anything else when you confronted her?" Alynna inquired.

"No ... I mean, she said she didn't do it, of course. Said she was at The Met during the Blood Moon attack, but had no alibi for this morning," Nick relayed. "She admitted her mother was a witch, yet claims she didn't have any powers of her own. I wouldn't be surprised if it was her mother who got her out. I remember one of the people who knocked me out was a woman."

Although Nick's face didn't betray any emotion, the tension in his body language was evident

"I'm sorry, Nick." Grant shook his head. "I should have told you. I knew about her mother. Dad told me and asked me to keep it a secret. He probably never thought she would do anything. And now two people are dead ..."

"It's not your fault, Grant," Alynna cried. "You were probably a kid when he told you that secret! Years ago! How could you know that this would happen!"

"You knew she was a witch?" Nick's voice turned angry.

Alynna gasped in shock, and Alex tensed. No one would dare raise their voice at the Alpha, least of all his right-hand man. Yet Nick could barely contain his rage.

Grant put his hand up. "It's okay," he said to Alynna and Alex. "He has every right to be angry at me. Her mother is a witch, Nick. Cady's is human and has no powers, as far as I know. And I don't think Michael or Luther would have kept her so close if they believed she was dangerous."

Nick's hands were balled into tights fists at his side. "You knew! And yet you let her come to me on Blood Moon!"

"What was I supposed to do, Nick?" Grant's voice was even, but the barely controlled anger simmered on the surface. "Let you transform in a hotel full of people? Let you go insane or die? Hurt or kill people, including Cady herself? Expose all of us?"

"Hold on, hold on!" Alynna put herself between

the two Lycans, who looked like they were ready to tear each other apart. "What are you talking about? Can you please explain –"

"It doesn't matter!" Nick crossed his arms and backed away from Grant and Alynna.

"Nick was caught outside during the Blood Moon without access to a safe room," Grant explained. "With Cady. There was only one way to control the shift, and Cady ..."

"Cady provided it," Nick finished.

Alynna's jaw dropped, realizing what he meant. "See! How could she betray us when she did everything she could to protect you!"

"To protect herself and their plan to destroy us!" Nick finished. "That's a moot point anyway. Cady is gone; we're obviously under attack. We need to inform the High Council."

"I'll call them right now." Grant fished his phone from his pocket with a defeated sigh.

"No! Wait!" Alynna put her hand on Grant's. "Please! Please Grant, don't do it. Not yet!"

"Why?" Nick asked, directing his anger at the young Lycan woman. "She's guilty. Other clans need to be warned. The witches need to pay. You know nothing about how this works and how we –"

"Don't talk to my wife that way," Alex warned

the Beta. "She's one of us and has worked damn hard to be part of this Clan."

Before Nick could say anything, Alynna touched her husband's arm. "Alex, Nick please. We can't tear ourselves apart right now. If the witches are out to destroy us, then we need to stick together."

Both Lycans seemed to stand down, moving away from each other. Alynna turned back to Grant. "Can't you keep a lid on this for a bit? Give me a few days."

"Alynna, I know you like Cady, but the evidence is all there," Grant reasoned.

"But there's something off about it! I can feel it!" Alynna looked pleadingly at him. "Do it, please. For me? For her? There must be part of you that's screaming that this is all wrong!"

Grant looked to Nick, who said nothing. The Alpha knew his stance though, seeing how he blindly hated all witches. Alynna, on the other hand, looked at him with such conviction in her eyes, he had to relent. "I can do forty-eight hours and no more. If the Lycan High Council finds out we deliberately withheld information from them, they will not look on it kindly. Especially if more Lycans are hurt."

"Thank you Grant!" She hugged her brother. "I'll get to the bottom of this."

"And if it turns out she did betray us?" Grant posed.

Alynna swallowed a gulp. "I promise, I'll let you know either way."

CHAPTER TWENTY-FIVE

Cady watched the landscape as they seemed to drive for hours, but the truth was it had only been about forty-five minutes. She recognized their route, and they were headed either upstate or to Connecticut. No one knew exactly where witch covens hid out - their kind was more of a loose association rather than an organized community like the Lycans. Not that witches hated each other, it was just the way things were. At least that's what she remembered. Luther had explained Victoria belonged to a small coven from upstate, composed mostly of her own family members.

The ride was silent, and neither Victoria nor

Daric had paid her much attention, even when she asked them questions. They kept driving on, farther and farther north until she couldn't keep track of where they were anymore. If only she had thought to slip her phone into her bra or something, but there was no time. Not when that blonde brute was ready to crush Nick's neck. *Nick ...oh god.* She would never see him again. She didn't know if she wanted to weep with sadness or joy. The way he treated her those last moments was too cruel, even for him. But couldn't she blame him. *Those awful witches, what they said about his parents.* Vasili must have told him, of course, as he witnessed the execution of his son and daughter-in-law's murderers. That bitter old man probably planted seeds of hate into the young boy.

The car slowed down, and they pulled into a gas station. "I need to fill up," Daric explained.

"Don't be too long, darling," Victoria flirted.

Daric ignored the witch, stopping the car in front of the gas pump. He opened the door and walked into the convenience store to pay.

Cady's heart began to pound. Her mother seemed distracted, typing out messages into her phone. Glancing at the door, she realized that Daric had left it unlocked. Was this it? Would this be her only chance of escape? They were the only ones at this station in the middle of nowhere. *I have to try.*

After hesitating briefly, she quickly grabbed the door handle, jerked it open, and jumped out of the car.

"Cady!" she heard Victoria scream behind her, but paid her no mind. She ran as fast as her legs could carry her, in no particular direction except away from the car. A burst of speed propelled her across the gas station, but suddenly, an invisible force slammed into her. She flew high into the air and was dragged back to the car, pinned against the metal body. She tried to wave her arms, but found herself unable to move.

"Where are you going, little one?" Daric asked as he walked toward her. He had his hand in front of her, as if he held her. "Tsk, tsk. There's nowhere you can run to, don't you see?" He moved his hand slightly, and she felt the invisible grip loosen. Still, she remained rooted in the spot. "Don't even try to escape. I may not be so merciful next time."

Cady's eyes widened with terror, and she nodded meekly.

"Now, get into the car." He motioned to the door, which swung open by itself. She slowly entered and the door closed, the locks clicking into place with a wave of Daric's hand. "I won't be making the same mistake."

She slumped in the back of the car in defeat.

———

Alex had to drag his wife to bed that night, but he simply couldn't stand by and watch while she ran herself into the ground. She ranted and raged against him, claiming she needed all forty-eight hours Grant gave them and didn't he think Cady deserved a fair shot? He reasoned that she needed rest, and the only way to help Cady was to come back to the problem with a fresh set of eyes in the morning. Alynna was so angry at him, she slept on the couch.

He lay awake in their bed, unable to sleep. He was conflicted. On one hand, the evidence was clear, but on the other ... well ... Cady was his friend, and he couldn't believe she would do such a thing. And Alynna was his wife, but also a brilliant private investigator with sharp instincts. She saw something they didn't. Sometime in the middle of the night, the door to their bedroom opened, and Alynna crawled into bed with him, seeking his arms and comfort, and cried into his chest. He felt his heart breaking, for his wife and for Cady.

They slept wrapped around each other until the sun was peeking out in the sky. It was late, but they needed all the rest they could get. They got up, got dressed, and went to Fenrir, which was deemed safe by the fire department since there was no structural damage to the building itself. The office was quiet despite being a Wednesday, but that was because Grant told everyone to take as much time as they needed to process the events.

The first thing they did was track down Dr. Jade Cross. It was easy enough, since she actually worked in the building, as Jared informed them. He put in a call to her office, and she replied that she would be up as soon as possible.

"Now," Alynna sat in front of her laptop, a cup of coffee in her hand, "I think we should try to find out more about Victoria Chatraine and what she's been up to between the separation and now. Can we track down the coven? Where are they hiding? And I should probably brush up on how witches work."

"We don't know much about them, unfortunately," Alex replied. "We don't exactly keep tabs on them, but if Dr. Cross is our expert on all things magical, then she should be able to fill us in."

"Good, now we need –" A knock on the door

made her stop. "Come in!" she said in an annoyed voice.

"Alynna!" Liam Henney walked in, briefcase in hand. "I heard about the gas explosion! Are you all right?"

Alex shot up from his seat. "My *wife* is perfectly fine," he said in a tight voice.

Liam squared his shoulders. "Well, good morning to you too," he said sarcastically. "I don't think we've been introduced."

"No, I guess not," Alex sneered.

Alynna rolled her eyes. "Alex, Liam. Liam, Alex. All done now? Can we do this pissing contest later?" Both men relaxed slightly, though Alex remained standing. "Ugh!" she let out a frustrated groan as she walked over to Liam. "What are you doing here? Oh shit!" She slapped her forehead. "We were supposed to have that meeting today! Someone should have told you that we cancelled!"

"It's all right," Liam assured her. "I assumed we wouldn't be able to meet, but I wanted to be here. To come and see what I can do to help."

"That's sweet of you." Alynna was about to place a hand on his arm, but from the corner of her eye, saw her husband tense. She put her hand down. "Um, we're kind of busy here with a deadline. I'm really sorry, Liam, for your wasted trip."

"Don't worry about it. It's not a wasted trip," he said warmly, which only made Alex growl softly. "I had some excellent results to show you, and I wanted to deliver them personally. But, I'll leave you to your work."

"Thank you, Liam," she said gratefully. "Why don't you head over to Grant's office? Or I can arrange lunch or something?"

"Thanks Alynna, I'll be fine. But I will pop in and see Grant, if that's okay?"

"I'm sure it'll be fine. Go ahead and talk to Jared." She led him to the door and closed it behind her. She sent her husband a warning look. "Don't even start with me," she cautioned as she sat on her desk.

"I wasn't going to say anything." Alex gritted his teeth.

"You're going to have to learn to get along with Liam," Alynna said.

A buzz rang through the room, and Jared's voice came through the speaker. "Mr. Westbrooke, Ms. Westbrooke, Dr. Cross is here. The Alpha saw her waiting outside, and he asked if he and Mr. Vrost could sit in on your meeting as well?"

"Of course, Jared," she answered. "Give me a second and send them in."

"No problem. I'll get some coffee for all of you."

———

When Alynna pictured Dr. Jade Cross in her mind, she imagined an older, matronly lady, maybe a female version of Dr. Faulkner. She didn't expect a pretty young Lycan who was maybe a year or two older than herself, with brown hair tied back into a ponytail and deep green eyes hidden behind glasses. She was dressed like a prim librarian in a long-sleeved polka-dot shirt, a gray tweed jacket, a pencil-cut skirt and ballet flats.

"You're Dr. Cross?" Alynna couldn't contain the astonishment in her voice. "Er, sorry ..."

The other woman laughed. "Don't worry, I get it all the time." Dr. Cross spoke with a slight posh English accent. "I graduated university at eighteen, and then took another two years to finish my two PhDs. Biochemistry and Bioengineering."

"Why have I never heard of you before?" Alynna eyed her suspiciously. "And I haven't seen you around, even at The Enclave."

"She's kind of our secret weapon," Grant explained.

"Dr. Cross is officially employed as a scientist in Fenrir's Food R and D division," Nick clarified. "But, she's actually our expert in all things magical.

We've been funding her research and studies for two years now."

"Secret, so ... no one knows Lycans are studying magic?" Alynna asked suspiciously.

"A precaution," Grant assured her. "And one I'm glad we decided to take, considering the current circumstances."

"It's an honor to meet you, Alynna. I've been wanting to study you and get up close ... I mean not study you like an animal or anything! Not that I think you're a zoo animal!" Dr. Cross turned beet red. "Sorry, you're not the only one who tends to put her foot in her mouth. But the fact that you're a True Mate Lycan offspring from a human-lycan pairing and a True Mate yourself ... it's a fascinating study! I've been asking Dr. Faulkner for samples from you to study any possible magical properties, but –"

"Dr. Cross, please," Grant interrupted, barely hanging on to his patience.

"I'll let you have any sample you want," Alynna joked. "If you can tell us more."

"Right." She took out her tablet and opened up her files. "I just finished my examination of the mailroom and the device itself. I can say with 90% certainty that it was Ognevaia."

"Only 90%?" Alex asked.

"Yes, well, Ognevaia leaves no traces, so I can't be 100% sure unless the maker of the bomb confirms it. But all the signs are there - the relative size of the device and the blast, the green color of the flames reported by some of the eyewitnesses, and I've basically ruled out all other possible explosive chemicals the bomb maker could have used. I could examine the bodies as well, but I don't think it's necessary at this point."

"What else can you tell us about the bomb itself?" Alynna asked, staring at Dr. Cross' pad.

"Well, nothing more than you already know, given the video evidence. The subject entered the premises sometime around 2:30 a.m. and planted the bomb on the southeast corner of the mailroom. The device was rigged with a timer, not a remote, to go off at eight a.m., perhaps to coincide with the morning rush into work."

"Right." Alynna tapped her fingers on the pad to get a closer look at the remains of the device. Satisfied, she continued. "What about witches? What can you tell us about them? Could they have done this?"

Dr. Cross took her glasses off. "Well, we don't know a lot about how their society works, I'm afraid, since they don't keep records and they don't exactly talk to us."

"But I thought that you studied magic and magic comes from witches?"

"Well, I study magic itself, not witches in particular," Dr. Cross explained. "Er, it's kind of a broad subject. The Alpha has given me free reign to research and learn as much as I can without sticking to one particular topic. Witches and warlocks are the main magic-wielders in our world, dealing with nature magic, but there have been studies and research that suggests we Lycans held magic once, too. But again, I'm still working on a few sources, but no witch will talk to a Lycan about these things."

"What is nature magic?" Alynna asked, curious.

"Well, it's difficult to explain in one sentence, but take Ognevaia for example. This substance comes from nature, a mixture of various ingredients, like herbs and elements like wind, water, fire, earth. The substance itself is inert, but once it's powered by a witch's magic - by saying the right spell or incantation - it becomes a powerful potion."

"So, aside from their general hatred of us," Alex changed the subject, "what motive could the witches, or whoever these people are, have to bomb us?"

The scientist shrugged. "I'm afraid that's not my

area, Mr. Westbrooke. I'm not very good with people and their motives."

"I think we know why," Nick finally spoke up. "They want to destroy us."

"But why us?" Alynna asked. "Why the New York Clan? Why not the High Council or even start small? Witches don't have a centralized organization, right?" Dr. Cross shook her head. "How could one coven even begin to mount an attack on a clan and so sloppily, too? Poisoning with Belladonna, then a bomb? It doesn't make sense to me."

"Maybe they're just trying to scare us ... or get ready for bigger things," Nick countered. "Primul, this is a waste of time. We need to alert the High Council, and we must all prepare for the next attack."

"I know how you feel, Nick," Grant sympathized. "But Alynna is bringing up good points."

"But the Council –"

"We will tell them we needed time to gather all evidence before causing a panic," Grant said in a firm voice.

"Primul, this is no time to let personal feelings –"

"If anyone is letting their personal feelings get in the way, it's you!" Alynna lashed. "I can't believe you wouldn't even give Cady a fair chance! What happened to innocent until proven guilty?"

"That belongs to the court of humans," Nick blurted. "Primul, I have more things to attend to. I'll take my leave."

Grant nodded, and Nick left without a word.

"I've never seen him like this," Grant sighed.

"What the fuck is the matter with him?" Alynna asked in an annoyed voice.

"Alynna," Grant began. "Nick's parents ... they were killed by witches."

Alynna's face fell. "Oh my god! I didn't know!" She buried her face in her hands. "That's why ... oh my ... Nick ..."

"It's okay," Grant assured her. "He's ... he'll need time. Speaking of time, Alynna I have to inform the Lycan High Council by tomorrow. Noon."

His sister nodded. "I understand. I'll keep working on it."

"Good, I should go." The Alpha stood up, bid them goodbye, and walked out the door.

"I should get going, too." Dr. Cross stood and picked up her things. "I'm sorry I couldn't be of any more help." She turned and walked toward the door.

"Wait!" Alynna stopped her with a hand on her arm. The young scientist looked at her curiously. "I saw you hesitate when you were talking about Cady. You called her 'the subject'."

The Lycan shrugged. "I don't deal in speculation. Only facts."

"Dr. Cross," Alynna pleaded. "Anything you can do to help us ... I won't mention it to Grant unless we can prove it. One hundred percent."

"Well, I've met Ms. Gray a few times," she sounded hesitant. "She was the one who found me and recruited me, actually. She, the Alpha, and Mr. Vrost are the only ones who know about what I'm really studying. She's adored by all Lycans in New York, you know? And wouldn't she be trying to prevent Lycans from learning and possibly getting their hands on magic? And ... there's something. I just don't know if it's my place."

"No, please, tell me," Alynna urged. "Just between us."

"Well, those videos. They seem off to me."

"Off? In what way?"

"Yes. One of the preliminary - very preliminary, I have to warn you - studies I'm looking into is how magic can affect technology. Glamour magic, that is. Magic that can fool the eye into thinking it saw something else has always worked on people, but apparently with some modifications these days it can work on cameras, too. Another witch will be able to detect it, but some of the rumors I've heard say it's easy to spot, if you know what you're looking for."

"Show me." Alynna pulled her toward her computer and pulled up the footage.

"Well, see here ... this footage from the CCTV from Blood Moon, look at Ms. Gray's face. Doesn't it seem like it's glowing and unusually clear compared to all the other faces?" She clicked on the other window. "And the Fenrir footage ... there it is again! You can tell it's clearly her. Scroll to the morning, when the employees came in. Sure, you can make out their faces, but only if you knew them really well. None of their faces are as clear as Ms. Gray's, even in daylight."

"Could it just be a trick of the light? She was always alone in those videos," Alex offered.

"Yes, it could be. But also, one of the theories is, if this was a witch or warlock, they maybe overused the glamour magic since they can't exactly calibrate the amount they would need to make it look realistic. But, I don't really ... I have some suspicions, but I can't back it up with evidence."

Alynna looked thoughtfully at the computer screen. "Dr. Cross –"

"Please, call me Jade."

"Jade, I could kiss you!" She smiled. "Thank you

so much. This ... this could be nothing, but it could be just what we're looking for."

"I'm glad I can help." Jade smiled back warmly. "I have to go, but please call me anytime." She handed them her card. With that, she left.

"I see the wheels in your head turning, wife of mine." Alex narrowed his eyes. "What's the plan?"

"Well, first I need to call some friends ..."

CHAPTER TWENTY-SIX

After the gas station, it was another hour of driving before they reached their destination. At this point, Cady really didn't know where they were, only that it was some decrepit old mansion in the middle of nowhere. Victoria had hauled her out of the car, dragged her into the house and then into a room upstairs, and locked the door behind her.

She looked around the room. It was pretty big, decorated in a gaudy, turn of the century style with lots of gold trim and red velvet. There was also no other door except the entrance, and it looked like someone had put steel shutters outside the windows. No form of natural light came into the room, but it was well-kept. An hour later, Victoria had come in with a plate of food, and she was so hungry, she didn't even think about what they served her and she ate everything.

She lay on the bed for hours, until she was just too tired to fight off sleep. In the morning, or what she assumed was morning, Victoria came again with breakfast.

"Hungy, dear?" she asked as she put the tray on a table near the door. "Eat up."

Cady's stomach growled so loudly, she didn't care. She sat down next to her mother and ate all the toast, eggs, bacon, and washed it down with orange juice.

"Glad you have an appetite," Victoria commented. "There are clothes in the dresser. Go and get cleaned up, then I'll take you downstairs to meet the Master."

"The Master?" Cady asked. "Who is the Master?"

Victoria gave her a wicked smile. "You'll find out soon enough. Now go and get dressed!" With that, she left.

Cady could hardly disobey. After all, she was effectively their prisoner. And she wanted to know what would happen to her now.

———

Although she thought there would only be long gowns and dresses in the closet, she was surprised to find an entire wardrobe with brand new underwear, bras, blouses, pants, dresses, and even shoes, which were around her size. After her shower, she chose to wear a blouse with long sleeves, khaki pants, and a pair of flats. Not knowing what else to do, she sat on one of the comfy armchairs and stared up at the ceiling.

She didn't have to wait for long, however, as the lock clicked and the doorknob turned. Victoria walked in. "Come, dear, the Master is eager to meet you."

Cady followed her mother as they left the room. The hallways were dark, with only a few candles providing light. They made their way into the main foyer and down the grand staircase, where a large oil painting of a lady wearing a white dress and a large ruby necklace stared down at her. Her eyes seemed to follow her until they turned into another hallway. Victoria opened the large wooden doors at the end, revealing a large, cavernous room. It was rundown and unkempt, like the rest of the mansion, but Cady could tell it was probably a ballroom of some sort, perhaps more richly appointed in its hey-day. One side of the room was all glass, with a gorgeous view of the autumn leaves and some mountains in the distance.

In the middle of the room stood a tall figure, dressed in black robes. The figure pulled down his hood, revealing long, thinning white hair, a pale, withered face, and red-rimmed black eyes.

"Welcome my dear Cady. Please, come closer."

Off to his right, Cady realized Daric was dressed in a loose white shirt, dark leather pants, and boots. He looked handsome yet menacing, with his unmoving blue-green eyes and long hair tied back in a ponytail.

Victoria pushed her daughter forward. "Here she is, Master Stefan," the older woman preened. "Isn't she perfect?"

Dark eyes looked at her, almost piercing right into her. "She is ... exquisite." Stefan moved closer, and when Cady looked away, he put his thumb and fore-finger on her chin, his long nails pressing into her soft skin. "Do not turn away from me, child," he ordered.

"Who are you?" Cady dared to ask. "What do you want with me? Why are you hurting the Lycans?"

"Lycans!" Stefan hissed, letting go of her chin and walking away from her. "Do not mention those vile creatures to me!" he spat. "They are the disease in this world! And we will only benefit when we exterminate every last one of them!"

"What does this have to do with me?" she asked. "And the witches ... they've lived in peace with the Lycans for decades now."

Stefan let out a haughty laugh. "Witches!? You mean those weaklings? The so-called Witch Assembly!" He stalked back to her. "They prefer to close themselves off from the world, keeping to their kind, while the Lycans continue to breed and pollute the planet with their presence. My dear, I'm no warlock!"

Cady looked confused and looked to her mother. "I don't understand! What is going on? I thought you were a witch!"

"I am my dear," Victoria said. "For now."

Stefan laughed again. "I am beyond nature magic, beyond witches and warlocks, and beyond the Witch Assembly. I am a Magus!"

Cady gasped. "A mage!" she breathed out. Witches and warlocks used elemental magic, found and forged in nature, enhanced with their own talent. But mages were essentially witches or warlocks who have broken with the laws of nature in order to seek more power. "You use blood magic!" she gasped. That meant Stefan had done the one thing witches and warlocks could never do - kill someone and use their blood.

"That's right my dear," Stefan confirmed. "I refuse to be bound by weak, elemental magic. I wanted more power, so I could destroy the Lycans."

"Mother," Cady cried, looking at Victoria. Did she not notice the change? Her mother seemed more gaunt, the brightness from her hair was fading, her eyes becoming a dark, emerald green instead of their usual bright color. "You didn't ..."

"I'm almost there, my dear," she said proudly. "I've already dabbled in blood magic, and I just need a few more spells."

"But why?" Cady's voice was anguished. She didn't bear any love for Victoria, but didn't want to see her turn into a truly evil mage. "Please ... you can't ..."

"Why not?" Victoria's voice was haughty. "You don't understand! You never had power, never felt it! And to be bound by stupid rules when you could change the world! Your father, he cast me aside for his precious Lycans and kept you away from me. I'll finally have my revenge and be rid of Lycans." Her eyes grew darker. "And now, my sweet daughter, you'll help us make that come true."

"But I told you, I don't have any magic!" Cady

whipped her head towards Stefan. "She told you that, right? I have zero magic or talent!"

"I know, my dear child," Stefan said. "But we don't want you for magic. We need your blood. Or rather, your bloodline."

"Charlotte Fontaine, your great-grandmother," Victoria began, "was one of the original witches from Europe who came to America to establish a coven here. She was part of the first Witch Assembly, and her ancestry goes back to the most powerful witches of all time, even to the possible first witch ever recorded, Judith."

"And so my dear, if it's not evident to you yet," Stefan loomed over her, "your bloodline, your progeny, will bear the same blood. If you were to mate with another powerful warlock, you could produce some truly talented children who we can train and eventually turn into mages."

Cady covered her mouth with her hand, unable to move or speak. Her eyes grew wide. "You're all insane! You're going to impregnate me and make me churn out your mage babies? Why didn't you do this on your own?" She looked at Stefan and Victoria meaningfully.

Stefan gave bitter guffaw. "Oh, no my dear, simply impossible. Once I transitioned from warlock to mage, I lost the ability to have children.

However," he looked at Daric, "my young protégé is still very much a warlock and himself from an impressive and powerful bloodline. He will make a fine sire."

Her eyes trailed over to the handsome warlock, but Daric remained stoic and unmoving.

"This is crazy!" Oh god, she was going to be a broodmare! And that brute! He would force himself on her until she got pregnant. "You can't possibly think you'll get away with this."

The old mage cackled. "Do you think your precious Lycans will save you? They only care about their kind! If they think the resurgence of the True Mate pairings will save their race, well ... I will obliterate them before that happens, just like I did with that old Alpha."

"Michael?" Cady's eyes widened. "The car wreck wasn't an accident?"

"Of course not. True Mate magic is powerful, and as soon as that spawn of his was born, it sent a shockwave through the magical world. I knew I had to get rid of him before they produced more True Mate children."

"Alynna!" Cady's eyes went wide. "You were responsible for all those attacks against her."

"Smart girl." Stefan nodded. "Being the only living True Mate spawn, we knew she could also find her own mate. We couldn't risk it. Unfortunately, one of my people bungled that up, and now we can't touch her. But, no matter." He eyed her meaningfully. "Soon you'll be mated to Daric, and the two of you will produce a fine brood of mages to wipe every last Lycan off the face of the Earth."

"No!" Cady didn't know what else to do except launch herself at Stefan. But with a wave of his hand he pushed her away, slamming her against the wall. She cried out in pain as she slumped back. "Mother ..." She reached out to Victoria.

For a second, she thought she saw a flicker of compassion in her mother's eyes, but it soon clouded over. "Do not defy the Master, Cady. It will only bring you more pain."

"Daric!" Stefan commanded. "Take your bride-to-be back to her room and lock her up. Make sure she's secure. Tomorrow, you'll be mated, and you'll produce your firstborn, my heir."

"Yes, Master."

Numbness followed the pain that spread through Cady's body. She followed Daric like a mindless zombie as he pulled her up and led her out of the ballroom. His grip was strong, yet gentle on her arm. He even walked slowly and took shorter steps to accommodate her smaller stride.

When they reached her room, she was about to

yank open the door when he grabbed her shoulder, turning her to face him.

"Would it be so bad, little one? To make love to me?" he asked, a finger tracing her jaw. "I could bring you pleasure and not pain. I do not and have never hurt women ... in that way. I do not want to start now."

"Then don't do this, please," she cried. "Because I won't go to your bed willingly."

"I must do this," he stated. "But you don't have to resist me. That will make it at least tolerable, and the Master will leave us alone. And maybe some-day, it could also be pleasurable for you." His hand went lower, to her collarbones and down over her arms, tracing along her skin ever so lightly.

She looked into his eyes, his handsome face. Daric was sinfully attractive, and he looked like he belonged on an underwear ad in Times Square. A lot of women would be fighting for a chance to climb into bed with him. But something about his touch made her recoil. Wrenching away from him, she ran into her room, straight into the bathroom, and lost her breakfast into the cold, porcelain bowl.

CHAPTER TWENTY-SEVEN

"Thanks dude!" Alynna said brightly into the phone as she watched the video she had just downloaded. "I owe you a million! No, seriously, do you want a million dollars? Hahahaha ... I can check my couch cushions. All right, just your usual fee then, but I'll be sending over a bonus!" When she hung up the phone, Alynna screamed in happiness.

"Sweetheart!" Alex burst into the room, his face panicked. "Who's in here? What happened?"

Alynna launched herself into her husband's arms, toppling him over until they were rolling on the ground. She leaned down and planted a long, passionate kiss on his lips. "I'm sorry ... I'm sorry I've been acting so mean and moody!"

Alex laughed. "It's okay baby. Shhh ..." He pulled her head to her chest. "Now, tell me what happened."

"I found it! Not just that, but I found three things that clear Cady."

"Really?" Alex sat up, nearly knocking over Alynna. "Show me!"

"I will. But we need to go get Jade and get this to Grant now. Cady may be in danger."

———

Grant sat across from Liam Henney, trying to concentrate on what he was trying to say. He nodded and smiled, but really, none of the words were processing in his brain. He was worried about the call to the Lycan Council he would have to make as soon as the San Francisco Alpha left. He could feel Nick, who stood in his usual corner, was even tenser than himself. The usually well-kept Beta was looking worse for wear, with dark circles under his eyes and his normally clean-shaven face showing some stubble.

"So, as you can see, we're ready to move into clinical trials sooner than expected –"

"GRANT!" a voice boomed from the door of his office as it burst open. Three figures strode in, the one leading them a bundle of energy Grant recognized as his sister. "I need to see you now! You haven't made that call to the Lycan High Council yet, haven't you? I found it! Cady is innocent, and she's in danger! Dr. Cross here will – oh, hey Liam," she greeted sheepishly. "I didn't know you were still here."

"Grant couldn't see me yesterday, but he said this morning would be good." Liam's brows knitted. "What's this about Ms. Gray? And the High Council?"

Grant slapped his forehead. "Can't this wait?"

"No!" Alynna dropped her laptop in front of Grant. "I'm sorry for bursting in, Liam, but this is life and death. Maybe you should go ... uh, this is Lycan business."

Liam crossed his arms. "If this involves the Lycans and the High Council, then I'm obligated to know."

The other Alpha groaned. "He's right. And now he'll have to report whatever we talk about here, Alynna, and I won't be able to protect *anyone*," he said meaningfully to his sister.

"You don't have to protect her from the High Council anymore!" Alynna said in an excited voice. She noticed that Nick moved closer to them. "All right Liam, if you need to know, then here's the short version: the explosion at Fenrir wasn't from a leaky gas line. Someone planted a magical bomb in our office and made it look like it was Cady, but she's innocent. Really she is! Dr. Cross, please show Grant what you found."

The young scientist came forward. "Primul, I've been doing some research about how magic affects technology. See, the way magic affects the electromagnetic fields have always been a source of —"

"Jade, please." Grant cleared his throat. "Can we skip the science speak?"

"Er, right. Yes, let me move on." Jade opened the laptop Alynna had placed on his table. "Now, only a real witch will be able to tell for sure, but I believe, with about 80% certainty, that these tapes have been affected by glamour magic. You can see how bright and clear Cady's face is. Now, I was able to dig up some videos from past investigations where witches used glamour." She pulled up a different file. "See in this convenience store robbery? It's from a few years ago, back before any such research was started. According to my sources, the perpetrator was a warlock. He put glamour on his face to make it seem like he was a rival warlock. However, once other witches and warlocks saw the footage, they immediately recognized the spell." She put the two pieces of footage side by side. "See? Same clear face, despite all other faces being fuzzy and that slight glow around the edge?"

"We know she's working with witches," Grant reasoned. "Of course they would use some type of magic."

"That's not all. I have three more pieces of evidence to prove she's innocent." Alynna took some papers she had printed out and handed them to Grant. "I had some of my hacker friends check out Cady's keycard. They said that on the surface it certainly looked like it was her card used to enter the building, but it was obviously spoofed."

"Spoofed?"

"Someone made a copy of the card and then used it to enter Fenrir." She pointed to the paper. "I had our IT guys double AND triple check it! They confirmed it was definitely a spoofed card. They said something about the codes being different, but something that would only be picked up if we were looking for it."

"So, she made a copy and gave it to someone. What are your other pieces of evidence?" This time, it was Nick who spoke up. His face remained stoic, but there was an urgency in his voice.

."Well, here's footage my hacker friends ... er ... acquired from The Met. It's from the same time Cady was on tape at Blood Moon." She clicked on play, and it showed Cady as she walked into the museum, paid for ticket, and began to walk through the rooms. "The Met was having late hours, and she didn't leave until they closed at ten p.m." She scrolled the video forward, which indeed showed Cady walking out the door at 10:05 p.m.

"So Cady –"

"I'm not done," Alynna interrupted him. "There's one more, one reason why I believe Cady is in danger. She didn't run away, but was taken by force. Wait." She took a deep breath and pulled up another video. This time, it looked like CCTV footage from a gas station. "My friends ... well, they're pretty good at what they do. Their services, which aren't always on the right side of the law, cost a fortune, but well worth it. They have some pretty sophisticated facial recognition software, and I paid them to search for any signs of Cady in the tri-state area. Here's what they found."

The footage showed a blue sedan pulling into the gas station and a tall, blonde man getting out of the driver's side. They could barely see the two other figures in the car. Suddenly, the rear passenger door flew open, and one of the figures came running out. It was Cady, really Cady this time. Her face in the video wasn't unusually clear, but she was wearing the same clothes from the morning of the attack. She sprung from the car and ran off camera, but a few seconds later, the blond man came out of the store and raised his hand. Suddenly, Cady came flying back into the frame, her body pinned on the body of the car. The blonde man came at her, his hands raised. The look on the red-head's face was that of pure terror.

"If they've hurt her, I swear to god," Nick growled furiously, his eyes glowing. "I'll wipe every damn one of them off the face of the Earth!"

"Nick, stand down." Grant put a hand on his Beta's arm. "Well, it's obvious now. Cady was set up to take the fall for this. Thank you, Alynna, for believing in her."

His sister beamed.

"The High Council will still have to be informed," Liam warned them. "They will not take an attack, especially one by witches, lightly."

"They will be informed," Grant agreed. "But we will also let them know Cady was framed."

"And now we need to get her back." Nick gnashed his teeth. "Whatever it takes."

"We will," the Alpha agreed. "Let's get to work. Alynna, what do you need? Can your hacker friends help us again? I don't care what it costs, just have them see if they can find traces of that car or of Cady." He turned to Nick, who sat on a chair, his body deflated and hands fisted tightly. "We won't stop until we find her."

———

Nick looked around Cady's apartment, watching as Alynna and Alex poured through her personal things, looking for anything that could help them find where the witches could have taken her. He could hardly believe it was just two days ago they made love on her bed and he was ready to give everything up for her. Anguish tore through him as he recalled how cruel he was later that evening, using her and then saying those things, using every single word to cut her down and hurt her. Her face when he called her a whore was etched into his mind, haunting him. And he did it on purpose, trying to break her and hurt her as deeply as he had been hurt by her supposed betrayal.

"Nothing here," Alynna said as she exited the room. She eyed Nick slyly. "You naughty boy." She wagged a finger at Nick.

"What?" Alex asked as he came back from the kitchen.

"Nicky-boy," Alynna tutted. "Who else would those tighty-whities in the bathroom belong to? I always knew you were a briefs and not boxers kind of guy! And, breakfast for two, her bed all unmade and," she sniffed at him, "*your* scent definitely all over her room. You've been keeping a secret from us. It wasn't just that one night, was it?"

"Are you happy? Satisfied to know you're right?" Nick asked sardonically.

"Hey, hey," Alynna's voice turned light. "I'm teasing, okay? And it was about time! Sheesh! I was getting sick of the two of you giving each other cow eyes all the freakin' time you were in the same room! I honestly didn't know if you two were going to start making out any second. And how the hell did you last a decade without jumping her bones or gouging your eyes out in frustration? Heck, *I'd* tap that! I'm just happy for you."

"How could you be joking at time like this?" Nick ran his fingers through his hair in a frustrated manner.

"Because, Nicky-boy," she took him by the arm and sat him on the couch, "we are going to find Cady, rescue her, and you will get down on your knees, grovel for forgiveness, declare your ever-lasting love to her, and she'll fall into your arms, right?" She patted his arm. "I totally shipped you guys from the beginning!"

Nick looked dejected. "If she's smart, she won't take me back." He frowned. "The things I said to her ... did to her that night ... uncalled for and cruel." He stood up and walked over the one of the shelves of personal trinkets Cady liked. He stared at one of the pictures, the one of her and Luther at her graduation, her smile bright and her father standing proudly beside her. "I appreciate the thought, Alynna, and I know we'll find her. But whether she 'falls into my arms' is another matter."

"Is that the reason for your glum face?" she asked. "Well, I know Cady. She'll forgive you for anything if you just ask."

"Right, well," he gave the place one last look, "if we can't find anything here, we may as well go back to Fenrir."

The trio left the apartment and went back to the garage. They climbed into Nick's car and drove back to Fenrir.

They went straight to Grant's office, and to their surprise, there was someone waiting there. It was Vasili Vrost.

"Nikolai!" Vasili called as soon as they entered. "Where have you been? Why haven't you been answering your phone? I've been worried sick! I was on my way to London when this happened and then I saw the news when I got there. I flew back as soon as I could!"

"I'm sorry, Grandfather." Nick hugged the older man. "I've been busy. Apologies for worrying you."

The older man sighed. "This ... things like this are dangerous! I know they are part of your job, but if something happened to you ..."

"I'm fine, Grandfather," Nick reasoned. "Please ... we have business to attend to, urgent business." He began to lead Vasili to the door.

"Nikolai, let go of me!" The older Lycan jerked his hand away. "I will not be ignored! You didn't like Madison, you didn't like Constanza, and now you are in danger! I insist you start courting the next eligible mate I send your way!"

"Grandfather," Nick's voice lowered. "This isn't the time." He glanced at everyone in the room - Grant, Liam, Alynna, Alex, and Dr. Cross. They stood, rooted in their spots, afraid to move as they watched the scene unfold.

"No, now is the time! What is this business you are going about? I demand to know!"

"We are under attack, Vasili," Grant revealed. "I just got off the phone with the Lycan High Council."

"Attack? By whom?"

"Witches, possibly," Alynna offered.

"Witches!" Vasili's eyes widened. "No!"

"Yes, I'm afraid it's true," Grant said with a nod.

"We are under attack, and they've taken one of our own. Ms. Gray. They're holding her somewhere, and we mean to get her back."

"I forbid it!" Vasili shouted at his grandson. "You will not risk your life and face witches for that human! I told you to stay away from her. Ms. Gray is not vital to our kind, and you should let the witches have her if that's what they want."

"Grandfather!" Nick roared at the old man, his face fierce. "You will not insult Cady and certainly not in this room! No!" he cut him off when Vasili opened his mouth. "You will speak no further of her, nor say her name, understood?"

Vasili's face grew red with anger. "You will never see the Hudson mansion again. I will give it and everything to your cousin. Every chair, every plate, every vase in the house will belong to him."

Nick looked defiantly at this grandfather. "Good. He can have it. I don't want it; I never wanted any of it!"

Vasili's face turned into an ugly mask of hate. "You will regret this, Nikolai!"

As he turned to leave, Nick called out to him one last time. "Grandfather."

Vasili stopped, but didn't look back.

"I only hope someday you can put this all aside

Nick collapsed on a nearby couch. Grant was already handing him a drink. "I'm sorry, Nick."

"I'm sorry, too." He took a sip. "I'm sorry I let him go too far."

"Enough dramatics," Alynna declared. "If we're gonna go find and rescue Cady, we need to start getting to work. Now."

The tension slowly eased out of the room and everyone sat down and found a chair as they gathered together.

"Any traces of that car?" Liam asked.

Alynna shook her head. "Stolen plate, for sure. They're smart. But we do know that the gas station was somewhere upstate, near the Connecticut border. Unfortunately, after that we haven't found traces of it at all. It's all backroads and single-lane highways out there, no traffic cams or CCTVs."

Nick ran his hand through his hair in frustration. "How else can we find her? Or find out who took her?"

A loud thump from the outside made everyone freeze, and then the large, heavy doors of Grant's office swung open, slamming against the walls.

"We may be able to help."

CHAPTER TWENTY-EIGHT

Nick felt the blood freeze in his veins and his knees buckled slightly. Beside him, he could hear Alynna's cry.

"Cady?!" Alynna shook her head. "No, wait ..."

He could understand why the young Lycan thought she was seeing her friend standing in front of them. The woman who stood off to the side was almost a carbon copy of Cady. However, it took him only a second to realize she wasn't his Cady. No, this woman was probably a decade younger, a few inches taller, and her hair was more strawberry blonde than red, her eyes light green instead of indigo blue.

There were two other women who came in with her. On the other side of the Cady-clone was a much older woman with white hair dressed in loose-fitting robes. In the middle was stunning redhead with blazing green eyes, wearing a white coat and white leather boots. While the younger woman looked like Cady ten years ago, the other woman could be Cady's twin a decade or so from now.

"I'm sorry, Alpha," the woman in the middle nodded to Grant. "I've been trying to reach you since the explosion. Your security and gatekeepers are top-notch."

"But no match for you, apparently," Grant quipped. "Witch."

"Yes, well, we were desperate," the woman explained. "And er ... sorry about your admin. He'll be fine. He'll wake up feeling fresh as a daisy in a few hours."

"I told you there was too much beech root in the potion!" the old crone beside them cackled.

"I'm still learning potions mixing, Estella," the younger Cady-clone retorted.

"Good thing you're a blessed witch then," Estella shot back.

"Please, Estella, Lara," the middle witch warned. Grant cleared his throat. "Sorry. Right ... Alpha, my name is Vivianne Chatraine. I'm Cady's aunt. Her mother's twin sister. And head of our coven."

"Of course!" Alynna slapped her forehead. "That's why you look so much alike!"

"Yes. And this is Estella Rodriquez, one of the senior witches from our coven and," she motioned to the younger woman, "my daughter, Lara Chatraine."

Lara smiled at everyone and gave them a shy wave, while Estella simply looked at her fingernails.

"No wonder she and Cady could be twins," Jade realized.

"Er, can we get on with it?" Grant sounded impatient.

"Of course. Again, apologies for bursting in like this," Vivianne continued. "Where do I begin? We saw the news footage of course, and some of the cell phone videos online. The explosion at your office was definitely made by Ognevaia."

"We knew that," Grant confirmed. "But what does this have to do with Cady?"

"Well, it's a long story."

Grant sighed. "Why don't you sit down? All of you?" He motioned for them to take a seat on the couch, and everyone made way as they walked to the center of the room. Vivianne sat in the middle, with the two other witches on either side.

"Thank you. Alpha," she began, "you're aware of Cady's heritage, right? My sister was ... well, she's always been very troubled and rebellious. She married Luther Gray without telling us. Not that my mother wouldn't have approved, but it was certainly unusual. But she just left our coven to be with him. We assumed she had a happy life with her husband and her daughter. She never contacted us after they got married." Vivianne sighed sadly. "In the last few years, the witch covens around the US and the Witch Assembly have been noting some strange occurrences."

"What occurrences?" Alex asked.

"Well, a few ... dark incidents. Traces of the use of blood magic, specifically."

Jade gasped. "Oh no! Blood magic!"

Vivianne trained her eyes towards the Lycan. "You know of blood magic?"

She nodded. "I'm studying magic." She paused and then looked at Grant. Her eyes grew wide, and she placed her hand over her mouth.

"Purely informational reasons," Grant explained.

Vivianne narrowed her eyes, but continued. "Blood magic is the opposite of nature magic. It's an abomination, something real warlocks and witches would never attempt. You need to take blood unwillingly, and it often involves killing. We've seen a rise in the use of blood magic in the last few years and, so far, we've narrowed it to one ex-warlock. Stefan Nemajic."

"What do you mean ex-warlock?" Jade asked. "I thought you could never take anyone's powers away?"

"Well," Vivianne looked apprehensive, "as you know, magic takes many forms. There is nature or elemental magic, which you already know about. Sometimes people are born with 'blessed' magic, like my daughter. She was born with the ability to manipulate air currents."

Lara smiled. She waved her hand, and a gush of air swept through the room, sending various papers scattering to the floor.

"Amazing!" Jade jumped up from her seat and rushed to the young woman. "What else can you do? How much control do you have?"

"Dr. Cross, please." Grant looked like he was going to have an aneurysm.

"Sorry!" The young Lycan scampered back to her chair. "Please, go on."

"There's Lycan magic, which for some reason your kind seems to have lost, but is retained in some other forms." She turned to Alynna. "Like when True Mate children are born. The power of it sends a beacon throughout the magical world."

"So you know about True Mates and my sister?"

Grant raised an eyebrow at the older witch. "Are you keeping tabs on us?"

"Purely informational reasons," Vivianne replied with an impish smile. "Anyway, when you use blood magic, it takes its toll on you. You become something different, and you lose your humanity – some say your soul. You also lose all connection to the rest of the magical world, becoming what we call a mage. Or in the case of Stefan, a Magus, or a master mage. He's the only one we know of who has reached that status, but we're quite sure he's turned a few other witches and warlocks into mages as well. Victoria too, possibly, as we believe she's been working for him for the last five years at least."

"How do we Lycans fit into all this?" Nick asked. "And what do they want with Cady?"

Vivianne narrowed her eyes at Nick. Her face suddenly changed, then she smiled, her eyes sparkling. Estella and Lara also looked at one another. "Mother," Lara began.

"Later, child." Vivianne put her hand over her daughter's. "Anyway, let me continue. Our kind and yours have never had easy peace, but to tell you the truth, many of us now simply prefer to live our own, quiet lives. Not all of us were taught to hate Lycans. But, Stefan was part of a coven that always despised your kind. They see Lycans as a threat to us, and he was obsessed with destroying all of you. We believe that when the first True Mate pairing of the last generation came about, he plotted to stop it, also beginning his rise to mage and Magus status. There was no way he was going to let Lycans increase in numbers again."

"Wait, you mean ..." Grant's voice dropped.

"I'm sorry, Alpha." Vivianne nodded. "He was threatened by Alynna and Alex, and as well as your father and her mother. Now that we witches have begun to connect the dots, recent evidence we uncovered suggests he likely caused the death of your father."

"I knew it wasn't an accident." Grant gritted his teeth. Alynna grew pale.

"So, the mages hate us," Grant said in a steely voice. "They killed my father and tried to kill Alynna. But what about Cady? Why her?"

"Several reasons, one being she was so close to you. Stefan loves to play mind games, cruel as he is evil. He wanted you to believe she had betrayed you, to catch you off guard and confuse you. Next," Vivianne's voice croaked slightly, "this is difficult to say, but there's no other explanation. Stefan wants our bloodline. We are descended from the Fontaines, a powerful and old witch family. Victoria, myself, Lara, and Cady are the last direct descendants and carriers of Charlotte Fontaine's blood."

"They're going to take her blood?" It was Alex who asked the question.

"If only, handsome," Estella chortled and winked at Alex. He gulped and Alyyna tried to hide a smile, amused by the cheeky old witch.

Vivianne cleared her throat. "Not just her blood. Her bloodline. They want her children. They will make her breed many witch and warlock children and turn them into mages as soon as they manifest any power."

Nick shot to his feet. "I'll kill them before they lay a hand on her!" he roared. This time, Alex and Grant had to hold on to him, as his eyes began to change and the muscles underneath his skin began to shift.

"Nick, please, calm down," Grant soothed. "We will find her before they ... do anything." He turned to Vivianne. "What do you know? How do we rescue her? Where is she?"

"Well, they won't just mate her right away. To guarantee powerful offspring, witches usually wait until certain times of the month or year to, uh, procreate, plus they will probably perform some type of blood ritual before then to make sure. If my calculations are correct, tomorrow night should be the next possible date for the mating ritual, assuming they've found the right candidate."

Nick calmed down and sat on one of the chairs. "How close are we to finding her?"

Alynna shook her head. "I'm sorry, the trail went cold after the gas station." Everyone else looked at each other, and silence filled the room.

"Alpha," Vivianne spoke up. "We can help. Or rather, someone close to Cady, who has formed a bond of sorts with her, might be able to reach out to her."

"I'm the person she's known the longest," Grant offered. "But we've never shared any sort of bond."

"Well, it's not about how long you've known her." Vivianne placed her hands on her lap. "Bonds are strange that way. They can form instantly, or maybe simmer on the surface. It could be something as simple as knowing how someone feels without saying it, or ..." She looked slyly at Nick. "Sharing dreams, perhaps?"

Nick shot to his feet. "I think I can reach her. Through dreams."

All eyes turned to him.

Vivianne looked like the cat that ate the cream. "Good. Beta," she looked at him, her green eyes piercing into hers. "Both you and Cady must be asleep for this to work, so we'll assume she'll go to sleep sometime before midnight. We can help en-sure you do reach her in the dream state, if you don't mind us performing a ritual of our own?"

"Whatever it takes," Nick answered. "If it means getting her back."

———

Cady was lying in the most amazingly soft bed, the linens soft and smooth.

"Cady," a voice called her. "Cady, please."

"Hmmm?" She opened one eye. She smiled as Nick's handsome face looked down at her. He was sitting on the bed. "Nick ... where did you go?" She stretched and yawned. "Come to bed, make love to me," she purred.

"Later, love," he said, stroking the side of her face. "I want to. I promise I will, but I need you to tell me where you are."

She sat up and looked around her. "I'm at home, of course." She smiled dreamily. Everything was beautiful and perfect and white. "This is our home, the way I've always imagined it to be. Isn't it perfect?"

"Yes, Cady." He touched her cautiously, as if he was afraid she would vanish. "But you need to tell me where they took you."

"They?" Her eyes suddenly cleared. She looked at Nick, and then scrambled to the edge of the bed, away from him. "You!" she hissed.

"Cady, love, I'm so sorry for all the things I said. If I could take them back –"

"But you can't!" she shouted at him. "I never want to see you again! Those things ... you called me a ..." Tears began to fall down her cheeks.

"I swear I will make it up to you. Or leave you alone, if that's what you want. But only after we rescue you! Please tell me where they're holding you."

She looked confused. "Holding me? Where? Nick?" The edges of the dream began to fade as she began to remember. Victoria. Daric. Stefan.

"They warned me about this." Nick grabbed onto her, crushing her against him. "You're starting to recall what happened in the real world, but that also means the dream state we're sharing will soon fade. It's really me, love. Don't you remember? The dream after the wedding. The car. It's real, we've been sharing dreams all this time."

"Oh god!" She pulled away and scratched her head. Her dream home was disappearing, the edges turning to black. Nick began to fade in and out. "It's some mansion. Abandoned. Probably still in New York, but near Connecticut. I remember ..." She wracked her brain, thinking of some clue. "The mansion was turn of the century, had a big ballroom with an entire wall made of glass, overlooking some mountains. There's at least two floors and there was a grand staircase and a large portrait of a woman in white with this gigantic ruby necklace! Oh Nick, I wish I knew more! They're keeping me in my room. I can't go out, and I can't even look out the window!"

"Have they ... did anyone hurt you?"

She shook her head. "Not yet. Tomorrow they said ..."

But the dream ended before she could continue. Cady's body was soaked with sweat as she woke up. She sat up, turning on one of the lights beside her bed. "Oh my god," she cried out. "Nick ..." It had felt real. *Wait, it was real.* Nick really was in her dream, right? Hopefully she had given him enough information to find out where she was being held.

———

Nick woke up with a start. He was back at The Enclave, in his own apartment and the three witches peered down at him as they sat by his bedside. Everyone else was waiting in his living room.

"Did it work?" Lara asked excitedly.

He nodded his head, and she hopped off the bed to call everyone in.

As the rest of them walked in, he reached for a bottle of water, trying to calm himself. His heart was beating fast, his anger rising again. It was his wolf, wanting to be released. He had never felt like this before.

"She's ... unharmed, for now." He took another swig of water. "She's being held by the mages in an old turn of the century mansion either upstate or in Connecticut. It's at least two stories and has a ball-room with one side that's entirely made of glass and view of some mountains and trees that have already turned."

Alynna was jotting down note furiously into her notebook. "What else?"

"There's a portrait of some sort, probably in the main foyer. A woman in white wearing a large ruby necklace."

"That's it?" Grant asked.

He nodded. "She faded away before I could get any more."

"It'll have to be enough," Vivianne sighed.

"My team and I will get to work," Alynna said as she raced out of Nick's bedroom.

CHAPTER TWENTY-NINE

In the small setup in Nick's penthouse, Alynna worked for hours, going back and forth with her hacker friends over video chat. There were three of them on the screen, but they only agreed to work for them if no one except Alynna saw their faces.

Alynna, except Liam. Much to Alex's annoyance, the Alpha took a seat across his wife and they worked together with ease, throwing research and computer jargon at each other.

They all waited around, taking turns assisting Alynna and Liam when they could and also finding spaces to take quick naps. Alynna herself stopped at around three a.m., cuddling up to her husband on one of the couches. By the time she was up again,

Liam was getting ready to crash in the guest room. The witches had long retired to one of Nick's spare bedrooms, and the Lycans lounged around the living room. Nick was alert and up, not even feeling slightly sleepy.

Finally, at around eleven a.m., while everyone was eating lunch, Alynna had a breakthrough. "I think I know where they're holding her!" she said, turning one of her monitors toward the others. "Gracie House in Upstate New York, about a three hour drive from here."

It was an old mansion on a sprawling estate near Connecticut. Alynna clicked through the photos, showing a large picture window in a ballroom overlooking some mountains. The next photo showed a portrait hanging in the foyer, with a woman in a white dress, a huge ruby pendant hanging over her chest.

"That must be it!" Nick urged. "Let's go now!"

"We should verify it first," Grant calmly added. "What if she's not there and we spend three hours driving and it turns out she's across the state?"

"How can we be sure then?" the Beta's hands curled into fists. "We need to act now."

"How about we start with satellite photos first? Guys," Alynna looked at her hacker friends on her screen, "any satellites we can borrow today?"

It was hours after her last meal, and Cady assumed it was probably nearing evening time. They didn't tell her anything, but she assumed, from what little she knew of witches, that there would be some ritual before they made her ... she shook her head. She mustn't think of that. Nick said they were going to find her, right? They would come for her and rescue her. She would just have to resist and stall as much as she could.

As time passed, Cady lost hope of a rescue. Finally, the door to the room opened and Victoria, plus two other women she'd never seen before came in with her. "Finish this meal." She placed a tray on the table. "Don't even think about disobeying me, child."

She was so hungry, she devoured the food quickly. Afterward, she felt lightheaded and the world around her became blurry.

"Now, be a good girl. Take off your clothes and get into the tub," Victoria ordered.

Cady made her way to the large bathroom, removed all her clothing and stepped into the tub. The other women must had filled it with warm water while she was eating, along with some scented oils that made her sleepy. Strangely, she felt calm, even as they helped her out of the tub and began to dry her and then dress her. They put her in a white linen dress that came down to her heels, but had a deep V that ended just above her belly-button, exposing the deep curves of her cleavage. They brushed her red hair until it shone, then arranged it artfully, pinning a few curls up while leaving some tendrils down. Finally, they placed a gold circlet around her head.

"You're ready," Victoria proclaimed.

Cady felt like she was floating as she was led out of the room, down the staircase and into the ballroom. There was a large wooden square dais in the middle of the room and a dozen or so hooded figures stood around it. Daric, dressed in white linen robes himself, was standing on the dais, a small table with a large gold bowl in front of him.

"Time to begin," Stefan proclaimed. He stepped toward the circle, and they parted as he went through, joining Daric.

Victoria brought Cady up to the dais, guiding her so she stood in front of Daric. She looked up at his cold, handsome face. Cady thought she'd be more scared, but instead, she felt dazed. Everything around her seemed to blur and shimmer. "Why ... why am I feeling so ..." She looked at her mother. "You drugged me!"

"For your own good, my dear." Victoria patted her arm and she flinched.

"Don't touch me!"

"Don't fight it, my child. This is meant to be. Years from now, you will be a hero. The mother of mages."

"No," she tried to protest, but she felt too weak.

"Get on with it!" Stefan ordered.

"Yes, Master," Victoria bowed. She took something from her belt, a long, sharp jeweled knife that she held up in the light. She took Daric's hand and then cut into his palm, squeezing it until drops of blood flowed out, dripping into the bowl.

"His blood, and then your blood." She grabbed Cady's hands and repeated the motion, slashing deep into the young woman's flesh and letting drops of blood fall into the bowl. "Your blood and his will mix together, and we will know you will be blessed tonight."

Victoria placed her hands on the rim of the bowl, closing her eyes and murmuring some words. Around them, the hooded figures began to chant. She opened her eyes, which had now turned fully black like Stefan's, and Cady gasped at the sight.

"Mother," she cried out. "No ..."

The witch looked straight ahead, unmoving as

she continued the chant and the others grew louder and louder as they followed her.

Suddenly, Victoria's eyes cleared and she was knocked back, toppling to the ground. "No!" she screamed.

"What happened?" Stefan hauled her up to her feet. "What did you do, Victoria?!"

"It wasn't me!" Victoria swore. "It's not ..." She looked down at the bowl, and then at her daughter. "You slut!"

Stefan pulled her aside and looked at the bowl himself, then at Cady. "What is the meaning of this?"

The cloud around Cady's mind cleared, and she shook her head. "What do you mean?"

Her mother grabbed her arm and yanked her toward the bowl. She cried in pain. "Look! Your blood!" Victoria shoved her head down, and Cady peered inside. The two pools of blood gathered on opposite sides, almost repelled from each other.

"I don't know what this means!" She yelped in pain again as Victoria dug her nails into her hair and yanked her upright.

"You're not compatible! In fact," Victoria removed her hand from her hair and grabbed Cady's abdomen. Her eyes grew wide. "You're already carrying a child!"

Stefan roared, sending the house shaking.

"You slut! You whore!" Victoria screamed at her daughter as she dragged Cady out of the ballroom. She shoved her against the wall. "Did you know you were pregnant? No, obviously not!" A loud crash came from the ballroom.

Cady felt the wind knocked out of her, and her first instinct was to place her hand on her belly. "How can you be sure?!" she asked. She couldn't have been more than two weeks pregnant. Oh god, was it the night of the Blood Moon? "I took precautions!" The morning after pills, she took them as soon as she could. Was she too late?

"Not good enough, I guess! Magic doesn't lie; your blood wouldn't mix with Daric's because you're already pregnant," her mother spat. "Who is it? Is it that Alpha!? You dare let a Lycan defile you and put a pup inside you!"

Oh my god. A child. A baby. Nick's baby. A rush of emotions went through her. She had to escape, do everything she could to protect it. "No!" she denied. "It was a human lover, someone I met at a bar!" If they knew it was Nick's baby, they might use it against the Lycans or worse, force her to get rid of it.

"You lie."

Victoria and Cady looked toward the doorway. Daric stood there, his arms crossed. "It's the Beta's child, isn't it? You lay with him just before we arrived at the hotel. You've been with him for a while now."

"No!" she protested. "It's not his! I've had dozens of human lovers; it could be any one of them!"

Daric walked to her and peered down at her. "Oh no, little one, another lie. You've only been with him."

She began to sob, and she covered her face as tears streamed down her cheeks. "No ... no please ..."

"The Master wants her back in the ballroom." Daric didn't wait and took Cady by the arm and guided her back in the room.

The ballroom was empty, though the wooden dais lay in the corner, smashed to pieces. Stefan stood in the middle, his arms crossed. "Bring the filthy Lycan whore here! I will take care of her." He pointed a finger at her.

Victoria seemed distraught, but unable to move. Daric cleared his throat. "Master, would it not be more prudent to keep her alive? For leverage?"

Stefan put his hand down. "What do you mean?"

"If she does carry the spawn of the Lycans's Beta, we can use her as leverage."

"No!" she protested. "Nick, he won't want me or

the baby! He hates witches! His parents were killed by witches, and he'll never recognize any child we had! His grandfather would disown him!"

Stefan looked from Cady to Daric. "You're sure she's carrying the Lycan's child?"

"I can't be sure until we see the child, but what would we lose if we waited?" Daric shrugged his shoulders. "We're already prepared to house her here until a child comes. Besides, it's early yet, we may still be rid of the child."

Cady gasped at his callousness. "You son of bitch!" she cursed.

"Hmm ..." Stefan looked thoughtful. "Take her away for now and let me think on this."

"Yes, Master." Daric bowed his head. He made a motion to grab Cady, but stopped as a loud crash came from outside.

"What was that?" Victoria whipped around.

"Master!" One of the mages wearing a hood rushed into the ballroom, shutting the door behind him and bracing against it. "They're here!"

"Who?!" Stefan asked angrily.

"The-the-the Lycans! And they've brought witches!" The mage cowered, then was thrown toward the wall as the doors flew open.

CHAPTER THIRTY

"Stefan!" Vivianne shouted as she entered the ballroom. Lara followed behind her, and the Lycan force filed in. Grant, Nick, Liam, Alex, and Alynna stood behind the two witches as Lara waved her hand, the door slamming shut behind them.

"Witch!" the Magus hissed at Vivianne. "And you brought these dirty creatures too!"

"What have you done, mage?" The witch's eyes flickered over to the side, where Victoria had taken hold of Cady, a knife at her throat. "And you, dear sister! You would harm your own child, our blood?"

"Stay away, all of you!" Vivianne screamed. "If you value her life, you will leave now!"

Stefan laughed. "You fools. You cannot stop me!"

Nick looked at Cady, his anger boiling and rage barely contained. "Let her go!"

"Silence, creature!" Stefan ordered. "You do not tell a Magus what to do!"

"Give up, Stefan," Grant bellowed. "We've got you surrounded. We have more forces outside, and all your mages have deserted you."

The Magus' eyes turned hard. "You lie! They would have stopped you!"

"Your pathetic force turned coward as soon as they saw the Lycans in wolf form surround the house," Nick declared.

"No!" Stefan screamed in anger, the house began shaking again. "Daric!" he called.

"Yes, Master!" Daric sprang forward, stepping in front of Stefan. "Go, Master!"

Before anyone could do anything, Stefan spun around and disappeared.

"No!" Vivianne cried as she leapt forward, Lara right behind her. With a flick of his wrist, Daric sent the two witches flying across the room. The women slumped against the wall, the wind knocked out of them as they struggled to get up.

Liam and Alex went at him next, a black and a brown blur launching at the warlock as they shifted into their Lycan forms. Daric was able to bat them aside, but not before Liam's paw reached out and clawed him on the shoulder. The blonde warlock staggered back as blood stained the front of his white robes.

Grant and Nick shed their clothes as they transformed, ready to attack the warlock. Grant's wolf was large and imposing, with thick black fur and over six feet tall when standing on its hind legs. Meanwhile Nick's wolf had light golden brown fur, and though not as broad, was just as tall and striking as Grant's. They circled Daric, covering either side of the warlock so he couldn't escape, snapping and snarling at him as they moved in close.

Meanwhile, Alynna had slowly walked over to Victoria and Cady. "You're done, Victoria. Give up now, and we may be merciful."

"Ha! Stupid Lycan!" She gripped Cady tighter, the knife cutting into her throat, a drop of blood forming at the tip. "If you come any closer, I swear I'll ..."

"You'll what?" Alynna asked. "Kill your own daughter?"

"Or maybe I could kill you!" Victoria aimed the dagger at her.

Alynna laughed. "Try it, witch. Belladonna

couldn't kill me. I'd like to see what your little letter opener can do!"

Cady took a chance and reached out, grabbing her mother's arm and twisting it away. Victoria screamed in pain and her other arm let Cady go. She staggered forward, falling into Alynna's arms, crying in relief.

"You're safe, now Cady," she soothed, stroking the redhead's back.

"Alynna ... you all found me ..." she hiccuped. "You didn't believe them, right?"

Alynna shook her head, tears springing in her eyes. "No way, Cady."

Cady hugged her friend, then turned around to face her mother. Her eyes widened in horror as she saw Victoria drag herself toward Nick, still in wolf form. He had his back exposed to her as he flanked Daric on the right side, opposite Grant.

"No!" Cady shouted as she ran, her legs sprinting toward Victoria. As her mother moved to stab Nick with her knife, she shoved her body between them, the knife plunging into her stomach.

Victoria screamed in anguish. "What have you done?" She grabbed Cady before she crumpled to the ground and the world went black.

———

Both Grant and Nick's wolf heads whipped toward Victoria's screams and sobs, Daric seemingly forgotten. Both wolves growled and ran toward the two women.

"Victoria!" Daric leapt toward the older witch, grabbing her by the shoulder. "Leave her! We must join the Master! Now!"

"I can't! Cady," she cried as blood oozed out of Cady's gut, staining her own hands and clothes.

The warlock paid her protests no mind as he pulled her into his arms and they disappeared into thin air.

"Goddamn you, no!" Nick howled as soon as he transformed back into his human form. Cradling Cady in his arms, he pulled her close. "No, love, please hang on!" he cried. Blood began to seep into her white linen dress, dripping down the front, the sticky substance covering his bare chest.

Alynna sobbed, and Alex, who had run toward the scene, wrapped an arm around his wife. She folded herself into him, sobbing uncontrollably.

Nick rocked Cady's lifeless body against his. "You can't ... no ... please, Cady. I love you. I never got a chance to tell you ..."

Grant's face was grim as he knelt beside his friend. "I'm sorry, Nick." He put a hand on his arm. "I'm so sorry."

Vivianne and Lara joined them, as well as Liam. The older witch looked down at them with sadness, and her daughter took her hand as she began to cry for her niece, the blood of her blood she had never known.

"Cady, Cady," Nick repeated over and over again. He refused to let her go, even as Grant tried to pull him away.

"Nick, please," Grant pleaded.

"We'll take care of her ... if you just let her go." He let out a deep breath as Nick remained rooted to the spot. "We'll give you a few minutes."

Everyone seemed to understand the Alpha's words as they all turned around, making their way toward the door.

Nick wrapped his arms tighter around her. "I'm so sorry, my love." His anguished words echoed in the room. "I'm so, so sorry for not believing you, for not telling you sooner how much I love you and always have, since that first moment I saw you."

A loud, gasping sound suddenly filled the room. The Lycans and the witches looked at each other in surprise, then sprang back toward the couple.

Nick scrambled away as Cady's body convulsed. She sat up, coughing and gasping for air. He knelt in front of her, stunned as Cady parted the front of her dress. Though covered with blood, the skin under her ribcage was completely healed.

"Nick?" She stared at the Lycan kneeling across from her. "Why are you naked?" She looked around, and her cheeks grew pink. "Oh my god, you're all naked!"

Nick half laughed and half sobbed as he pulled her toward him and kissed her fiercely on the lips, tasting her as if he'd never get a chance to kiss her again. Cady squeaked in surprise but moaned as he continued to devour her lips.

A cough interrupted them and the couple looked up at the others, watching them. Alynna and Alex were grinning, Grant looked relieved, while Liam and Lara seemed embarrassed, both of them suddenly finding the moldings on the wall interesting. Vivianne, meanwhile, had a knowing look on her face.

"What are ... oh my god!" Cady looked at her mother's twin. "You're ..."

"Vivianne Chatraine," she introduced herself. "I'm Victoria's twin sister. Your aunt."

Cady's eyes swung to the other redhead. "And you?"

"I'm your cousin, Lara."

With Nick's help, Cady stood up and then

walked toward mother and daughter. "You're my family," she declared.

"Yes." Vivianne smiled, her eyes shining with tears. "We are your family."

"Hold on. This is great, but," Alynna interrupted, "Cady, what happened? Are you really a witch? Do you have magical resurrection powers?"

"I thought this would be quite obvious, especially to you." Vivianne looked at the young Lycan woman. "Cady and Nick are True Mates. She's carrying his child, and now nothing can harm her."

Nick turned to Cady, his face in shock. She smiled and nodded, and he hugged her to him. "I love you, Cady Gray," he whispered.

"And I love you, Nick Vrost," she replied and pulled him down for another kiss.

CHAPTER THIRTY-ONE

"Well, according to our tests," Dr. Faulkner took off his glasses and placed a file in front of them. "You definitely are pregnant. Very, very early stages."

"Two weeks exactly." Nick kissed Cady's cheek. "Blood Moon."

"If you need some time to talk, I'll be outside with the others." With that, the older Lycan left the room.

After they rescued Cady and made sure there were no other mages or surprises hiding in the mansion, the Lycan and witch force drove back to New York. They arrived shortly after three a.m. Everyone was exhausted, though elated at their victory over the mages. Liam accepted Grant's offer to sleep in one of the extra suites in his large apartment, while the witches stayed at Nick's penthouse. Cady just wanted her own bed, and so she and Nick went down to her place after helping the witch trio settle in. Nick slept with his arms around Cady all night, as if he was afraid she would disappear. In the morning, they went straight to the medical wing of The Enclave to have Dr. Faulkner administer a pregnancy test.

Nick turned to Cady. "Cady, my love, I'm so happy to have you back, I haven't apologized for the things I've done. I'm so sorry." He took her hands in his. "Can you forgive me? For the things I said a few days ago? Calling you —"

She kissed him soundly on the lips. "I forgive you. For everything."

"So easily?" he teased. "Aren't you going to make me grovel at least? Alynna said there should at least be some groveling on my knees."

Cady laughed, a sound that made Nick's heart soar with joy. "If you want to grovel, go ahead, but it's not necessary." She lay her head on his chest. "I thought I'd never see you again."

He took a deep breath and held her tight. "Me, too." He kissed her hair, inhaling the deep scent.

"I've always wondered why you smell so good to me, like caramel apples." He paused, thinking of his conversation with Grant after the Blood Moon. "Apparently, I'm the only one who can smell your scent. You just smell human to everyone else."

"Really?" she asked. "Oh, you smell good to me, too. Like Christmas or winter. My favorite time of the year."

"Strange, huh?" He stroked her hair. "True Mates, you and me?"

"I didn't even think it would be possible. First, Alynna and Alex, and now you and me."

"I meant what I said, if you heard me last night." He smiled down at her. "That first moment I saw you, I was a goner. I fell in love at first sight."

She wrinkled her delicate brows, trying to remember. "Oh my god! At the airport?" Her face went red. "I remember treating you poorly because I was so mad Grant wasn't there!"

He laughed and kissed her nose. "You were adorable. And stole my heart right then."

"I don't believe you." She smirked at him. "You're teasing me. All these years I thought you couldn't stand me! You were always so distant."

"Well, it was difficult." he confessed. "Grant used to call you his little sister and well, I took my job seriously. And he would have kicked my ass if I seduced you the same day I met you."

"And so you waited ten years ..."

"Ha! You walked into my room that night!" he retorted.

"To prevent you from tearing up that hotel!" She swatted him playfully on the arm.

"Well, believe it or not, it's true." Nick took her hand and threaded his fingers through hers. "I'll just have to keep proving it to you, now, won't I?"

He kissed her again, softly and gently this time. She sighed when he pulled back. "I didn't instantly fall in love with you that moment, but all these years, well ... it took much longer for me, but here I am. I love you, Nick Vrost."

After a few more kisses, Cady stood up. "C'mon, let's go and join everyone." She turned toward the door, but felt a tug on her hand. When she looked back, Nick was down on one knee. "I said you didn't have to grovel!"

Nick smiled up at her and took something out of his pocket. She gasped. "What?"

"Cady Elise Gray, love of my life, my True Mate, and future mother of my pups ... will you marry me?"

Her jaw dropped, and it wasn't just because of

the huge rock sparkling in front of her. "How did you ..."

"It was my mother's," he explained. "I took it out of the safe before we came to get you. Just in case."

"Just in case?"

"Just in case you maybe hit your head and got amnesia, went insane, or got hit with confusion potion and agreed to take me back," he said sheepishly and pushed the ring closer to her. "I mean, I knew there was a small chance you would forgive me, but still ...What do you say, Cady?"

"Yes," she choked as he slipped the ring on her finger. "Yes. Always."

———

After a few minutes, the couple went out to the waiting room, where everyone was waiting for news, including Estella and Jade, who had stayed behind in Manhattan during the attack. The raid on the mage lair was relatively easy, with Nick bringing most of his security forces as backup. Aside from one minor injury, everyone was safe and unharmed.

"Well, it's confirmed," Nick announced as the entered the waiting room.

"Oh my god, you're knocked up too!" Alynna

shouted happily as she bounded forward, hugging her friend. "Yay! Are you hungry? I am! We can go raid buffets together! I love watching the waiters squirm when they see me!"

"Two pregnant True Mates?" Alex slapped his forehead dramatically and looked at Nick. "Hope you're ready to have your food budget go up." Alynna punched her husband on the arm playfully.

"And! Holy smoking cracker jacks!" Alynna took Cady's left hand and held it up to the light. "I hope you have an armed guard for that thing!"

Cady blushed and Nick put an arm around his new fiancée.

There was some excitement and confusion, but when everyone realized what was happening, they all came forward to offer their congratulations to the happy couple.

"Wait a minute." Alynna looked at Vivianne. "You knew, didn't you? About them being True Mates? I saw you looking strangely at Nick."

"I knew that Nick had a special bond with my niece." The witch smiled mysteriously at Nick. "We all felt it." She motioned to the other witches.

"But how?" Nick asked.

"Well ... most magic is connected in some way," Vivianne explained. "When major events happen in the magical world, it sends a kind of shockwave, sometimes small, sometimes big. I felt this major shift about a month ago. I think it was when your bond as True Mates began to form." She looked at Nick and Cady.

"The wedding," Cady remembered and looked at her mate. "You asked me to dance. It was the first time we ever touched."

Nick nodded. "Yes and after that night, we started sharing dreams."

"What kind of dreams?" Jade asked in a curious voice.

Cady blushed, and Nick grinned. "Nothing we can share, unfortunately, Dr. Cross. At least not in polite society." Jade turned red when she realized what he meant.

"I felt a magical shockwave once before," Vivianne continued. "Twenty-two years ago, when you were born." She looked at Alynna. "The magic of True Mates is quite distinct, I can tell you that. Nick and Cady finding each other though, that's what brought me here. You see, when Victoria began her transformation into a mage, one of the effects is that she severed her connection to the rest of the magical world. Nature magic and blood magic are incompatible, after all. I lost all connection to her about five years ago," she said with sad eyes. "But the moment the two of you touched, I felt a new connection to you, Cady. You are the blood of my blood, after all."

Cady paused and closed her eyes. "I can't explain it, and I don't have any powers myself, but I can feel it."

Vivianne embraced her niece. "Yes, it's there. You may not be magical, but the blood in our veins is powerful. That is why Stefan wanted you."

Cady looked at her cousin with concern. "Won't he try to get to you then, Lara?"

The young witch frowned. "He can try, but he probably knows I'm too well-protected."

"Well, he's still out there." Nick turned to Grant. "We have to stop him."

"I agree." Grant nodded at Vivianne. "Stefan is still a threat to us. To all of us. I suggest it's time the witches and Lycans have more than a truce, but rather, forge an alliance."

Vivianne nodded. "A wise move, Alpha. It will be difficult and it will take time, but what choice do we have?"

"Our High Council and your Witch Assembly must be informed. Everyone must be warned. Stefan was able to grow in power because he operated in the shadows. If we force him out into the open, into the light, he'll be vulnerable. But you're right, it won't be easy. Lycans can be stubborn and stuck in their ways."

"Yes, as are witches." Vivianne looked at Nick and Cady. "But our bonds have begun to form. It's a good start."

CHAPTER THIRTY-TWO

"I think we should definitely buy out the apartments below and then maybe have some stairs put in," Nick's brow furrowed as he looked at the blueprints spread out on the dining room table. "Or a big loft? We're definitely going to need more room."

"More room? Your penthouse takes up half the floor! What would we need the extra room for?" Cady asked in an exasperated tone.

"Well, the nursery, of course, and once the first one outgrows that, he or she will need their own room and then the next one can take the nursery, then that one will need a bedroom as well. Maybe we'll need several bedrooms. And a library for studying. A music room, too. My grandmother was an amazing piano player; I'm sure one or two of our children will inherit that."

"Exactly how many babies do you think True Mates can have?"

"I don't know, but we'll have to try for as many as possible." Nick gave her a lascivious smile.

"For the good of the species right?" She smirked.

"Of course. For the good of the species."

"We'll have to try real hard then."

Nick gave a growl and stood up, then took her hand. "C'mon. We need some practice. Let's take a break."

"Oh no, mister!" She swatted his hand away. "You said we'd do some wedding planning after looking at the blueprints!"

Nick groaned. "Let's elope, please? Grant will let us borrow the jet. How about Vegas? Or Paris?"

Cady laughed. "Don't make me sic Callista on you."

Callista Mayfair, Grant's mother, who had over the years appointed herself as Cady's surrogate mom, was once again livid she wasn't going to get to plan a grand wedding. Cady and Nick wanted a small affair at The Enclave, much like Alex and Alynna, but they had to appease the older lady.

Grant begged them to go along, as Callista was perhaps the only person that brought fear into the Alpha's heart. Grant offered any bribe of their choice, and Nick was thinking the apartment in Rio would make a nice wedding gift.

So, they agreed to a ceremony and reception at The Plaza Hotel with under fifty guests, and it had to take place in two weeks. Callista took that as a challenge and was a fiend in her planning, needling, cajoling, and prodding wedding vendors to get everything done on time to make everything perfect. The banquet manager at The Plaza was probably going to consider a career change after this wedding. Cady had already planned to gift the poor woman with a very nice spa trip. Nick had suggested therapy sessions as well.

Though Nick tried to put her tablet aside – Callista had already sent twenty Instant Messages in the last hour – she pointed to the chair. "Sit, Mr. Vrost." With a defeated sigh, he sat back on his chair. The doorbell ringing made both of them look up.

"Saved by the bell!" Nick declared as he stood up again. He didn't bother checking through the peephole and opened the door, grateful that anyone or anything would save him from wedding planning. He secretly hoped it was a mage, as that would probably cause a really long delay and he could release some pent-up frustration and anger, but he was more surprised at who he saw on the other side.

Vasili Vrost stood in the hallway. "Hello Nikolai," he greeted softly.

"Grandfather." He crossed his arms. "What are you doing here?"

"Nikolai. I ... you see ..." The old man fumbled with his words, wringing his hands. Nick said nothing, but stared him down. "Will you give me a minute of your time, please? You won't even have to let me in."

"Nick!" Cady called from behind Nick. She peeked around his tall frame. "Who is it ... oh, Mr. Vrost! I didn't know we were expecting you."

Nick had given Cady a short version of what happened with Vasili the day she was rescued and how he had broken ties with his grandfather. "Nick, sweetie, why are you standing there?" She rubbed his arm in a soothing manner. "Why don't you let your grandfather in? I'll have tea ready. Would you like some, Mr. Vrost?"

The old man looked gratefully at her. "Thank you, Ms. Gray. I would very much like that."

Nick, who would do anything for Cady,

shrugged and opened the door wider, leading Vasili to the living room couch as Cady busied herself in the kitchen.

"I'm ... I'm glad Ms. Gray is safe, Nikolai," Vasili said, sitting down on the black leather couch.

"Yes, she is safe." Nick sat down across from him in the love seat. "And I'll make sure no other harm comes to her." The two man sat in uncomfortable silence for a few minutes until Cady returned.

"Here we go. Good thing I already started a pot." Cady breezed in and put a tray on the table. "Sugar or milk, Mr. Vrost?"

"Yes, both please." He nodded at her. He took the cup she offered and waited for Cady to finish serving, who then sat next to Nick with her own tea cup.

"Now, what do you want?" Nick asked gruffly. "Have your say and then you can leave."

"Nick!" Cady admonished. "I'm sorry, Mr. Vrost. I don't know why he's in a foul mood."

"I'm afraid it's because of me." Vasili looked down at his tea with doleful eyes. "All right, let me say this and you can decide." The old man seemed nervous, something Cady guessed he'd never felt before. "Nikolai, you are my family, the last of my line. I ... I was wrong to say those things to you, and I came here to make amends."

"Even though I've made my choice?" Nick looked at Cady meaningfully. She squeezed his hand.

"Yes. It's your life and it was wrong of me to dictate how you should run it and who you should spend it with." He looked at his grandson straight in the eye. "And everything - the businesses, the estates, the house, it's all yours. No conditions. Even if you still decide that you want me out of your life."

"I don't care about that, I told you," Nick reminded him. "But it's not me who you should be apologizing to."

He immediately turned to Cady. "Of course. Ms. Gray. I'm sorry for the way I treated you and for the things I said. I have nothing to say in my defense, except that the grief of losing a child never really leaves you and makes you say things you don't mean. But, will you forgive this foolish old man, even though he has treated you ill? Or at least let me try to make amends?"

Cady paused, then took a breath. "Of course, Mr. Vrost. Yes, I accept your apology."

Vasili's face turned from sadness to relief. "Thank you so much, Ms. Gray. I want to start healing this rift between us. All of us." He looked warily at Nick, who seemed satisfied at his apology.

"There is one other thing you can do to to make

amends. Not for me, but for Nick." Cady switched over to the couch and sat next to Vasili. She reached out and placed her hands over his. "Will you stand by Nick's side when we get married next week? I'm sure he'd very much like you to be there."

"Next week?" The old man seemed surprised. "I mean ... of course I'll be there. I don't mean ... next week seems a little soon, eh? But then again," he gave Nick a warm smile, "when I met your grandmother, I wanted to marry her the very next day and I told her so. But my dear, did you not want to have time to make arrangements? Have a proper trousseau, order flowers, find the right venue, send out invitations?"

Cady shot Nick a look. "You didn't tell him?"

Nick shrugged. "I haven't spoken to him since last week."

"Tell me what?" the old man asked.

"Mr. Vrost —"

"Vasili," he corrected. "Or grandfather, or you can save that for after the wedding, if you wish."

"Then you must call me Cady. But Vasili," Cady continued, "Nick and I are True Mates. And we're expecting a baby. A Lycan pup." She patted her belly instinctively.

Vaili's mouth dropped open, and he looked from Cady to Nick, who nodded at his grandfather with a small smile. Tears started to fall down the old man's eyes, streaking his cheeks. He wiped them away with a handkerchief and took both of her hands in his, kissing them. "That is ... I'm ..." He stood up and embraced his grandson. "I always thought that when this day came I would be relieved and happy, but now that it's here ... I can't even begin to describe what it feels like." He took a deep breath and composed himself. "Nikolai, my child, if you would have me, I would happy to be by your side when you marry this amazing woman."

"That would make me happy as well, Grandfather." Nick put his arms around Vasili. "Though god knows why she would have me."

Vasili looked at Cady with shining eyes, his face reminiscent. "Yes, only god knows why these women want us, but bless them, they do. You'll make a beautiful bride, just like my Ana," he said. "Now, wedding plans ... I must insist you have it at the Hudson mansion ... I mean if you want to, that is ..."

"We'd be honored," Cady said before Nick could interject. "I'll talk to Callista. She's been fighting the The Plaza coordinators all day. Believe me, she'll be over the moon. And we don't have to pay for therapy for their banquet manager!"

"Good. Now, your pup ... do you have a doctor?

Are you talking vitamins? When is your next appointment? And what about your nursery! You can't be raising a child in a place like this!" Vasili looked around. "This is good enough for a bachelor, but look at these sharp edges! All this glass! Not good for the baby!"

"Grandfather, the baby's not going to be walking anytime soon!" Nick slapped his hand on his forehead.

"But it's never too early!" Vasili stood up and looked around Nick's apartment, carefully examining anything that could harm a baby.

"Actually, we're making renovation plans." Cady took the blueprints from the table. "Would you like to see them, Vasili? And I suppose we'll have to make another addition. A larger guest room, so great-grandfather can visit anytime?"

Vasili's face lit up even more. "And then maybe in a few years, when more pups have arrived, you'll just have to move into the Hudson mansion. We'll get you both a chopper so you can get to work on time and be back by supper!"

Cady laughed. "Sounds like a plan! Now, Nick thinks that this wall should go down, but I said ..."

Nick watched his grandfather and future wife pour over the plans, and his heart soared. The two of them talked excitedly about the blueprints and, much to his relief, forgot about wedding planning. He couldn't believe how lucky he was, not just having Cady as a True Mate, but also as his future wife. He joined them as they sat at the table, making notes on the blueprints.

EPILOGUE

It seemed like it was just yesterday the New York clan was celebrating a wedding, and now they were having another one. The Vrost Hudson mansion and the river provided a beautiful backdrop for Nick and Cady's special day. Callista Mayfair had taken up residence in the Hudson mansion as soon as possible, making sure every detail was perfect. She also found an unlikely ally and assistant in Garret, the Vrost's faithful butler, who was just as ruthless as the Lycan lady in making sure all the arrangements were suitable and perfect. He also supervised the dinner service, inspecting everything to ensure every piece of silver was perfectly polished and every table napkin was pressed and folded. When the day of the actual wedding came, some people thought Callista and Garret controlled the weather too, as even Mother Nature seemed to cooperate with them, providing a crisp and clear day with no sign of rain clouds.

The lawn was bursting with the gorgeous reds, oranges, and yellow of fall. Two groups of white chairs in rows of ten were set up on the massive space, and an aisle covered in a rust colored rug ran down the middle. At the end was a beautiful fall-themed trellis made of fir branches, pine cones, and apples swathed with caramel-colored ribbons.

When the ceremony began, Nick stood in front as he waited for his bride, flanked by his grandfather and best man, Alex Westbrooke. As the music started, the lone bridesmaid, Lara Chatraine, walked down the aisle, followed by the maid of honor, Alynna Chase-Westbrooke, both of them wearing rust-colored gowns. Finally, the music changed and the bride walked out of the main house, looking radiant in a beautiful white gown in lace and tulle with a long train, carrying a fall-themed bouquet. The groom looked in awe at his beautiful bride, and as she approached the middle of the aisle, she was joined by Grant Anderson and Vivianne Chatraine, and they walked her down the rest of the way.

Nick shook hands with Grant and kissed Vivianne on the cheek before offering his hand to Cady, then they faced the judge. The ceremony was quick, and the aunt of bride was asked to say a few words of blessing. The kiss lasted much longer than necessary, and all the guests cheered as the happy couple walked down the aisle together, now man and wife.

Although they wanted an outdoor ceremony under the moon, it was much too cold. They had it inside the grand ballroom, which was decked out in the same fall colors as the ceremony area, with the addition of lanterns and fairy lights. The guest list doubled, seeing as Vasili now had to invite all his extended family, friends and colleagues, and the bride, of course, had a whole extended family of witches.

Nick and Cady opened the dance floor, impressing everyone with their dance moves, although the bride had to give most of the credit to her groom. They danced two more songs together and switched to other partners, Cady dancing with Grant, then Vasili, and finally Alex before she was back in her new husband's arms. Nick himself danced with Alynna, Vivianne, and nurse Ellen, who was one of their special guests. Although Cady wasn't able to visit Mercy Hospital since she was discharged, she personally delivered the invitation to her former nurse, who was thrilled that Nick had finally popped the question.

"Aren't you glad we didn't elope?" Cady whispered into her husband's ear.

"If only to see that." Nick motioned to the dance floor off to their right. Alex was dancing to the slow song with Estella, who was not-so-subtly trying to grab his ass. The young Lycan kept trying to push the older witch's hand up higher, but she was not having it and continued to slide her hand down his backside. Off to the side, Alynna was giggling uncontrollably with Lara and Jade as they watched the poor Lycan get groped by the wily old witch.

"Did your ass escape nurse Ellen's fingers?" Cady snickered.

"Nurse Ellen respects that I'm now a married man," he declared. "Which is why she started ogling Grant's assets."

Cady threw her head back and laughed out loud. Nick thought she was the most beautiful woman in the world.

"I'm glad everyone's getting along," Cady observed as Nick spun her around. "Look at that!"

Nick turned his head to the left and saw Vasili talking to Vivianne, and he laughed at something she said while placing her hand on his arm. The older Lycan gave the witch a nod, then offered his arm to lead her to the dance floor. "Well, we might have hope yet."

"We'll need it." Her brow furrowed. "The mages _"

"We will defeat them," Nick declared. He held her closer. "I won't let anything happen to you or our child. Not after I almost lost you."

She laid her head on his chest. "I know you will. And we will defeat the mages together."

Nick swept her up, making her laugh as they spun in circles, the rest of world turning into a swirl of lights around them.

———

Dear Reader,

Thanks for reading Cady and Nick's story! I hope you enjoyed it.

So, who's next?

Why, it's (my) favorite Alpha, Grant Anderson.

The New York Alpha finally meets his match.

Like spoilers? You can get a sneak peek at the first two chapters by turning to the next section.

Oh, and those pesky mages will be back for sure. Stefan's not done yet.

By the way, do you want to read a **bonus** chapter of Nick and Cady's first meeting ten years ago, **plus** their special holiday novelette, "The Bells of Christmas"?

Then subscribe to my newsletter - it's free and you can opt out any time, plus you get **ALL my bonus content** including a FREE Book - The Last Blackstone Dragon. Head to this website to subscribe: http://aliciamontgomeryauthor.com/mailing-list/

You'll also get a three free books - My paranormal book, **The Last Blackstone Dragon** and my contemporary romance, **The Billionaire's Heart: The Combustion Series**.

It's my gift to you.

Happy Reading!

All the best,

Alicia

SNEAK PEEK: ROMANCING THE ALPHA

BOOK 3 OF THE TRUE MATES SERIES

F rancesca Muccino let out a long, tired sigh and rubbed her eyes as she sat back in her chair. It was another Sunday night and she could hear the kitchen crew finishing up outside, cleaning and scrubbing away, making sure everything was spotless. Meanwhile, she had just finished with the books.

Another depressing month, she thought glumly, trying not to look at the spreadsheet on her screen.

As manager and part owner of Muccino's Italian Restaurant, it was her job to make sure all the books were balanced. While they weren't going under, profits were down for the fifth straight month and they barely broke even again for this one.

At least everyone gets paid, she mused. She herself had taken a pay cut to make sure all the employees could at least get their full salary this month, but the servers were definitely balking at the lack of tips. Hopefully, the Spring Break slump would be over soon and the students from the nearby colleges and universities would soon be packing Muccino's on weekend nights.

"Yo, Frankie!" Dante, the oldest of her younger brothers and co-head chef, popped his head into her office. "I'm headin' home. And so's Matt," he said, referring to their half-brother.

"And Enzo?" she asked, crossing her arms over her chest as she mentioned the name of Matt's twin.

"Where do you think he's headin'?"

Frankie rolled her eyes. "Right. He's going out clubbing with his friends until morning. Tell him I said to drink plenty of fluids before he goes to bed!"

"Yes, yes!" a voice from behind Dante called sarcastically. "See ya Tuesday, Frankie!" Enzo shouted right before the back door slammed shut.

Frankie shook her head. "That boy!"

Dante chuckled. "C'mon Frankie, give him a break. He's young and he's got no responsibilities yet, what else is he gonna do?"

"I know, I know," Frankie sighed. "I just hope he keeps out of trouble."

"You know him," Dante sat down in front of his sister's desk. "The last time we had to bail him out, he got into a fight protecting some girl. He loves girls, can't stand to see 'em in trouble."

"And the women sure do love him back," she smirked. Her middle brother was a true charmer, which was why he was the perfect host for Muccino's. Enzo could effectively talk little old ladies into ordering the evening's specials as much as he could charm the younger ones out of their pants. No woman between the ages of 18 and 90 years could resist his handsome face, tall, toned body, sandy blonde hair, and those chocolate brown puppy-dog eyes. "I just wish he'd grow up. Like Matt." Despite their identical looks, Enzo's twin brother Matt was his complete opposite. He preferred to stay at home and tinker on his computer in his free time, though he did help out in the kitchen on busy nights.

"We all know Matt's your favorite!" Dante joked.

"He's not!" Frankie tossed a wadded up post-it at him. "I hate all of you equally!" she joked.

While growing up with four younger brothers wasn't easy, Frankie took her role as oldest sister seriously. Matteo had always been a painfully shy and awkward child, overshadowed by his more boisterous and outgoing twin. That said, she paid him a lot of attention to make up for it. She even encouraged him to go to college and take up computer engineering. He was the first one in their family to graduate from college, just last year and on a full scholarship. Frankie was so extremely proud of him. He was currently working for a startup in Jersey City, but he still helped out at the restaurant out of loyalty.

Dante glanced over at the screen and then looked at his sister. His mismatched eyes - one blue, one green, a hereditary quirk in their family that he shared with Frankie - looked worried. "Not another good month, huh?"

She shook her head. "Afraid not."

"How bad is it?"

"Bad enough to worry," she confessed.

"I told you, Frankie, we gotta start using the Internet to bring in more people! Set up a website, go on social media and stuff! Matt could help!"

"Matt is busy and he should have his own life," Frankie stated. "Besides, the college kids will be coming back soon, we don't need to advertise or go online! People already know us and we'll do it like Ma did and Nonna did, by making great food!"

Dante threw up his hands. "Frankie, we can't just stay stuck in the past! Yes, Ma and Nonna were able to start and build up Muccino's all those years ago! But we need to take it into the future! We'll get some reviews and--"

"*Basta*! I don't wanna talk about this now!" She slammed her palm on the table.

Her brother sighed and shrugged, then glanced at the spreadsheet on the screen.

"I'm sorry, Dante...I'm just worried," she slumped back in her chair in defeat. "Fine. Talk to Matt, but only if he has time! We can get one of those Facethingys."

"Facebook," Dante corrected. "Jeez, are you really 28 or 68? Are you gonna start talking about that time when soda pop was 10 cents?"

"Yes, Facebook," she stuck her tongue out. "Whatever. You guys work on it."

"Thanks, Frankie!" he leaned over and kissed her on the cheek. "Oh and by the way, cousin Eddie called again."

"What is it now?" she asked in an irritated voice.

"He keeps saying that Gary Fontana is encroaching on his land again, poaching his chickens."

"And why is this my problem?"

"Well, he says he caught Gary in Lycan form on camera this time."

"Argghhhhhh!" Frankie let out a frustrated groan. Aside from being head of the family, she was also Alpha for the entire New Jersey Lycan clan.

There weren't many of them and most were related to her, and so there wasn't much to do except settle small disputes like this. Of course, she also had to send "incident reports" to the Lycan High Council whenever there were any problems. They had to keep the lid on their secret, after all. She wondered how many of the reports the council actually read and if they were as tired of her redneck cousins as much as she was. "Fine, fine, I'll deal with it tomorrow. Now go," she shooed him away. "You've been on your feet since three, go home and rest."

"Yes, Primul," he joked, and then ducked another flying object before heading out the door.

Frankie let out another sigh, leaned back in her beat-up leather chair, and looked at the two portraits hanging on the wall on her right. The first was a beautiful older woman with white hair and the second a middle-aged version of the other. Both had the same features - thick, wavy hair, dusky olive skin, an oval-faced shape, and thick, arched brows, plus of course, the startling mismatched blue and green eyes. Frankie herself was a third doppelgänger for the two women, though she always thought her features weren't as striking and her hair was more curly and unruly. Her mother especially was a great beauty, and she remembered all the men who would flirt with her and try to date her when she was a single. "Oh Ma, Nonna, I miss you both," she said sadly.

———

After locking up the restaurant, Frankie got into her ancient Honda and drove back to her house. She lived close to the restaurant, just a ten-minute drive away. Barnsville, New Jersey was a typical small college town, usually bustling with activity during the school year. Since it was Spring Break, though, the town was much less busy.

Frankie knew the route home from the restaurant by heart, having worked there since she was fifteen and basically growing up at Muccino's, either playing in the office by her mother or grandmother's feet or hanging around the kitchen and pantry since she could walk. Drive down Main Street for about two miles, go past the old mill and then turn into the driveway of her childhood home.

She still lived in their old, five-bedroom Victorian-style house, which had belonged to her grandmother, then her mother, and now, to her and her brothers. Dante, Enzo and Matt had moved out a while back, preferring to have their own bachelor pads, but their youngest, Raphael or Rafe, was still living with her at home while he finished his political science degree at the nearby NJU. Tonight though, he was staying at a friend's house, studying for a test. He would be the second Muccino ever to graduate college, and while Matt was naturally brilliant, Rafe was hardworking and whip smart, determined to go to Harvard Law School as soon as he finished his degree, and then become a lawyer.

Frankie slowed the car down as she approached the driveway. As she turned in and her house came into view, she suddenly slammed on the brakes. *"Cazzo! Madre de dio!"* she cursed aloud as a figure suddenly appeared out of nowhere, bounced off the hood of her car and rolled down to the ground.

She bounded out of her car and rushed to the front. There was a large man - a very naked man, she realized - slumped down on the ground.

*No, wait...*She sniffed the air. "Lycan!" she gasped aloud.

She grabbed her purse, took her phone out and dialed Dante's number. It rang a few times before it sent her call to voicemail. "Dante! Where are you? Please come to the house now! I think...I ran over a Lycan and I think I killed him!" she shouted, her voice panicked.

A low groan made her gasp. "Wait, I think he's alive! But anyway...I'll call you back!" Tossing her phone back into her purse, she ran back to the man.

Stranger, a voice from deep inside her said. Her inner wolf, normally silent, growled softly at the unfamiliar presence.

As Alpha of her clan, she was much more in touch with her Lycan side, at least that's what her mother and grandmother said. It was a part of her, after all. Over the years, aside from learning to control the she-wolf, she also learned to listen to it like a second gut instinct.

Kneeling down, she inspected the figure on the ground. Taking another whiff, she sought to identify the scent. *Ocean spray, sea salt, sugar and fried dough, like going to the boardwalk.* She froze, stunned as the image the scent brought her felt almost real, with the ocean roaring in her ear. *Strange,* she thought.

Yum.

"Yum?" Her wolf never had that reaction before.

She placed a hand on him, hoping to shake him awake. He was hot, normal after transforming back from Lycan form, which explained his naked state. Touching his naked skin sent tingles of heat through her own body and she nearly jumped back in surprise. However, she kept her hand on his shoulder, squeezing it and shaking him.

"Hey...you! Mister!" she called. "Wake up! What are you doing here? You're not one of us! This is Jersey territory!" She flipped him over onto his back. Knowing he was Lycan, his body would heal much faster, even without medical attention.

When his face came into view, she bit her tongue, trying not to gasp. From what she could see, the Lycan was handsome, with dark hair, high cheekbones, a straight nose and sensual lips. His muscled, well-defined chest was covered in a soft matt of dark hair, a line trailing down a tight six-pack, teasing to what lay below. Frankie blushed and turned her head away, but not before she glanced at his impressive package. He let out another groan, his lids opening for a moment, revealing emerald green eyes.

"Hey! Are you awake?" she asked.

The man opened his eyes, but they were unfocused.

Frankie paused, gathering her thoughts. There was no way she could call 911, as the police and the ambulance would ask her tons of questions she wasn't prepared to answer, like what a naked man was doing in her driveway and why was he healing so fast after being run over. Of course, she couldn't just leave him there where her neighbors would see him. Squaring her shoulders, she decided she'd have to take him in for now and figure things out later.

"Ok, if you can get up, let's get you into the house, ok? What happened?"

He seemed to nod, but his eyes remained glassed over. "Hurt...can't see..." he managed to moan. "Drugged..."

"You were drugged?" she asked. "Ok, well you can shake it off at my house." She helped him get up, placing her shoulder underneath his left arm. "Jesus, you're huge!" The man was probably around 6 feet tall and towered over her own petite, 5'1 frame. His upper body was broad and compact, his shoulders bunched with well-defined muscles. It was difficult, but she managed to brace him as they walked towards the house.

It was a feat to get him up the porch and prop him up against the door while she opened the lock with her key, but she somehow managed it. There was no way he was going to get up to the second floor, so she guided him to the guest bedroom on the ground floor. She foisted him off her and onto the bed, then opened one of the lamps on the bedside.

Looking at him in the soft lamplight, she realized just how much more handsome he was. His eyes were closed again, but she could clearly see all his features, and his tanned skin, the slight stubble growing on his strong jaw. Something in her was mesmerized at the sight of him and her hand caressed his cheek gently, brushing away a streak of dirt.

A strong hand caught hers, and she instinctively pulled back, but he was much stronger. He pulled her down, and then rolled her under him, pinning her on the mattress with his body.

Frankie gasped as his nose nuzzled the spot under her ear and he breathed deeply. "You...almond cookies..." he said incoherently. She opened her mouth to speak and struggled to get out from under him, but was silenced as his lips captured hers.

At first, she remained frozen, unable to move from shock. But soon, desire and heat shot through her body and she wasn't resisting at all, but was returning his ardent kisses. His lips moved over hers, devouring them, his tongue seeking entrance. As soon as she parted her lips, he delved his tongue into her mouth, warm and delicious, seeking hers out.

Hands slipped under her shirt, yanking down the cups of her bra. Large, warm palms cupped the generous globes of her breasts, squeezing gently, fingers playing with her nipples until they turned into hard little buds. Something hard pressed against her hips, and he shifted his body so he was cradled between her legs. He was definitely fully erect, his naked and engorged penis pressing into the seam of her jeans.

A deep, appreciative growl came from deep within her and Frankie pushed her hips up at him instinctively. Moving his hands away from her breasts, he trailed lower, over her belly, and his fingers clumsily clawed at the buttons on her jeans. She pushed at his hands impatiently, and unbuttoned them herself. He yanked her hands away and pushed his own under the thick fabric and her panties, his warm fingers seeking out the wet folds of her sex. Slowly, he probed a finger inside her and finding her already wet, let out a low, feral growl as he continued his fervent assault on her lips.

Suddenly, the sound of the front door unlocking and opening brought Frankie to her senses. "Fuck!" she cursed and tried to push the man away. It wasn't an easy feat, but she braced her hands on his chest and then mustered all her strength to push. She must have caught him by surprise, because he quickly rolled over and fell back on the floor with a loud thud.

"Frankie! Frankie where are you?" came Matt's

voice from the main hallway. She heard footsteps run up the stairs.

"Frankie, what happened?" Dante called.

Fuck! Frankie buttoned up her jeans, straightened out her bra and shirt, then tried to brush her long, black hair back into some semblance of order. "I'm coming!" she said, scrambling quickly out of the guest bedroom

Matt was running down the stairs and she nearly collided with him. "Frankie!" he grabbed her by the shoulders to steady her. "Dante said you called in a panic and that you killed someone! What happened?" Matt's brown eyes were filed with concern.

"Frankie, there you are!" Dante called as he entered the main hallway from the kitchen.

"What are you guys doing here?" she asked, her voice high and tense.

"You leave that message on my phone and then don't call back? What were we supposed to do?"

"Er...sorry, I got distracted."

Dante's eyes scanned her from head to toe, his nose wrinkling and when she blushed at his gaze, his eyes widened. But before he could say anything, Matt spoke up.

"Tell us what happened! Where's the guy you ran over? Is he dead?"

She shook her head. "No, no...he's ok...just drugged." She sighed and then relayed to them what had happened, at least up until the part she got him into the house.

"A Lycan? Here in Jersey? Aren't they supposed to ask you permission before entering your territory?" Matt asked. Although he was one of her fully human half-brothers, he knew how Lycan society worked.

"Usually, but it looks like he was drugged and maybe dumped here. He was uh, naked, which makes me think he shifted to escape the people that drugged him, and then wandered off," Frankie thought aloud.

"Where is he?" Dante asked.

"I put him in the guest bedroom," she explained.

"Is he dangerous?" Matt asked, a worried look on his face. "Did he try to hurt you?"

"He's too weak to do anything, I think," Frankie assured him. Dante shot her a knowing look and she looked at him with silent, pleading eyes. "Matty, can you please uh...go and get him some clothes, please? I think he's about Dante's height, but a little broader in the chest."

"Check my old room," Dante instructed. Matt nodded and bounded up the stairs.

Dante turned to his sister. "Too weak, huh?" he sniffed the air around her. "You know you can't hide anything from me. Not when you smell like sex and—"

"Shush!" she held her hand up. "Can we please not...I'm ok, he didn't hurt me...we just..." she stammered and Dante raised a brow at her. "Let's not do this now, ok? I'll explain later." *If I can find a logical explanation*, she thought to herself. *Except I've gone insane from lack of sex all these years.*

"Fine. Let's go take a look at this guy."

The two of them went to the bedroom and Dante flipped on the main light switch so he could get a closer look. The large man, still naked, had somehow hoisted himself up onto the bed and he lay on his back, his eyes closed.

"Huh," Dante moved closer, peering over man. "He looks...oh mother of god!" Dante turned his head slowly to his sister. "Jesus, Frankie, don't you know who this is?"

She shot him back a look and shrugged. "Am I supposed to?"

"Frankie...jeez, you're supposed to be our Alpha!"

"Just tell me who he is!"

"This is Grant Anderson. *The* Grant Anderson,

billionaire industrialist, CEO of Fenrir Corp, and New York's Alpha.

Get **Romancing the Alpha: Book of the True Mates Generations Series** at your favorite online book retailer!